ALCHEMY OF FIRE

ALCHEMY OF FIRE

Gillian Bradshaw

This first world edition published in Great Britain 2004 by
SEVERN HOUSE PUBLISHERS LTD of
9–15 High Street, Sutton, Surrey SM1 1DF.
This first world edition published in the USA 2004 by
SEVERN HOUSE PUBLISHERS INC of
595 Madison Avenue, New York, N.Y. 10022.

British Library Cataloguing in Publication Data

Bradshaw, Gillian, 1956-
    The alchemy of fire
    1.   Ex-prostitutes - Turkey - Istanbul - Fiction
    2.   Istanbul (Turkey) - History - To 1453 - Fiction
    3.   Historical fiction
    I.   Title
    823.9'14 [F]

    ISBN 0-7278-6097-6

Typeset by Palimpsest Book Production Ltd.,
Polmont, Stirlingshire, Scotland.
Printed and bound in Great Britain by
MPG Books Ltd., Bodmin, Cornwall.

For Jenny
Who wanted a book dedicated to her

PART I

Constantinople

AD 672

One

It was early in June, and for three weeks the workshop had been making attar of roses. Rose petals were everywhere: floors, tables, even the workshop latrine. Trodden upon and swept aside, their delicate pink had become a damp brown litter which squashed into wads on the workers' shoes. The heady fragrance of the fresh blooms was almost smothered by the cloying smell of the darkening cakes removed from the presses. The workers breathed rotting rose, and the thick sticky scent flavoured everything they ate.

'I hate roses,' Theodosia declared mutinously, shortly after lunch. She was twelve, and this season was the first time she'd joined in the work of processing the roses.

Her mother Anna regarded her with a tolerant smile. How tall the girl was getting, only half a head shorter now than her mother! And how pretty she was, her eyes bright with resentment, and her flushed face framed by wisps of fair hair that had strayed from under the plain worker's headscarf. Still smiling, Anna tucked one of those blonde locks gently back under its restraint. 'You're just tired,' she said.

They were all tired: Anna, who owned the workshop; her daughter; the two slaves and one hired worker employed to help. They'd all been working late since the season began. The rose growers picked the blossoms soon after dawn, when their scent was strongest, but the farms were all outside the city, and the carts never arrived at the workshop until the evening. By then the blooms were wilting, already past their peak, and had to be rushed into processing immediately. More than a hundred pounds of rose petals a night had to be stripped from their flower heads by lamplight, and any mildewed or spotted blooms discarded. The workers' hands became covered in scratches from thorns, stray thistles and straw, and black with dirty rose sap. Once the rose heads had been stripped, the petals had to be arranged to extract their scent. The workshop was crammed with racks of ceramic plates, each one covered with oil, and every inch of that oil had to be covered with rose petals. In practice only a third of the racks were treated on any one day, but even so it was late at night by the time the last handful of petals was shaken out over the waiting oil. The next morning, however, work had to begin again early. Every day, a third of the racks had to be cleared of old rose petals; the petals washed and pressed to remove all the oil; the oil strained off the water, filtered and reapplied to the trays – and all the regular work of the perfume manufactory and shop still had to be done.

'But it's so *stupid*! Just *look*!' exclaimed Theodosia, waving a hand angrily at the towering racks. 'How many hundreds of pounds of roses have we done since the season started? And in the end, how much attar do we get? Four or five pounds?'

Anna smiled. 'Less. That's why the stuff sells for ten nomismata an ounce.'

Theodosia stuck her lip out. 'It's not *worth* it!'

Anna stopped smiling. She was very proud of her business, and could never bear to hear it slighted. 'Hush!' she exclaimed reprovingly. 'There are plenty of people who have to *live* on two or three nomismata a *year*. They work this hard or harder all year round and never earn more than a few coppers! You should thank the blessed Virgin that we have such a good livelihood!'

Theodosia made a face. 'Why?' She tilted her head back and gazed at her mother resentfully, green eyes full of challenge. 'I shouldn't need a *livelihood* at all. I ought to be a *lady*. *Ladies* don't have to work.'

It was a very sensitive subject, and she knew it, and, thought Anna, had brought it up *now* because she knew her mother was tired and would react. Anna lowered the hand she'd raised to slap her daughter: the girl was too old for that now. In the silence, a small bell jingled: someone wanted admittance to the shop.

'No,' Anna agreed, collecting herself with an effort. 'But

4

maybe you should remember that young *ladies* aren't allowed to stand around at public fountains giggling with their friends, or go running into the market to watch acrobats. *Ladies* aren't allowed out of their houses without an escort. They sit on their backsides doing embroidery and going mad with boredom. What's more, they get married off, at your age, to foul old men. You think you'd like that better than making perfume, do you? The bell in the shop just went: go see who it is.'

Theodosia scowled and stalked off. Anna watched her go, noticing the rose and sweat stains on the linen undertunic, wondering if she should order the girl to pick up a cloak to cover herself up, then deciding that it was too hot, and that Theodosia was still enough of a child to appear in an undertunic without attracting any comment.

Not for much longer, though. Anna herself had been only thirteen when men started to whistle after her every time she walked down the street, and Theodosia took after her mother in her looks: tall and golden, with a long straight nose and green eyes. Already her straight body was beginning to fill out with a suggestion of curves: the child was growing up. Wistfully Anna remembered Theodosia as a warm bundle in her arms, and as a skinny little girl darting happily around the workshop. What was she to do, now that her baby was threatening to become a young woman? God and his saints, had Theodosia *really* taken it into her head to want to be a lady, or had she said that only to annoy her mother?

Martina, the free employee, came over shaking her head. She was a middle-aged spinster who lived with her married sister and worked in the perfumery in the afternoons. 'That girl should have more respect for her mother!' she said disapprovingly. She could be relied upon to disapprove of most girls and all men.

Anna raised her eyebrows, and Martina ducked her head in hasty apology: the comment was impertinent, offered from employee to employer uninvited.

'She's young,' Anna said, relenting, 'and we're all tired.' She remembered her own childhood. Had *she* always completed her chores cheerfully and without complaint? Absolutely not: she'd sulked, sneered and complained with the best of them. *Probably I was even worse than Theodosia*, she thought, with rueful amusement. *Poor Papa!*

Theodosia came back into the workshop. With her was a man.

Anna stared. Martina drew in a deep breath of outrage. Over in the corner, Zoe and Helena, the two slaves, abruptly stopped their chatter, fifteen-year-old Zoe with a little shriek and old fat Helena with a simper. All the women were in their undertunics, with laces undone and hems kilted up because of the heat, and what was acceptable in a child was indecent in a grown woman.

Theodosia smirked with mischievous pleasure. The man – a workman, by the look of his dirty clothing – lifted his eyebrows as he looked around. He grinned appreciatively. His gaze fixed on Anna and became one of frank admiration. She was, of course, identifiable as the person in charge by the ring of keys at her belt, but the workman's look was not the kind a man gives the person in charge.

'Theodosia!' exclaimed Martina indignantly. 'Why . . .' Words failed her.

Anna took five quick steps over to the cloak she'd hung in the corner and flung it around herself in a swirl of black linen and a jingle of keys. 'Theodosia,' she said warningly, 'we'll discuss this later.'

Theodosia's smirk vanished. Anna gestured imperiously at the door to the shop, then followed the workman through it.

The perfume shop formed the front of Anna's house; the workshop and storerooms occupied the rooms behind it, which were arranged around a small courtyard, and the household slept in the rooms on the upper floor. The shop faced out on to the street – which, as Anna liked to remind customers, was the Middle Street, the main thoroughfare of Constantinople . . . though not, unfortunately, its fashionable end. The shop's large windows were ordinarily open during the morning, so that passers-by could see the rows of gleaming flasks and bottles for sale inside. In the afternoon, however, when everyone was normally busy in the workshop, the windows were shuttered and latched and the door bolted to keep out thieves. Anna noted with approval that Theodosia

6

had bolted the outer shop door after admitting the workman, and not left it open: the perfume shop was dark, dim and marvellously fragrant. The centre of the room, however, was lit well enough for convenience, since light shone through the door from the workshop and courtyard behind.

Anna moved over to the counter in the middle of that space of light and set her hands on it, the image of black-swathed respectability. She inspected the workman severely. Severity and respectability were her usual means of putting men in their place. She didn't actually *like* behaving like a strict matron, but she'd found that if she was pleasant and friendly, men got ideas that led to trouble. She was still suffering from the consequences of a few relaxed and cheerful discussions with an influential member of the perfumers' guild: he'd been most offended when she refused his offer of marriage.

To her annoyance, the workman looked back boldly, his bright black eyes and broad crooked-toothed grin reminding her that he'd just enjoyed the sight of her in her undertunic. Still more irritating, he didn't look worth the interruption to her work: he plainly didn't have the money to buy expensive perfume. Aged about thirty – her own age – with curling black hair and an unkempt beard, he was wearing a leather apron over a plain linen tunic, much worn and covered with black stains. His hands were stained, too, and covered with the puckers of old burn scars. Another burn scar interrupted the beard on one cheek.

It was – unfortunately – bad for business to tell a customer to take his stupid grin out of her shop. The man might not be rich enough to buy expensive perfume, but that was true of most of her customers. Here at the unfashionable end of the Middle Street she sold the cheaper scented oils which both men and women used after bathing, along with scented soaps and the occasional flask of more expensive perfume for a special occasion. It was all too obvious that this man needed something to wash with: he smelled. It wasn't so much body odour as an acrid, unpleasant smell that nagged at Anna as familiar, though her rose-sodden senses couldn't identify it. 'You want to buy some perfume?' she asked resignedly. 'Or some scented soap?'

7

'No, good woman,' said the workman, politely enough. 'I was hoping for help in another matter, which is why the girl decided I needed to speak to her . . . I suppose I should say, speak to her *superior*, though she said, to her mother. Are you the proprietor of this establishment?'

Anna raised her eyebrows. *Proprietor of this establishment*? Very educated phrasing for a workman – but then, from the sound of him, the fellow probably wasn't a workman after all. He was a refugee: if the combination of poor clothing and educated speech hadn't been enough to give him away, his strong Syrian accent would've betrayed him.

It was, actually, surprisingly strong, that accent. Most of the refugees arriving in Constantinople now were Asiatics, from Smyrna and Cyzicus: the big Syrian influx had been a generation before. Maybe this fellow was merely the son of Syrian parents – but if he'd been brought up in the city, why did he talk like a man who'd just stepped off the boat? If he'd arrived recently, though, why had he fled his home at all? Syria might be under the government of the enemies of God, but it was peaceful and secure. Constantinople – God and his saints protect it! – was threatened with attack. The war against the Arabs, which had been going badly since before Anna was born, had at last reached the point where it would be lost altogether unless the battered empire could scrape up a victory. All the provinces which had formed a buffer against the storm had fallen, and now Constantinople itself lay exposed to the blast. The citizens still continued with their business day to day, but every now and then the terrifying awareness would strike: the assault would surely come within the next few years, and it might mean the end of the empire.

'God will not permit Constantinople to fall!' some of the more devout declared fervently, but Anna had doubts. Terrible things happened all the time, so God obviously did permit them. Jerusalem had fallen, after all, and Edessa, which had had a letter from Christ himself promising that no barbarians would ever take it. Like the rest of the citizens, Anna prayed every Sunday that God would preserve Constantinople, but, like the rest, she was afraid. Why would

8

anyone leave peace and security to flee into the heart of a terrifying war?

Maybe this Syrian was so devout a Christian that he intended to die a martyr in the defence of the capital of orthodoxy. That was, undoubtedly, very noble, but Anna hoped it was not the case. Zealots were nothing but trouble. They denounced perfume as sinful and tended to blame any pretty woman for their own lustful thoughts.

'Yes, I am the "proprietor",' Anna replied, putting her curiosity aside for the moment. 'What is it you want?'

The man nodded, unsurprised. Female proprietors might be unusual in most businesses, but in perfume-making they were fairly common. 'A fitting mistress for such a sweet and fragrant trade,' he remarked, with another look of admiration.

Anna, who'd heard the compliment at least a thousand times before, rolled her eyes in contempt. The Syrian, slightly crestfallen, went on more pragmatically, 'I was wondering, good woman, if you had any distilling equipment you're not using just at the moment. I don't have much money, but I could afford a small rental fee.'

'You're a perfume-maker?' Anna asked with cautious sympathy. Distilling equipment was rare, and only a few trades made use of it. She didn't like grinning flatterers, but a perfume-maker who'd arrived in the city penniless was entitled to some assistance from his fellows in the trade.

The Syrian, however, hesitated a moment before replying, and Anna's eyes narrowed with a sudden suspicion. The acrid smell which had nagged at her found a name.

'Median oil,' she said.

The Syrian instinctively glanced down at the black stains on his tunic, then looked up again quickly. 'What?' he asked, with false surprise.

'That's Median rock oil you've got all over your tunic,' Anna insisted. 'I know the smell. They use it to heat the water at the Kaminia baths, and they use it at the Arsenal to make incendiaries. What would you put in my distilling equipment if I let you borrow it?'

The Syrian hesitated again. 'You're right,' he admitted at last, with a nervous smile of appeasement. 'It's true I'm

9

working at the Arsenal, but that's to get a permit to remain in the city. I'm not trying to borrow distilling equipment for them, though. I want it for a *private* use. I thought . . .'

'What would you put in my pots if I rented them to you?' Anna demanded again, cutting him off. 'What, exactly, is this "private" use, if it isn't perfume-making?'

The Syrian floundered.

'Are you an alchemist?' she continued relentlessly. Alchemists employed distillation, and presumably someone accustomed to smokes and stinks wouldn't mind working with Median oil.

The man winced and admitted it with a reluctant nod.

'I suspected as much!' exclaimed Anna, in indignant disgust. 'Is that honest? Asking to *rent* perfume-making equipment, when you intend to fill it up with sulphur and dung?'

'I'd clean it up afterwards!' the Syrian protested. 'And—'

'Hah!' exclaimed Anna. 'There's no cleaning away the stink of sulphur. It eats itself right into the vessel. Suppose I took the pot back and used it to steam sweet marjoram without realizing what you'd used it for? The sulphur smell would come out the moment I heated it, and the result would end up smelling of rotten egg! It would cost me as much again as the value of the pot!'

The Syrian was downcast and chagrined. He ran an oil-stained hand through his dirty hair and grimaced. 'I don't even have any sulphur!' he protested. 'I can't afford it now. I just wanted to . . .' He stopped himself with a heavy sigh. 'Never mind!'

Anna felt sorry for him despite herself. He was an educated man: that was clear from the way he talked. He must have come from a good family. It must be hard, to lose home, family and wealth; to flee to a strange city, and do menial work at the Arsenal in exchange for a permit to remain. He couldn't be a religious zealot, either: zealots liked alchemy even less than they liked perfume. Whatever his story was, it probably involved hard luck. It must be humiliating for him to haggle with a shopkeeper over the rental of a few pots – and more humiliating to be refused.

She'd been planning to buy some new distilling equipment for the workshop once the rose season was over. The pot she had was so old that the embedded grime was starting to taint what was brewed in it. She'd have to dispose of it *somehow*.

'I won't *rent* you any pots,' she told the Syrian firmly, 'but I might be willing to *sell* you one, and let you pay for it in instalments. What sort of equipment are you wanting?'

He immediately looked up again with a grin. 'God bless you!' he cried eagerly. 'I need a tribukos, or else an ambix with a phiali, and . . . do you have a kerotakis?'

She was taken aback. 'A what?'

'A kerotakis. It's a vessel you can seal up, with a kind of shelf inside it, so you can expose objects to vapours . . .'

'No,' said Anna, so impatiently that the Syrian stopped short. After a moment of silence she went on, 'I don't have a tribukos, either. But I could sell you an ambix with a phiali and double boiler.'

'Wonderful!' cried the Syrian enthusiastically. Then he sucked his upper lip down between his teeth anxiously. 'How many instalments of how much? No, wait! Can I see the pot first?'

Anna went back into the workshop storeroom, collected the whole assembly, and lugged it through. The ambix was a high-sided pot used for distillation. Simpler ones had an overlapping lid with an indented lip running round the outside: vapour from what was cooked in the pot would condense on the lid and collect in the lip. The phiali, or cucurbita, was a more elaborate lid, with a projecting spigot to drain the condensate off into another vessel. She was not surprised that the alchemist was interested in these particular items; she'd heard that alchemists had invented them. He was lucky she had them: not all perfume-makers used them. Old-fashioned members of the perfumers' guild considered steam distillation an unnecessary new-fangled gimmick. There'd been some heads shaken when Anna bought her ambix.

She set the assembly down on the counter with a clatter. The ambix was a large one, made of a thick, heavy ceramic, three feet high, stained with use. The double boiler that went with it was copper, green with tarnish and black with soot.

The Syrian sucked his lip again and picked up the ambix to examine the base. He picked up the double boiler. He frowned. He tipped the ambix on to its side and ran an oily finger over the base. He frowned harder. 'This can't ever have been put on the fire!' he said accusingly, holding up a finger that was now green from tarnish and unmarked by soot. 'Is there something wrong with it?'

Anna snorted. 'Why would I be such a fool as to set an ambix on the fire? Oh, I suppose *you* might. What does an alchemist care about smells? I can tell you, though, that direct heat will kill a scent in minutes. Even with the double boiler, I can only use steam distillation for the more robust materials – marjoram, and wild grape and the like. It would never do for roses or jasmine.'

'Why?' asked the Syrian, looking into her face with a sudden direct interest that took her aback.

'Flowers are too delicate for steaming,' she replied impatiently.

'No, I mean why does heat kill scents?'

'I . . . I don't know,' she stammered. She'd never thought about it. 'It just does.'

The alchemist looked down at the tarnish-stained base of the ambix thoughtfully. 'Perhaps scent is a property of liquids and moist things? When it's exposed to the fiery element, its *atomoi* are converted into air, the way water is converted into steam – and then they cease to be scents?'

'Perhaps,' agreed Anna, off balance. After a moment she added, 'Not everything used to make perfume is moist, though. There's myrrh, for example. It's dry, and the doctors say that its effect is heating and astringent.'

'Ah, but myrrh is a resin, the dried sap of a tree!' exclaimed the Syrian, smiling at her eagerly. 'So it, too, must be related to the element of water. Perhaps its drying properties are because it was the sap of a tree that grows only in dry places.'

'Perhaps,' Anna said doubtfully. She and the Syrian looked

12

at one another for a moment. Then she sniffed and asked briskly, 'Do you want the ambix?'

'It's old,' objected the alchemist.

'If it wasn't old, I wouldn't be willing to sell it,' Anna told him tartly.

'True,' agreed the Syrian, and grinned. 'And if it was new, I couldn't afford to buy it. I'll take it.'

They haggled over a price and the number of instalments, agreeing at last on a mutually satisfactory arrangement. The Syrian picked up the pots.

'Not so fast!' Anna objected, and he put them down again.

There was a lesson she'd learned young which had served her well all her life. She'd learned it in two forms, but they were both essentially the same: never trust a man's promises, and never accept payment by credit.

'I need some security,' she told the Syrian.

'Security?' he repeated, baffled.

'Something to pledge against the value of the pots! If you walk off with those and never come back to pay me a copper, what am I supposed to do?'

'I'm an honest man!' he protested. 'Here: my name is Kallinikos of Heliopolis, I have lodgings at the House of Theodore, near the Platea Gate, and I already told you that I work at the Arsenal, in the Caesaria quarter. My superior is Stephanos Skyles, Magistros of the Arsenal. If I cheat you, you can complain to him. He'd be glad of an excuse to get rid of me.'

Kallinikos, Anna thought, without surprise, was decidedly an upper-class name. All the compounds of *nike*, 'victory' – Aristonikos and Nikephoros, Nikias and Nikomachos – were the sort of name aristocratic fathers foisted upon their sons in the hope of procuring them a notable military career. 'Beautifully victorious' seemed a bit top-heavy for this scruffy workman, but presumably the man had been rather better dressed when he lived in Heliopolis. This fellow was probably an aristocrat – and aristocrats were notoriously casual about paying debts to tradesmen.

'How do I know you're telling the truth, "Kallinikos"?'

13

she asked suspiciously. 'After all, an "honest man" wouldn't have tried to rent pots for something that was likely to ruin them.'

He grimaced. 'I didn't realize that I could ruin the pot for perfume-making. The only reason I didn't want to mention that I'm an alchemist was because I was worried you might be one of those people who think that alchemy is impious. I wasn't trying to cheat you. Why would I want to cheat such a beautiful woman?'

She raised her eyebrows. 'You would cheat an ugly one?'

'No, no! I just meant that I wouldn't want you to think badly of me . . .'

'This is honest? To admit that you'd cheat some poor girl just because she was ugly?'

'I didn't mean . . .'

'God witness it! You're not taking away this ambix until I have something of yours as security against a default.'

Kallinikos sighed. 'All right, all right! I'll find something or other to put down as security against the cost of the ambix. I'll come back with it this evening, and collect the pot then. All right?'

'Fine,' agreed Anna, smiling, and let him out.

Still smiling, she took the ambix back to the storeroom and returned to the workshop. She slid one of the ceramic plates out of the rack and shook off loose rose petals into a basin. 'I've sold that old ambix,' she announced to the workshop at large. 'The buyer doesn't have enough to pay for it all at once, though, so I'm going to let him pay in instalments. He'll come back this evening with something to pledge as security against payment in full.' She tapped the plate against the rack, then began picking the remaining rose petals out of the oil.

Martina grunted. 'Get a good price?'

'Unlikely to get a better one,' Anna said contentedly. A petal stuck to her finger. She pried it off, dropped it in the basin, ready to be pressed to extract the excess oil – then paused and sniffed her oily finger.

It smelled of roses. She was suddenly struck with the marvel of the thing. Rose petals contained a scent, but that scent was something that seeped out of them and could be trapped in refined oil. What was it? Was the alchemist right to think it might be a strange form of water?

In two or three weeks she'd see the fragrance she was smelling now. At the end of the rose season they would pour as much of the oil off the trays as they could, then wash the plates and collect the film of oil from the water to add to the rest. They would bottle it, and sell it for twice its weight in gold.

Heat didn't really *kill* scent, she realized. It released it. When the trays were being washed in hot water, the whole workshop would be incandescent with fragrance. Incense in grains smelled sweet only when you picked it up and sniffed it, but let the same quantity smoulder on a fire and the aroma would fill a church. A perfume might keep for years, safely bottled in a cool place; apply it to the warmth of living skin, and it woke, and breathed, and faded away. Perhaps scent was a property of air, and it was merely trapped in a liquid, until it was freed by the element of fire.

'It must have been a very good price,' Martina said slyly, 'to make you smile like that!'

Anna stopped smiling. 'I was smiling at a thought,' she said sharply. 'And what I was thinking about was attar of roses – which *we* are supposed to be producing. We need to get these trays clear and the petals pressed.'

'I have a music lesson this afternoon,' announced Theodosia smugly. 'I have to go soon.'

Anna almost snapped at her – but it was true. What was more, Anna had paid for the lesson in advance. The instructor had insisted on it. 'Very well!' Anna conceded. 'But it's not *that* soon. There must be another hour at least before you need to leave, and I want you to spend it working! And come straight back here afterwards. I want you here when the roses arrive.'

The lesson was part of a course in lute playing for girls. It was being taught, three days a week, by an instructor at a local boys' school; it took place in the school hall, but late in the afternoon, after the boys had left. Theodosia had been attending with her two best friends for six weeks. The three

15

girls' families had clubbed together to buy one instrument for the students to share, since none of them was convinced that their daughter would persevere and practise. At the moment, however, all three girls professed a burning devotion to music. They hadn't missed a lesson, and they were always running over to one another's houses to practise – though Anna strongly suspected that this was only because it gave them an excuse to skip chores, meet together and giggle. Certainly they never seemed to come straight back from the lessons. She was annoyed, but not really surprised, when Theodosia did not come straight back to the workshop this time, either.

'That girl needs a whipping!' muttered Martina, when Theodosia was nearly an hour late. Anna did not respond, but she sympathized with the sentiment. The next load of roses was due any minute, and every pair of hands was needed.

The shop bell rang. Anna cursed. It was too late now for anyone to want to buy perfume: it would be the cart with the roses. She tossed her black cloak on again and went to open the door.

It was not the cart with the roses. It was the Syrian alchemist, Kallinikos, pale and out of breath. He braced himself against the door frame with one hand and panted, 'Mistress Anna . . .'

She was about to ask sternly who'd told him her name when, 'Mama!' Theodosia called weakly from behind him.

Anna looked, saw her daughter lying limp on a stretcher improvised from a cloak, supported by two unknown men.

For so many years, any quarter-hour delay in Theodosia's return home, any fall, any fever, had caused Anna a sense of pressure upon the heart: her child, her only child, might be in danger. She had always tried to suppress the feeling: no child wanted a clinging pest as a mother. She had succeeded too well. Now her daughter had been carried home on a stretcher, and no premonition had touched her. She had even cursed because the girl was late.

'Oh, God!' she exclaimed, partly in horror and partly in real prayer. She thrust her way past the Syrian and bent over Theodosia, seizing the girl's hand as it reached up for her own. She smelled the vomit even before she

16

saw the splashes over Theodosia's thin tunic and the stretcher.

'She was lying in the street by the Church of the Holy Apostles,' Kallinikos explained breathlessly. 'I recognized her, I told them to bring her here . . .'

'Get her inside,' Anna ordered sharply.

The stretcher momentarily got stuck in the doorway before Anna could force herself to relinquish her daughter's hand, but eventually it was inside. The perfume workers, who'd come out from the workshop at the first commotion, were all standing in the shop goggling. Zoe gave a little wail. Anna turned on her. 'Go fetch Simeon the Doctor,' she commanded. 'Now!'

Zoe gave another little wail and ran to obey. Anna escorted the stretcher through the workshop and upstairs to the room she shared with her daughter. She ordered the men to set the stretcher down on the bed.

When they'd done so they stood rubbing their tired hands. Anna pushed one of them out of the way and knelt over her daughter. Theodosia was very pale and tearful, but there didn't seem to be any blood. Anna caught her hand again. 'What happened, darling?' she asked gently.

'My head hurts!' Theodosia moaned. 'And I feel sick, I feel really sick!'

'She was sick while we was carrying her,' one of the men confided – unnecessarily, as the fact was only too obvious.

'But what happened?' Anna asked impatiently. 'Was she attacked?'

'I think it was an accident,' Kallinikos supplied. 'When I came up she was lying in the street, half conscious, with a crowd around her trying to decide who she was. Somebody said she ran out of the church without looking and was knocked over by a horse.'

'I didn't see it myself,' put in one of the stretcher-bearers, 'but my neighbour did. He said that it was some rich gentleman on a big stallion, a huge bad-tempered jumpy horse nobody should be using in a crowded street anyway, and when the girl got knocked over he didn't even stop, just rode away fast. The rich don't care.'

17

'My head hurts!' sobbed Theodosia again.

Anna untied her daughter's scarf and examined her head. The lump was easy to find, on the side of the head above the right ear. There was some blood matted in the fair curls, but not much: the scarf, and the thick hair itself, had cushioned the worst of the blow. 'My poor lamb,' Anna told her lovingly. 'I'll get you a compress for it. I've sent for the doctor.'

Theodosia relaxed, obviously much happier now that she was home in bed with her mother looking after her. She smiled weakly and turned her face away, closing her eyes.

Anna got up and started downstairs to fetch the compress. The men followed her. When she reached the kitchen at the back of the workshop, one of them coughed and said, 'I hope the poor girl will be all right. Beautiful girl. The man with the horse was a bastard!'

'Didn't look too bad,' said the other. 'She'll probably be running about again tomorrow.'

'God send it!' Anna said fervently. 'Thank you for bringing her home.'

The first man coughed again and added, 'The man said you'd give us something for it.'

Anna gave him a hard look, and he looked back, embarrassed but determined. The two might have helped anyway – but they might not have. Theodosia wasn't one of their own, a known child of the neighbourhood, entitled to care and protection by right: she was a stranger. They wanted to be paid for helping her.

Anna went into the shop, unlocked the strongbox, and took out some coins. 'Here,' she said.

The men, both looking embarrassed now, took the money and shuffled out. Anna looked at Kallinikos. He flung up his hands in defence. 'I had to say *something* to persuade them to help!' he protested. 'It was too far to carry her by myself, unless I tossed her over my shoulder, and I was afraid that might hurt her more.'

Anna wrestled down the surge of gratitude. It wasn't safe to show gratitude to men: they always tried to take advantage of it. 'Hmf!' she said, and went back to the kitchen. She folded a linen napkin, poured a little cold water from the large storage amphora over it, then went back to the shop. She chose a bottle of spikenard and poured a little on to the damp cloth, then added a dollop of a compound of lavender, wine and honey. She went back upstairs.

Kallinikos had followed every step, but he stood discreetly in the doorway of the bedroom while she knelt down beside Theodosia and gently placed the compress on the girl's head. Theodosia drew in a deep breath of the fragrance.

'That's nice,' she murmured. 'It's nice and cool.'

'Yes, darling,' her mother said tenderly. 'Dr Simeon will be here soon.' She began to unlace the vomited-upon tunic, then turned to give Kallinikos a reproving look.

She found him watching her with an expression of longing and grief so intense it shocked her. They stared at one another for a long moment, in desire and recoil. Then he ducked his head and went out.

Simeon the Doctor arrived a few minutes later, very out of breath. Zoe had apparently told him that Theodosia was dying. He was an old friend of the family – a stout man with a greying beard and five children of his own – and he had known Theodosia ever since she was born. He was relieved to discover that he had been misinformed.

'There's some concussion, but I don't think the skull is cracked,' he told Anna, after examining and cleaning the injury. 'Do you remember what happened, Theodosia sweetie?'

Theodosia made a face: she hated it when people called her 'sweetie', as though she were still a little girl. She put the compress back on her lump. 'No. All I remember is running out of the church. I was in a hurry because Mama wanted me back by the time the rose cart came.' She paused a moment, then added, in some puzzlement, 'Next I was lying on the ground with a lot of people around me. I didn't know where I was or what had happened. I felt horrible.'

'One of the men who helped carry her back said she was knocked down by a horse,' put in Anna. 'He said the rider didn't stop.'

'Well, at least she doesn't seem to have been unconscious for very long,' said Simeon comfortingly. 'From the sound

19

of it, she woke up only a little while after the accident, which should mean that she didn't take any serious harm from it. Still, with head injuries one must always take great care. She should stay in bed for at least three days, no matter how well she feels, and she should have a low diet of broth and gruel.'

'I hate gruel,' said Theodosia in disgust. She sounded much more her normal self, and Anna smiled.

'You can have some honey in it,' Simeon told her, also smiling. 'I think it's delicious with honey.'

Theodosia made a face.

'How is your stomach now?' Anna asked her. 'Would you like a little broth? Or some water?'

The girl began to nod, then winced and said, 'Water, please,' instead. Anna stroked her head again, then started downstairs to fetch it. Simeon went with her.

The workshop appeared to be very busy. They went into the shop, and Anna unlocked the strongbox again.

'Send for me at once if she gets worse,' Simeon told her, taking his fee. 'If she falls asleep suddenly, for example, and you can't wake her, or if she starts vomiting again. Otherwise, I'll come back in three days to check on her. With God's blessing, though, I think she will be all right.' He smiled at Anna, then reached out, caught her hand and pressed it. 'Truly, neighbour. I truly, honestly believe that your lovely little girl is in no danger.'

'Thank you,' Anna told him, and swallowed.

She let him out, then went back into the workshop to get to the kitchen. This time it registered that the staff were stripping rose heads. 'When did the rose cart come?' she asked Martina, not really caring.

'A little while after the doctor,' was the reply. 'We didn't want to disturb you. The driver agreed to take payment for this load with the next one.' Martina hesitated, then asked, in a rush, 'Will Theodosia be all right?'

'Yes,' said Anna, and was aware of a tremor beginning in her legs and a sudden need for tears. 'Yes, Simeon thinks she'll be fine. She's to stay in bed for three days, but he says that's mostly just to be careful.' She smiled weakly. 'I'm just going to get her some water,' she added, with forced briskness, and started on towards the kitchen.

She stopped again, however, as she noticed Kallinikos of Heliopolis, hands buried in roses like all the rest. 'What are you doing here?' she asked in surprise. She remembered the expression she'd caught on his face when she was putting Theodosia to bed. She owed the man a debt of gratitude, but an emotion that sharp and keen was dangerous.

There was no hint of the passion now, though 'My ambix,' he reminded her gently. 'And anyway, I wanted to hear if the girl would be all right. I thought I'd help out while I waited.'

Anna studied him a moment. He didn't look like he was hoping for any immediate return for his helpfulness, though she was sure he was trying to impress her; men always were. Many of them, she thought sourly, would envy him his rescue of her child, and would cheer on any attempt to take advantage of her gratitude.

Well, she was grateful: the thought of Theodosia lying hurt and confused in the street by the Church of the Holy Apostles, with no one knowing who she was and no one trying to help her – that thought was agonizing. She was very glad that Kallinikos had chanced to come along. There could have been many reasons for that look she'd caught on his face: maybe the sight of a woman putting a child to bed made him homesick. She would allow herself to be grateful. She wasn't going to give him her body or her reputation, though. He would have to be satisfied with the ambix.

'You can take the ambix,' Anna told him. 'You can take it, and I won't ask any security. Thank you for helping my daughter.'

He grinned. 'I'm glad I could. But I'd like it if you could launder my security before you give it back.'

She frowned in confusion.

'My cloak,' he explained. 'It's the only thing I still have that's worth as much as the pot. It's a good one. I put it under your daughter to help move her, and I think it's still upstairs.'

'Oh,' she said, not sure whether or not to smile. 'Oh. Yes.

21

Well, I'll have it laundered and returned to you at . . . you said you lived near the Platea Gate?'

'I'll collect it, if that's all right,' he told her. 'I have to walk past here every day anyway to get to the Arsenal.' He stood up and shook rose petals off his hands, then looked down at the fragrant pink drifts. 'They smell a lot better than Median oil,' he admitted, looking up at Anna with another grin. 'I'd ask if you want to hire another worker, but I don't think I'd fit in.' He made a sweeping gesture of deference to the workshop staff, who had, Anna suddenly realized, done up all their laces and dropped all their hems.

'You wouldn't fit in,' agreed Anna, and this time did smile. 'Martina, fetch him his ambix. I'm going to get Theodosia some water.'

He was gone by the time she came back through the workshop with the cup. She nodded to the others and climbed the stairs.

The bedroom was growing dark; dusk had come. Anna set down the water and lit the lamp, then brought the cup over and sat down on the side of the bed. She helped Theodosia sit up and supported her while she drank. Theodosia was naked now under the sheet. The knobs of her spine pressed against Anna's supporting arm, and the softness of her skin provoked a rush of memories. She had cradled this body as a helpless infant, fed and dressed it as a lively toddler, comforted it as a young child. It was more precious to her than life.

The prospect of the approaching war hovered at the edge of her awareness: what would become of Theodosia, or of herself, if Constantinople fell to its enemies? She thrust the thought aside. However much war threatened, it had not yet arrived. This day held grief enough, and relief enough, without borrowing sorrow from the future.

'I feel a lot better now,' Theodosia volunteered, lying back into the pillow. 'It just hurts if I move my head.'

Anna bent over and kissed her forehead. 'What were you doing at the Church of the Holy Apostles anyway?' she asked. It puzzled her. The great church was less than a mile away, but it was situated in the Constantinianai district of the city. People from their own neighbourhood of Philadelphion

22

usually went there only for the feast day of some apostle to whom they were particularly devoted.

Theodosia looked back at her uncertainly, green eyes huge and shadowed in the lamplight. 'I went to see my father.'

'Your father?' repeated Anna in surprise and bewilderment. 'What do you mean?'

'There's a statue of him. Over in the side part of the church, to the left after you go in. It has his name on it.'

'Oh, my darling!' exclaimed Anna, touched and exasperated. 'That must be the *Emperor* Theodosius. He lived hundreds of years ago!'

Theodosia frowned. 'There are *two* statues labelled Theodosius!' she objected. 'One's old, but the other isn't. He's young, and he's wearing a purple cloak. He looks noble and nice.'

'Darling, I'm sorry, but your father is not buried in the Church of the Holy Apostles, and there certainly isn't a statue of him there – particularly not one in a purple cloak! Nobody would *ever* have allowed that. He was buried in the Monastery of the Studion, very quietly. Maybe there were two Emperors Theodosius.'

Theodosia sat up carefully, clutching the sheet to her chest with one hand and her cold compress to her head with the other, gazing at her mother with shock. 'In the Monastery of the Studion?' she asked. 'You told me he hated it there!'

Anna made a small helpless gesture with both hands. 'He did. Darling heart, lie down, please. Don't hurt your head!'

'But you said—'

'Theodosia, your father doesn't care where he's *buried*. His spirit is free, in heaven with Christ and his saints; I do believe that.'

Theodosia lay down, blinking at tears. 'Can I see where he's buried?' she asked after a silence.

Anna shook her head. 'The Studion is a monastery, my love. They don't let women in. I asked once if I could see his grave, but they said no.'

'You said you visited him there after I was born. You said he got to hold me.'

'And he did! It made him very happy, and he said that you

23

were the most beautiful little girl in all the world. But that wasn't in the monastery itself. They have a room where the monks can meet visitors, and the abbot decided to let your father see us there. The grave is somewhere further in, where women aren't allowed.'

'I hate the Emperor,' whispered Theodosia.

'Shhh!' Anna told her severely. 'My lamb, you must never, *never* say things like that. It's treason. And anyway, Our Lord Constantine wasn't emperor when it happened. He was just a boy. He couldn't have stopped it even if he tried. For all I know he *did* try. You mustn't blame him for something that was his father's fault.'

Theodosia subsided. She kept blinking, however, and eventually the tears overflowed her eyes and ran down her face and into the pillow. 'I wish my father was alive,' she whispered. 'I wish I could remember him. I don't even know what he looked like!'

'I've told you about him,' Anna pointed out gently.

'Yes, but it's not the *same*!' Theodosia wiped her face with the sheet. 'I wanted to see him *myself*.'

Anna could think of nothing to say to that. She stroked her daughter's hair off her face. 'Who told you there was a statue of your father in the Church of the Holy Apostles?' she asked at last.

'Maria,' Theodosia replied at once. Maria was one of Theodosia's fellow-lutenists, a gawky, elbowy thirteen-year-old with straight dark hair. Her father was a baker.

'She went to church there at the Feast of St Andrew, and she saw this statue labelled Theodosius, and she asked her father if it was my father. He said he thought it was. So we all went there, and we agreed that it had to be him.'

Anna knew that 'we all' undoubtedly meant Theodosia, Maria and the other member of the trio, Sophia. She nodded, suddenly aware of Theodosia's separate life, of conversations about fathers and mothers, chores and ambitions, which would never be disclosed to a parent. It was natural that Theodosia's father should form a subject for the girls' discussions. He was by far the most exciting topic available to them. Everyone in Constantinople knew about him: Theodosius, son

24

of Constantine and grandson of Heraclius, a prince born in the purple, forced into holy orders and then unjustly put to death by his jealous older brother. All the neighbourhood knew, too, that Theodosia was his daughter, born out of wedlock. Of course the girls were fascinated. Of course Theodosia longed to know more.

'You went there today?' Anna asked in concern. 'Didn't Maria and Sophia stay with you after the accident? They weren't hurt as well, were they?'

Theodosia wiped her face again. 'They weren't there today. It was days ago when the three of us went. Today I was by myself. The music lesson was cancelled, see: the tutor left a message saying he was ill. Maria and Sophia went home, but I was tired of the roses, so I decided to go look at my father again. So I went up to the church, and I looked at him for a bit, and then I realized I was going to be late and ran out.' She looked at her mother. 'And now you say it isn't him at all.'

'It isn't him,' Anna agreed sadly. 'I wish it was.'

Two

Theodosia was feeling much better next morning, and by evening was eager to get out of bed, even if it meant having to strip rose heads. Anna, however, insisted that she wait out the full period recommended by the doctor. When Theodosia's friends came to visit the following afternoon, though, she relaxed her strictness enough to allow them upstairs with the lute.

The sound of lute-playing, interspersed with giggles, was drifting down from the bedroom when Kallinikos turned up late in the afternoon. Anna let him into the shop, and he looked up at the ceiling with surprised interest. 'Is that your daughter?' he asked.

'Her and her friends,' said Anna, with a resigned smile. 'As you can hear, she's feeling better.'

'I was going to ask how she was. I'm glad to hear her laughing.' He beamed at Anna as though he'd worked the cure himself.

She found his smile presumptuous and irritating. 'Your cloak's clean,' she told him shortly. 'I'll fetch it.'

She had noticed when she dropped it off at the fullers' that it was, as he had said, a good cloak – heavy wool, dyed a dark red, and decorated with patterned medallions and borders in yellow and black. It was unmistakably costly, and probably worth more than the ambix. She came back to the shop with it folded carefully over an arm, but when she gave it to the Syrian, he slung it casually over an oil-stained shoulder. *Not used to looking after his things*, she confirmed to herself. *Used to having servants.*

'I've got the ambix set up in a spare room at the Arsenal,'

he told Anna, with the air of a man imparting important information.

'Not at your house?' she asked, without real interest.

He rolled his eyes. 'I don't have a house. I have a room. I'm not allowed to *cook* in it, and if the landlord caught me setting up to practise alchemy he'd probably pitch the ambix out the window, and me after it.' He laughed, but with an edge of bitterness. 'Or rather, he'd have his man do it: he wouldn't dirty his own hands on a *tenant*. I tell you the truth, I never appreciated the misery of the poor until I left home. This room I have . . . no, you don't want to listen to me complaining, do you? I won't.'

'"Home" is . . . Heliopolis, you said, didn't you?' asked Anna, and ventured the question that had intrigued her from the moment she heard his accent. 'When did you leave Syria?'

'Last autumn,' he told her. 'Got through the Hellespont just ahead of Mu'awiya's fleet.'

She had heard the name of the Caliph before, but never pronounced like that. 'Mauias' was what most people said. But, of course, the Caliph ruled Syria. His subjects *would* know how to pronounce his name properly.

'The shipping up the coast was all to ruin,' Kallinikos continued. 'I got to Cyprus, but I couldn't find anyone to take me north. Eventually I had to enlist as an oarsman on a naval supply galley. That got me as far as Smyrna – I reached the city about a month after it fell. Then I deserted and hiked up into the hills until I met some imperial troops who were retreating north.' He laughed. 'I tell you the truth: they almost killed me. They thought I was one of the Caliph's men, and the only reason I didn't get an arrow through the heart was because they wanted to question me.' He shook his head, grinning. 'When I told them I was a deserter trying to get to Constantinople, they didn't believe me. Eventually I managed to convince their captain, but even so they insisted on tying me up every night, just in case. Mother of God, it was cold, too! It was winter by then, and we were up in the mountains. I was afraid my hands would freeze off. Anyway, we marched across country as far as Pergamum, and then we took the road to Cyzicus. We stayed there until the spring, helping out with the preparations for the Caliph's attack. Then my companions put me on a ship to Constantinople, and I thought my troubles were over.' He laughed again. 'The officials at the docks here almost put me straight onto the first ship out. "We don't need any more Syrian beggars here," they said. "You can go fight the Slavs in Thessalonika." But I showed them my letters from Cyzicus and from the Smyrna captain, and I told them that I was an engineer specializing in incendiaries, and eventually they agreed I could work at the Arsenal.'

Anna was off balance, impressed despite herself by the story. '*Are* you an engineer specializing in incendiaries?' she asked, grasping at the last item in the flood of unsolicited information.

Kallinikos nodded vigorously. 'That's the intention, anyway. In Baalbek – Heliopolis, I mean: most people there use the country name these days – in Heliopolis I mostly worked on irrigation systems, like my father, but I wanted to work on fire. I've always loved fire. The trouble is, incendiaries are military engineering, and I couldn't very well offer to help the Caliph kill Christians. So . . .' He spread his arms sweepingly. 'Here I am!'

The freshly cleaned cloak, jarred by the movement, fell off his shoulder on to the floor. They both bent to pick it up, then both stopped, each waiting for the other. Kallinikos moved first: he grinned, picked up the cloak, and flung it once more over his shoulder, even more untidily this time. Anna decided that his chances of getting it home clean and unstepped-upon were slim.

He 'wanted to work on fire'? Of all the reasons she could imagine to leave a home where you had money and comfort and undertake a desperate winter journey through the middle of a war to a strange city, that was surely the most bizarre. She supposed, though, that to an aspiring military engineer, wars were opportunities, and sieges were where you had to go to get advancement. It was a repellent thought. She tried not to think of the approaching war, but whenever her efforts failed, she was gripped by a sick, helpless panic. A generation before, the Arabs had swept out of disregarded desert to attack the empire. For nearly forty years the empire had fought – and for nearly forty years, had lost every battle. Two-thirds of the empire had fallen, including Syria and Egypt, the richest and most populous provinces. Now the Arab fleet had reached the Hellespont, and only Constantinople and the impoverished and beleaguered north were left to oppose them. Give them one year, or perhaps two, to consolidate their position and build up supplies, and then the siege would begin. How would it end?

She had so many hopes for the future. She wanted to see Theodosia married to a handsome, good-natured young husband; she wanted to compound a new perfume and maybe see it sold in the grand shops on the Milion; she wanted to live happily in the respect due to a successful businesswoman and the grandmother of a loving family. What would become of all her hopes and plans if the city fell? Would she live to become a slave in her own shop, and see Theodosia, raped by soldiers, dying young in a public brothel?

It suddenly occurred to Anna that she was speaking to someone who had lived his life as a subject of the Arabs, who knew what they were like. She had never spoken to anyone like that before.

'What are they like?' she asked abruptly.

'You mean the Muslims?' Kallinikos hesitated. 'Everyone asks me that.' He spread his hands. 'And then when I answer, people get angry.'

'I won't get angry,' Anna promised.

'Very well, then.' The Syrian flashed her another grin, this one nervous. 'They're not monsters. Despite what you may have heard, they don't eat babies—'

'I didn't believe they did!' Anna said impatiently. 'The only people who tell stories like that are the ones who don't know anything. What are they *like*?'

He shrugged. 'They're people. They love their children and their wives; they lose their tempers about the same things we do, and the same sort of things make them happy. People here call them heretics and enemies of God, but—'

'They *are* heretics, aren't they? Aren't they Arians?'

29

Kallinikos grimaced. 'Everyone says that, but I've never seen it. You have to be a Christian to be a heretic, even an Arian heretic, and the Muslims never were. They worship the same God as us, the God of Abraham, but they think Jesus Christ was just a prophet, and that their own prophet Mohammed was more important. They're very devout, though: *they* certainly don't see themselves as being enemies of God! Look, to me Constantinopolitans are stranger even than the Khawarij out of the desert: you people bewilder me all the time. We Syrians are Arabs ourselves, really, for all that we were part of the empire for so many centuries. We learn Greek, but Arabic is much easier for us: it's very similar to our own Aramaic. For us it's actually *easier* to answer to a caliph instead of an emperor.'

'I heard that a lot of Syrians are converting to the Mohammedan sect.' Anna, mindful of her promise not to become angry, kept her voice carefully neutral.

Kallinikos shrugged. 'That's true. Well, they *won*. Most people believe that God is the giver of victory, don't they? Me, I think wars are human things from start to finish – but there aren't many who agree with me. Even here they believe God chooses the victors, only here they say that God is punishing the Christians for some impiety or other. People in Syria look at all the Muslim victories and draw their own conclusion. On top of that, as I said, the Muslims are mostly very devout. They give alms generously, they don't drink wine, and they pray five times a day. People are impressed with it. Nobody's forced to convert to Islam, though. In fact, that's actually *discouraged*, because Muslims don't have to pay taxes. The Arabian Muslims even get a salary from the state, paid for by taxes on infidels. They're human: they're not eager to convert infidels if it means they lose money! They don't try to tell Christians how to worship, either: everyone's free to believe whatever theology he thinks is best. Not like here, where anyone who doesn't believe what the emperor believes can be charged with heresy. The Arabians aren't oppressive rulers, either. Heliopolis is still run by our own city officials, and we're judged by our own magistrates. There are plenty of Christian officials even at the Caliph's court.

Most people in Baalbek say things are *better* now than when we were ruled by the Emperor.'

If that was his usual answer to the question, thought Anna, it wasn't surprising that people in the city got angry with him. 'If life under the Mohammedans was so good,' she remarked sourly, 'I'm surprised you left it.'

'Oh, well,' he said dismissively. 'As I said, I wanted to work on fire, and I couldn't help them kill Christians. I was raised orthodox, and I'm not going to convert just because the Muslims won a war. And besides . . .' He paused, then went on, in a rush, 'And besides, what right do they have to rule the *world*? All their wars have been to seize lands that don't belong to them. Nobody even pretends otherwise! They're not interested in peace or negotiations: all they want is conquest. They think Islam is *entitled* to the whole world, that God himself has decreed that everyone on earth should be subject to the Caliph and pay the Faithful their big fat salaries. They believe that any city or province that resists that fate deserves a worse one. I said they're not oppressive rulers, and it's true, but their wars are . . . are *worse* than oppressive. Cities are being sacked and people are being killed and enslaved, and farmers and their families are dying of starvation because their crops have been burned – I saw it in the hills round Smyrna. God! People were eating grass, and one family we met had buried all their five children, one after another. The poor mother had gone mad: she just sat there hugging a bundle of rags and singing lullabies to it. It was horrible. They do all these evil things, but they think that God is on their side, so they don't need to feel any shame or guilt. They think that they are the only ones in the world who are virtuous, and everyone else is a villain. They think the fact that they keep winning proves that they're *right*. They're wrong.'

'Winning doesn't prove anything,' Anna told him, remembering the death of her lover Theodosius with a flare of the old rage. 'I agree with you about that, even if no one else does. If the strong defeat the weak, it doesn't mean they're right, it just means they're strong. God's justice – real justice – doesn't depend on worldly good fortune.'

Kallinikos' eyes lit. 'Exactly! If God was on the side of

31

whoever's stronger, he'd be nothing more than the friend of whoever's the biggest bully.'

They looked at one another a moment in agreement and approval.

'Do you think the city is strong enough to withstand them?' Anna asked. Even as she spoke, she knew that she was asking purely in the hope that he would say, *Oh, yes, easily!* Then she could take his words out in the dark of the night sometime, when she lay awake worrying about the future, and use them for her comfort.

'When I first saw it, I thought it was strong enough to withstand the devil himself!' exclaimed Kallinikos. 'I'd heard about the walls of Constantinople, but I'd always thought the stories were exaggerated.' Then he hesitated, frowning. 'I wish there were more people, though. I never imagined there could be so many empty houses in a living town.'

It was not the unconditional reassurance she'd hoped for. Anna made a face. She rarely thought about all the empty houses in the city. She had grown up with them. It seemed only natural and convenient that between the bustling main streets the land should be given over to ruins and open fields. Where else would people grow vegetables or pasture their goats? 'Surely Heliopolis has empty houses too?' she protested.

'Not to speak of,' the Syrian replied at once. 'Property inside the city walls is worth money, and if a house *is* standing empty, somebody's sure to buy it for something. In this city, though, the people rattle around inside the walls like . . . like a baby's foot in a man's boot! If the Arabians manage to get a force established on this side of the Bosphorus, it will be hard for the city to find the troops to man the whole extent of the walls.'

Anna tried to imagine a city with no empty houses in it, no fields. It was difficult: she had never been out of Constantinople in her life. 'My grandmother once told me,' she said slowly, 'that the city used to eat bread baked with grain from Egypt. She said it was given away free to all the citizens! Then, when Egypt fell, there wasn't enough to eat, and people had to leave or starve.'

'That's what I heard,' Kallinikos agreed, and sighed. 'Well, the city is what it is. It will have to be strong enough.' He met Anna's eyes and added, 'If it isn't, I'm dead. The Caliph executes deserters. But we shouldn't be talking like this, Mistress Anna. I came to collect my cloak, and to tell you that I can pay the first instalment on the ambix at the end of the week.'

She stared at him, nonplussed. 'I *gave* you the ambix.'

He stared a moment. 'You did? I thought you just meant I didn't need to leave the cloak.'

'I gave you the ambix,' Anna repeated patiently. 'In thanks to you for rescuing my daughter and bringing her home.'

Kallinikos beamed. 'I'm in your debt.' Then he stopped smiling again suddenly. 'No, no! I can't take a valuable gift like that from a poor widow.'

Anna raised her eyebrows. 'I am not a "poor widow". I am a successful businesswoman. And *you* are no longer . . . whatever it is you were in Heliopolis. You're a penniless refugee. You're the one in need of charity, not me!'

Kallinikos struck his forehead with the heel of a hand. 'Ouch! I forgot!'

She laughed. 'Take your cloak and go! I have work to do.'

'Oh, Mistress Anna, no!' he exclaimed, suddenly laughing back. 'Not yet, anyway! I have to ask you about scents!'

'What about them?' she demanded impatiently.

He spread his hands helplessly, then hastily caught his cloak before it fell off again. 'This is what happened,' he began eagerly. 'Last night I put some water in the ambix and set it on the fire, just to see how well it worked. And the room – the *whole room* – began to smell of hot marjoram!' He paused, then added diffidently, 'At least, I *think* it was marjoram. I'm not good with scents. It might have been some other herb. But you said you'd used the ambix to steam marjoram, didn't you?'

'It would have been marjoram,' Anna told him. 'So?'

'It was a clean, empty ambix!' exclaimed Kallinikos. 'The water was from the cistern at the Arsenal; all it smelled of was mud. Where did the *smell* come from?'

'The ambix,' Anna replied at once. 'It's old and scratched, and you can't get it completely clean any more. If you put your hand inside it and rub, the scent will come off on your fingers. I expect, though, that if you've boiled water in it, all you'll smell next time is mud.'

'I was *amazed*!' the Syrian told her. 'I had no idea that scented materials were so powerful, that a film on a scratched pot can still perfume a whole room. I'm still amazed! But you obviously knew that smells are like that. You told me the ambix would be no use for perfume-making after it had been used for alchemy.'

Anna shrugged. 'If you anoint yourself with oil after a bath, you don't have to use much, do you?'

'No!' he agreed, grinning with delight. 'I didn't think of it, but a couple of palmfuls of oil rubbed over a man's body must amount to much the same thing as a film of grease on the inside of an empty pot – and with scented oil, everyone would be complaining if that amount *didn't* leave them smelling good.'

'I'll tell you something more,' Anna went on, warming to the topic. 'When you buy that perfumed oil, there will only be a spoonful or so of real scent in the whole bottle. Half an ounce of myrrh or balsam, a few drops of mint or marjoram essence – that's all it needs. The rest will be ordinary olive oil – or almond or balanos oil, if your perfume is expensive. Or take rose water: a few drops of attar of roses in a quart of plain water will be enough to scent a whole banqueting hall!' She gestured at the workshop behind her. 'You saw how many roses we process, but at the end of the season, the fragrance of all of them will fit into a single large jar!'

'Really?' Kallinikos asked, his eyes shining. 'Could I see it?'

Anna shrugged, now slightly embarrassed. 'If you like.' She frowned. 'Why are you so interested, anyway?'

'Because it's *interesting*,' the Syrian replied at once. 'I never knew scented materials were so powerful.' He scratched his beard, then continued earnestly, 'When I came before, you said that heat kills scents – but that can't be right. I never noticed any scent from the ambix until I put it on the fire.'

'I realized that, too,' Anna admitted. 'After you left. I was wondering if scent is really something that's trapped in a liquid, and gives off its fragrance when it's warmed and becomes air.'

Kallinikos beamed at her. 'That was my hypothesis, too! You'd make a good alchemist.'

'Hah!' exclaimed Anna. 'Why in the world would I want to be an alchemist? I've never yet seen one who was rich. Why should I struggle to turn lead into gold, when I can turn rose petals into gold much more easily?'

He laughed delightedly. 'Rose petals into gold? I like that!'

She curtsied. 'Now, get out. As I said, I have work to do!'

'Yes, Mistress,' he said. Still grinning, he took himself off.

Anna went back into the workshop and found all the workers regarding her with wonder.

'What's the matter?' she demanded impatiently. Even as she asked it, she knew: they'd all heard her laughing with the Syrian. Respectable women never laughed in public, and Anna rarely laughed with anyone even in private. She wasn't in the habit of chattering to acquaintances when there was so much work to do, either. More than that – she *certainly* wasn't in the habit of chattering to men.

'We were talking about scents,' she informed her staff – then despised herself: she had no need to explain herself to them.

'Oh,' said Martina doubtfully.

Anna cursed herself silently. Why in the world had she allowed herself to talk to the alchemist so freely? Now the fellow would become a pest. It had been plain enough that he admired her, and it must have occurred to him that the situation of a penniless refugee could be vastly improved by a liaison with the owner of a successful perfume shop.

She hauled a tray of rose petals out of the rack, banged it angrily against the floor, and began picking off the trapped petals with impatient pinches. Men were a damned nuisance: that was the truth of the matter. They ran everything, and yet a woman could never even *talk* to them without getting into trouble. If she was beautiful, they were always trying to make her their personal property; if she was ugly, they treated her like an animal. Marry one, and the others might leave you alone, but then you were stuck with a master. Worse, all your household and your children would be stuck with him, too.

She glanced up at her household. Zoe was hard at work pressing the last of the oil from the used petals; Helena was sneaking a break, sitting in a corner and fanning her round pink face with an empty tray. She had raised Zoe from childhood, and she'd known Helena for years. She rarely thought of them as slaves, but that's what they were. If she married, her husband would become their master, and he could sell them if he wanted to.

He couldn't sell his wife's children – but he could easily decide that he didn't want to pay for lute lessons or new dresses for another man's bastard. He would barely need his wife's consent to dispose of her children by apprenticeship or marriage. A wife might be able to contest an arrangement she opposed, but it wouldn't be easy, and her protests might be in vain.

No, Anna thought fiercely. *This household doesn't need a master: it has a mistress!* If Kallinikos came back – as she strongly suspected he would – she would be very sharp with him, and send him off. She would tell him she was far too busy to stand about chatting with someone who didn't even have enough money to be a customer. If he was hurt and disappointed – well, it was his own fault for expecting things to which he had no right. Her obligations were to her household and to her daughter, not to some stupid Syrian with crooked teeth.

He turned up again two days later, this time during supper. It was shortly before the rose cart was expected, and the workers were sitting about in the courtyard eating bread and olives and drinking watered wine. Theodosia was with them, so pleased to be allowed to get out of bed and eat real food again that she didn't even complain about the roses. When the shop bell rang, she jumped up and went to answer it without being asked. She came back in a few minutes, smiling.

'It's Kallinikos,' she told her mother. 'You remember, the man who helped me after my accident? He says he wants to talk to you about perfumes.'

Anna frowned. 'Tell him I'm eating supper,' she commanded.

Theodosia gave her a look of surprise and disapproval. '*Mama!* He was really nice to me.'

'Theodosia, I really don't have time for him and his questions!' snapped Anna. 'I want some food before the rose cart gets here. Tell him that.'

Theodosia scowled and stalked back into the shop. Anna looked down at the chunk of bread in her hand. She felt suddenly vastly annoyed and dissatisfied with the world, and she had completely lost her appetite. She forced herself to take a bite anyway. She chewed the bread slowly, then picked up an olive.

Theodosia came back into the courtyard. 'He says can you just tell him how you distil marjoram,' she announced, 'and he wants to know when he can come and see the attar of roses.'

'When he can come and see *what*?'

'He says you promised to let him see the fragrance of all our roses fitting in a single jar,' said Theodosia.

Had she promised that? She supposed she might have done. She stood up, brushing crumbs from her tunic. 'Oh, I'll speak to him!' she exclaimed in disgust. '*Briefly.*' She picked up her cloak on the way through the workshop. As she muffled herself, she was vaguely aware of Theodosia, following behind her, glaring disapproval.

Kallinikos was studying the flasks and bottles that lined the shelves of the perfume shop. The street door behind him was cracked open to the late afternoon sun, and the level golden light showed that he had bathed before coming over: the oil stains on his hands were only faint, and his hair was damp. Anna shook her head in disgust: who did he think he was trying to impress? He turned to her, beaming.

'There you are!' he exclaimed. 'I understand that you're

37

very busy, but please can you tell me how you distil mar-joram?'

'Why?' she demanded, in exasperation. 'Are you planning to make perfume, after all?'

He shook his head. 'No, no, I just want . . . it's just that I'm not actually doing alchemy right now. I don't have enough money to buy the supplies, and anyway, I really wanted the ambix because I have this idea about distillation, and I wanted to check it out. So I thought it would help if I knew all the different ways distillation can be used.'

'What's the idea?' asked Theodosia. She was still behind her mother, and now stood watching from the workshop door.

'It's about fire,' Kallinikos said, turning towards her eagerly. 'About what happens to liquids when you expose them to fiery heat.'

'They boil,' said Anna impatiently.

'Yes, but then they condense into liquid again as they cool,' Kallinikos said enthusiastically, 'only the liquid isn't the same as the one you started out with, not unless it's pure water. Heat salt water, and the condensate is fresh; heat water with lime and sulphur, and you get holy sulphur water; heat resin, and you get turpentine. In each case the condensate has been purged of its earthy parts, and is of a purer and more fiery nature than the material you started out with. We've always known that, of course: alchemy's always relied on repeated heating and distillation to purify base substances. What I don't know is where scents fit in.'

'What good would it do you to know?' asked Anna.

'Maybe none at all!' exclaimed the alchemist happily. 'I can't be sure unless I *do* know. Please? I know you're busy, but can't you tell me *quickly*?'

'You put water in the ambix, pile the marjoram on a rack above the water, put it on a double boiler, and collect the condensate. Part of the condensate is a greenish oil that floats on top of the water: that's what contains the scent. There.'

'You put the marjoram on a *rack*?' the alchemist repeated, frowning intently. 'Not in the water?'

'No. Not for perfume. You can soak herbs in water to

38

make scented water as a hair rinse, or to sprinkle over the floor before a banquet, but then you have to use it within a few days of making it or it goes off.'

He clicked his tongue against his teeth. 'But if you steam the herb and collect the condensate, it doesn't go off? Why's that?'

'*I* don't know!' snapped Anna. 'You asked me a question and I answered it. Now let me eat my supper!'

'No, but it's *interesting*! Where does the herb keep its scent? You said it was an oil, didn't you? If that's part of the watery component of the plant, why does it last when the herb is dried? But if it isn't watery, why does it come out of the leaves along with the steam, which is?'

'I don't know,' said Anna again. 'Maybe it's a mixture.'

He beamed. 'That would be my theory, too! That it's a mixture of elements, like most things, but that scent has more air or fire in it than the rest of the plant. That would explain why it separates when it's exposed to heat.' He nodded to himself. 'That would fit.'

'What are you planning to distil?' Theodosia asked curiously.

He smiled at her. 'Median oil. I think distilled oil might prove to be more flammable than the ordinary sort. It makes sense, see, if repeated distillations really do purge liquids of their earthy parts and make them partake a little of the nature of fire.'

'But Median oil's already flame-able,' objected Theodosia, repeating the new word with a slight hesitation. 'I mean, it burns really well. They use it to heat the Kaminia baths.'

'Yes, but I think if you distil it, it should be *even more* flammable,' Kallinikos told her. '*That* would shut Stephanos up!'

'Who's Stephanos?' asked Anna.

'Magistros of the Arsenal,' said Kallinikos. 'My superior.' He grimaced. 'He's trying to tell me I can't set up the ambix at the Arsenal.'

'I think he has a point!' said Anna. 'The Arsenal must be full of incendiaries, and you're talking about filling my ambix with *Median oil* and bringing it to the boil in the middle of them! What if it catches fire?'

'It'll be on the double boiler!' protested Kallinikos, hurt. 'Over a *low* fire, in an empty storeroom. With a horn attached to the phiali, so that nothing can drip into the flames! And you're wrong anyway, actually. The Arsenal is the safest place in the city to distil the oil. It's the only place that's designed to hold flammable materials safely.'

There was a knock on the open door behind him, and they all looked round to see that the rose cart had come and that the driver was waiting impatiently to unload. Kallinikos sighed. 'I've made you miss your supper,' he told Anna contritely.

'It's all right,' Theodosia reassured him. 'She'd almost finished anyway.'

The Syrian helped them to unload the roses – an easier task than on previous days, since the rose season had passed its peak and the supply was beginning to peter out. As he carried the baskets from the cart into the shop, Theodosia held the doors for him. To Anna it seemed as though they were both talking at the same time.

'We've picked the petals off *thousands* of roses!' said Theodosia, and, 'Your mother says she turns them into gold,' said Kallinikos.

'It must be much *easier* to turn lead into gold!' said the girl, giggling.

An earnest shake of the head. 'Oh, no, no, very much harder, and much more expensive, too. You'd have to make the elixir, and there are only a handful of people who've ever done that.'

'The elixir?'

'It's supposed to be a sort of ferment, like yeast, a thing that renews life in whatever it touches. It can turn base metals into gold, or heal illness or reverse decay . . .'

'Can you really do that?'

'Me? No, not at all! I've never got anywhere near. As I said, hardly anyone has ever made the elixir. I have to admit, most alchemists spend a fortune on supplies and never have an ounce of gold to show for it. Rose petals, I fear, are a much more reliable source of money. They smell better, too.'

Theodosia laughed.

'That was *most* improper!' Anna scolded, when he had

gone and the two of them were back in the workshop stripping rose heads.

Theodosia scowled. 'Mama, he was really *nice* to me! And he's *interesting*!'

'Theodosia, all he wants is—'

'You're just scared that he might fall in love with you!' Theodosia declared loudly. 'When I had my accident he was really kind to me. I was sick and scared, and he held my hand and told me everything would be all right and he'd get me home straight away. And he doesn't know hardly anyone in the city; he's only been here a couple of months. All he wants is some friends to talk to! You don't have to be *mean* to him, just because you're beautiful!'

Anna swallowed, startled and strangely ashamed. At heart she knew that she was often 'mean' to men, just because she was beautiful – and she hated it in herself. As a girl she'd been open, eager and affectionate, and she still felt that way *inside*, but knew that to the world she was guarded, suspicious and severe.

She remembered the way the Syrian had begun to complain about his lodgings, then stopped himself; she thought of the eagerness with which he'd launched into his idea about fire. Theodosia was right: the man was lonely, and wanted someone to talk to. He *was* interesting, too. What he had said about the Arabs was something she'd found herself repeating to other acquaintances, and his questions about the nature of scents fascinated her. She . . . yes, she would admit it, she *liked* him. She wouldn't mind seeing more of him. She just didn't want him in love with her.

'Theodosia!' exclaimed Martina indignantly. 'That's no way to speak to your mother!'

Theodosia stuck out her lower lip and glared at the pile of roses in front of her. 'Sorry,' she muttered, not sounding it.

'You have a point,' Anna told her softly, and the girl looked up again in surprise.

'You have a point,' Anna repeated. 'I think he does mostly just want friends to talk to. But, love, I don't think unmarried men and women *can* just be friends.'

'You don't know that he's unmarried,' objected Theodosia.

41

'Maybe he's got a wife in Heliopolis, who's going to join him as soon as she can.'

Anna, surprised, wondered if Theodosia was right. Men of Kallinikos' age were usually married – unless they were monks or very devout, which he clearly wasn't; or too poor to afford it, which might be the case now, but which she doubted had been true in Heliopolis.

She found, though, that she did not believe there was any wife waiting to sail from Heliopolis. She remembered the alchemist's account of his desperate journey to Constantinople: no, there would be no woman arriving that way. And now the Arabs had reached the Hellespont, there would be no ships coming from the Mediterranean at all, not for many years to come – not unless the city fell, and if that happened, Kallinikos would be executed as a deserter. If Kallinikos had a wife, he had abandoned her – but it was more likely that she was dead.

If he had recently lost her, his decision to abandon his home city and his family and set out for Constantinople to 'work on fire' suddenly made a lot more sense.

'Anyway,' said Theodosia, 'even if you don't want to be friends with him, *I* like him. I hope he comes back soon.'

In fact, he turned up again the following evening. The visit was even later than the previous one: they were all in the workshop stripping rose heads when there was a most tremendous jangling of the bell, followed by a thumping on the shop door. Theodosia went to answer it and gave an exclamation of alarm.

Anna jumped up and hurried into the shop. Standing in the doorway, clinging to the frame, was a black-faced red-eyed creature stinking of singed hair. As Anna came in, it grinned at her, and at the flash of crooked teeth she recognized Kallinikos.

'Merciful Mother!' exclaimed Anna, shocked and concerned. 'You're hurt! You didn't set fire to the Arsen—'

'It worked!' he shouted, in a voice so hoarse that she was unsure whether the tone was one of anguish or of disbelief.

'Come and sit down!' Anna ordered. Gingerly she took hold of his grimy arm and led him into the workshop, causing the workers to drop their work in horror at the sight.

'It worked!' Kallinikos exclaimed again, thumping down on a three-legged stool. 'The distilled oil worked *perfectly*! It went WHOOMPF!' He flung both blackened hands out so enthusiastically he almost tipped the stool over. 'The *vapour* caught, just from the lamp! And then it set the condensate on fire, and it all blazed up. All of it at once! It was like a lightning bolt!'

'Are you hurt?' Anna asked uncertainly.

'No, no! Well, maybe a little. I thought it would be flammable, but I never expected it to be so flammable it all went up at once! WHOOMPF! It was amazing!'

'Fetch some water!' Anna ordered Helena.

'Oh, I didn't come here to . . . to ask for help!' exclaimed the Syrian, showing his teeth again. 'You don't have to . . . it's just that it was so *fabulous*, the way it burned, and . . . and I couldn't think of anyone else to tell about it!'

'What happened to your beard?' asked Theodosia in awe. 'Did it catch fire?'

'Just singed,' he told her, with a dismissive wave.

Helena hurried over with a bucket of water and a sponge. She scuttled up to the alchemist sideways, like a crab, set the bucket down, and backed off hastily. Kallinikos pulled the bucket in front of himself and began mopping his face with the sponge. He glanced down as he rinsed it, then stared at the black grease that covered it and exclaimed, 'Oh, the holy martyrs!' He looked up at Anna ruefully. 'I'm a mess, aren't I?'

'Yes,' agreed Anna, fighting an urge to laugh.

'Sorry.' He wiped his face with the sponge again, smearing the grime without removing much of it. 'No wonder people were staring. Sorry. I just didn't know anyone else to tell.'

'Theodosia,' ordered Anna, 'fetch some oil. Plain olive oil, to help the gentleman clean up, and some soap as well – and a little lavender oil for his burns.' As the girl hurried to obey, Anna glanced around her workers, all of whom were regarding the Syrian with horrified wonder. She knew that Martina, at least, had decided that the man was quite mad.

43

'The gentleman is an engineer at the Arsenal,' she told them, defending him, 'and he was devising a new sort of incendiary to use against the enemies of the city. We should all be pleased that it works.'

Kallinikos looked back at her quickly, reddened eyes not merely grateful, but full of hope, and Anna cursed herself silently. Why in the world had she given him that encouragement? She'd never be able to get rid of him now.

Three

S he later decided that encouraging Kallinikos hadn't been as much of a mistake as it seemed at the time. He was perfectly capable of making a nuisance of himself without it: like a devoted dog, he would thrust himself in unless he was actively pushed away. Anna would have considered it an act of hostility to send away an acquaintance who'd arrived at the workshop with a burned face, but Kallinikos seemed to take the gift of a sponge and a flask of lavender oil as signs of true friendship. He turned up at the shop almost every evening after that, full of the progress of the Median oil distillation project and questions about scents. He seemed to assume now that he was welcome, and need no further evidence to confirm it.

It wasn't entirely his fault. It was clear that as far as Theodosia was concerned, his assumption was entirely correct. She was always glad to see him: she listened to his alchemical theories with every sign of interest, and in return told him all about her music lessons. It emerged that he'd had music lessons himself for many years – a fact that again confirmed Anna's belief that he came from a good family, and had had the usual upper-class education. When Theodosia showed him the lute, he denied that he'd ever been very good. He was, however, still able to give her a few pointers.

'It's very improper!' Martina hissed at Anna when he provided the pointers, on his third or fourth visit. 'You should order him to leave at once, or he'll seduce your daughter!'

Anna looked at her incredulously, then looked at Kallinikos and Theodosia, who were sitting in a corner of the workshop with the lute. The Syrian had given up trying to make himself presentable once he saw that his efforts failed to impress, and he had, as usual, come to visit on his way back from work. He was dressed in his oil-stained tunic and leather apron, which were gradually becoming even shabbier and more disreputable from being worn every day and rinsed out evenings. The burns on his face, though not serious, had begun to peel, and he looked as though he'd trimmed his singed hair and beard with pruning shears. He demonstrated something on the lute, then handed the instrument back to Theodosia. She rubbed off the neck of the instrument with her scarf and made some comment about oil that made him grin in apology.

'I don't think so,' said Anna. 'Martina, how can you think that scarecrow is seductive? And anyway, she's a *child*!'

'Not for much longer!' said Martina darkly.

Anna shook her head impatiently. 'I'm quite certain that he sees her as a child. If I order him to leave it will simply hurt and bewilder both of them. Then, in a year or so, if I had to warn her of a real danger, she wouldn't take me seriously.'

She did not add another thing she was certain of: that if Kallinikos tried to seduce anyone, it would be herself. She'd seen the signs too often to be mistaken: the silent looks of admiration, the smiling leaps to assist, the thousand small attempts to impress her with his intelligence and his strength and his helpfulness. She strongly suspected that Theodosia had noticed it too – and that she was *deliberately* encouraging the man. *What was the girl about?* she asked herself impatiently.

In answer, a horrifying possibility occurred to her: the girl might have decided that Kallinikos would make a good stepfather.

After all, Theodosia was at a difficult age, too old to take things for granted but not old enough to be properly suspicious: she might well believe a stepfather would be a good thing. Her friends all had fathers, and those fathers – and their wives – had often made it clear that they regarded an all-female household as vulnerable and weak, and never mind the fact that Anna's business was the most profitable in the neighbourhood. Oh, the neighbours were never unpleasant about their opinion; in fact, it usually emerged when the men

46

offered help or protection – but still, the assumption was that a household headed by a woman was inferior and unnatural. Of course Theodosia would notice; of course she'd mind. She was perfectly capable of deciding that her mother ought to marry, and she liked Kallinikos. She had no idea, Anna thought grimly, of how much power a stepfather would have over her. The fact that he was likeable *now* meant nothing. Likeable men could become monsters, once they had authority.

I'm not having him, Anna promised herself, *whatever Theodosia thinks she wants*.

Fortunately, the question didn't arise. Kallinikos did not make any overt advances, despite all his smiling attempts to impress and all of Theodosia's encouragement. Anna guessed that he was too embarrassed about his poverty.

Because of that, she made a point of reminding him, in various small ways, that yes, he *was* poor – far too poor to approach a beautiful and successful woman like herself. If she offered him food during a visit, it was always with a suggestion that he couldn't afford it at home; when she gave him advice about the city, she included directions about what was free or very cheap. She made sympathetic enquiries about his lodgings, and jokes about his shabby clothes and his ragged haircut. He laughed at the comments, but he always winced as well. It did gall him, she was sure of it, but she hardened her heart. He made an interesting friend, but she was determined that he would never become anything more.

She was uncomfortably aware, though, that Kallinikos' poverty really did seem to be unjust. He was not, as she'd first assumed, doing menial work at the Arsenal. Apparently he'd demonstrated so much understanding of incendiaries that he'd been appointed to take charge of their production. He had not, however, been given the title and salary that should have gone with his responsibilities: those were kept by his superior, Stephanos. What was more, Stephanos had insisted on a large bribe before supplying the refugee with the necessary permit to remain in the city. Since Kallinikos had arrived penniless, he had to pay this in instalments from the meager salary he did receive. In consequence, he was unable even to afford

47

lodgings near the Arsenal, like most of his fellow workers. Instead he had taken a single room in a tenement near the Platea Gate, and walked two miles across the city every day to reach his place of work.

'Oh, the *walk* is all right!' he told Theodosia, when she commented on it. 'I *like* the walk.'

'It's the cheap lodging he hates,' Anna supplied. 'A pity you can't afford something better.'

Kallinikos duly winced, though he smiled gamely. 'I like seeing the city,' he said, sidestepping the thrust. 'All the monuments, and the magnificent churches full of holy relics. Besides, if I hadn't had to walk to the Arsenal every day, I would never have met you. I noticed your shop every day as I walked past it, and so when I had the afternoon off I thought, well, why not go in and ask about distilling equipment?' He smiled widely at both Anna and her daughter. 'And now, when I start home, I look forward to seeing my friends along the way.'

By the middle of July, the Syrian had firmly established himself as a friend of the family. Even Martina had stopped urging Anna to send him off, though she still regarded him with suspicion and disapproval. Zoe and Helena, in contrast, had decided that he was an eccentric who could, on occasion, provide useful advice. When the rose season ended and he came to see the attar collected, he had suggested a new collecting tool, a funnel-shaped spoon, which made it easier to separate the last drops of oil from the water used to wash the trays. He helped Anna choose a new ambix to replace the one she had given him, and bullied the glass-maker to improve the design of the phiali.

In the middle of July Anna even found herself giving Kallinikos' family-friend status public recognition. On the Emperor's birthday, a public holiday, there was racing in the hippodrome. Kallinikos expressed a desire to see it, and Theodosia at once declared, 'You can come with us!'

Anna hadn't been planning to go at all, and certainly wouldn't have invited Kallinikos, but she allowed herself to be persuaded. ('Oh, *Mama*, you know it's *fun*! Sophia and Maria are going! And Kallinikos says he's never ever *seen* chariot racing!') On the morning of the races, however, as she packed a basket of food for the day, she regretted her stupidity. True, she'd mentioned to some of the neighbours that she'd befriended the Syrian who'd helped her daughter – she'd told them that, poor man, he was a penniless Christian refugee and had no other friends in the city. Still, what would they think when they saw him escorting her to the races? She hadn't had a man escort her anywhere since her father died: a woman who had borne a child out of wedlock had to be twice as careful of her reputation as anyone else. She hoped that the Syrian would turn up in his usual ragged state, so that everyone would understand that she was only being charitable.

He did not. When he arrived at the shop, slightly early on the sunny July morning, he had made another attempt to improve his appearance. His tunic was almost clean, and his hair and beard actually seemed to have been trimmed by a barber. He was, moreover, wearing his good cloak and a gold ring. For once he looked, as well as sounded, like a gentleman.

Theodosia, who'd been arguing with her mother over whether she should wear a cloak, broke off, then applauded. Kallinikos bowed.

'You're going to be terribly hot in that, though,' Theodosia told him. 'It's wool!' She had been insisting that it was far too hot for her to wear more than a tunic.

'I have no choice except to wear it,' he replied. 'I have to look my best in the company of two such beautiful women.'

Anna snorted, and Theodosia laughed. 'Mama's trying to make me wear a cloak, too,' she confided.

'She's right, you should,' he agreed at once. 'A girl as pretty as you, in just that tunic? It would distract the chariot drivers. It could cause a nasty accident.'

She giggled and rolled her eyes, but put on the cloak. It was a summer cloak, of fine bleached linen, little more than a shawl: Anna, who was already muffled in heavy black, rather envied her.

Anna handed the basket of food to Zoe, who was coming

49

along to attend them while Helena remained at home, and they set out.

The Middle Street was already crowded with people jostling along to the same destination as themselves: well-dressed families carrying small children; ragged boys darting between sturdy labourers; rowdy groups of young men chanting the slogans of the racing factions; demure young women holding the arms of their fathers or brothers. Theodosia glanced around constantly until she spotted Maria and her family ahead of them, then pelted through the crowd to join her friend. Maria's family obligingly stopped to wait for Anna's party.

'Good health,' Anna said politely to Maria's parents as she caught up with them.

'Good health,' echoed Johannes and Eudokia. They looked curiously at Kallinikos.

'This is our friend Kallinikos,' Theodosia informed them. 'He's never seen chariot racing.'

'Never?' exclaimed Johannes the baker, horrified, and at once began explaining the sport, to Kallinikos' bemusement.

'So, that's Kallinikos,' said Eudokia, falling into step with Anna. 'Theodosia's told us about him, but she didn't mention that he was a gentleman.'

Anna shrugged, embarrassed. 'He doesn't usually dress like one. He's a poor refugee, new to the city, and he doesn't have much money. I think that cloak's the only valuable thing he owns. It's an act of charity to take him to the races, really.'

Eudokia, a plump pink woman, dimpled shrewdly. 'Don't worry, neighbour, I never for a moment thought there was anything *improper* going on. Everyone in Philadelphion knows that you're a respectable woman!'

Anna bit her lip, annoyed that her worry had been so obvious. 'My reputation matters to me,' she admitted.

'Of course it does!' agreed Eudokia. 'I don't see any harm in your refugee, though. Why, from what Theodosia's said, he's a good Christian, to come here to the city to help us against the heretics, and I'm sure it's good and charitable of you to befriend him. And I'm not surprised that your girl's

50

adopted him. She doesn't have any uncles, does she? Mine adore their uncles.'

This view of things had not occurred to Anna. She had had an uncle herself, and a brother – both dead now, the uncle in the wars, the brother while young, of a fever. She had adored both of them. She glanced at Theodosia, who was now chattering happily to Maria and Maria's two young brothers, and wondered whether that might not, after all, be what the girl wanted: a male relative to liven up a dull female house. 'I used to love my uncle,' she admitted. 'He used to come back from service with the fleet and tell us stories.'

'Mine used to give us sweets,' said Eudokia, and they walked on happily discussing families.

The street grew still more crowded as they proceeded, and more people poured into it from the different neighbourhoods of Constantinople. Thin whores and their pimps slunk out of the alleys near the Amastrianon Market and solicited the men in the crowd; well-to-do shopkeepers from the Breadmarket and the New Town strolled arm in arm with their wives; rich merchants from the Forum of Constantine strutted in brocade, surrounded by their slaves. Hawkers sold fruit and bread and sausages; water-sellers rattled cups against the amphora that held their wares; filthy holy men denounced the vanity of the world and called on the holiday throng to repent and give alms. The whole great noisy crowd poured down the Middle Street – past the markets; past the Tower of the Winds; past the porphyry column where the golden statue of the emperor Constantine the Great stood gazing proudly down on the city he had founded; through the marble splendours of the Augusteion Market – and finally, swinging right in a great noisy throng, through the dark arches of the towering hippodrome.

As always, the huge crowd seemed to dwindle once it passed through the colossal entranceway. Anna, crowding along with the others to the spot near the turning posts where the people from Philadelphion usually sat, looked up at the rows of empty places suspended above her, and wondered if once the city had filled them. She supposed it had: otherwise, why build so many? She remembered again what Kallinikos

51

had said about the population of Constantinople being like a baby's foot in his father's boot, and felt an odd, disturbing sense of diminishment.

Rumour said that the armies of the Caliph were as numberless as the stars of heaven. Constantinople couldn't even fill the hippodrome. What would happen when the Arab fleet sailed to the Bosphorus?

No one else seemed to feel small. Theodosia and Maria spotted their friend Sophia, sitting with her family in the middle of a crowded bench near the front of the section claimed by the neighbourhood. They called to her eagerly, but there was no space on the bench for them to join her. Sophia waved, then spoke to her parents. Her father, Theodore, looked a question at Johannes and Eudokia; Johannes grinned, cupped his hands round his mouth and bellowed, 'Let her join us! We'll look after her!'

Sophia was duly allowed to scramble over five rows of spectators to reach her friends. The girls embraced and at once began chattering together. The rest of the party began unpacking cushions, drinks, and fans, and settling itself on the bench.

Below them on the great racetrack, attendants were still sweeping the packed earth and checking the mechanism for the starting gates. The imperial box above the finish line, halfway down the stadium on their left, was still empty, though attendants were busy there as well, and the seats around it were beginning to fill up with courtiers: even from a distance the onlookers could see the glitter of jewels and the flutter of silks. Kallinikos stood up to see better, then jumped up on the bench to gaze about himself in awe and delight. 'This is magnificent!' he cried. With a sweep of the arm, he indicated the crowd, the shining monuments that lined the spine of the racetrack, the majestic piles of the hippodrome itself. 'This is what I *thought* Constantinople would be like!'

People on all the benches around turned to look at him. 'Yes, yes!' exclaimed Anna, embarrassed. 'Sit down!'

He sat down beside her, smiling, and began to ask about the monuments.

More people trickled into the hippodrome; entertainers appeared. A pair of clowns made their way around the circuit of the track, performing bawdy tricks with a basket of eggs; a stunt rider galloped past doing handstands and somersaults on his horse's back; a juggler strolled by, tossing brightly coloured balls high into the air. Then, at last: a stir, a sudden silence, and the Emperor walked into the imperial box to a flourish of trumpets.

The whole crowd got to its feet and cheered: 'Constantine! Invincible Victor, Lord of the World, Pious and Fortunate! King of the Romans, you reign!'

The tiny, distant figure in purple and gold graciously inclined its head, and the crowd cheered again. The Empress came to join him, carrying their small son, and there were more acclamations. At last the imperial party was seated, and there was a stir around the starting gates: the races were ready to begin. An attendant gave a signal, and the Emperor got to his feet again, holding up the white napkin that was the sign for the start. He suspended it out over the racetrack – then let it fall.

There was a roar from thirty thousand voices together, and the starting gates flew open. Four chariots, two blue and two green, drawn by four horses apiece, thundered out on to the track, and the crowd jumped to its feet screaming with excitement.

The chariots circled the track seven times – clipping the turning posts, hammering down the long sides of the oblong course, swerving across each others' paths as each driver tried to get ahead on the turn – and the crowd shrieked encouragement to the Greens or the Blues, depending on allegiance. At the seventh lap the second green chariot managed to slip in front of its rivals, and galloped across the finish line convincingly ahead of the others. The citizens cheered or howled, and flopped sweating back into their seats.

'Oh, I'm hot!' exclaimed Kallinikos, pouring himself a drink of water. 'What a race! I feel as though I've run it myself!'

'There are another seven races to come,' Anna warned him, and he laughed.

The races continued until early in the afternoon, inter-spersed with more clowns, jugglers and acrobats. By the end of the last race the crowd was hot, happy and exhausted. When the Emperor rose to leave, they cheered him to the echo.

'How does he get in and out?' asked Kallinikos, when the imperial box was empty and the applause had died into the buzz of conversation.

'That whole side of the hippodrome is built into the palace,' Anna told him. 'There's a stairway leading directly to the imperial box. The archives use the space under the arches to store documents.'

The Syrian looked at the long sweep of the bleachers surrounding the imperial box and whistled. 'That's a lot of documents.'

'It's records for the whole empire,' she said defensively. 'Not just the city. And they go back for generations.'

He thought about that, then shook his head in amazement. 'There must be tax records there for Baalbek from my grandfather's day. People probably believed then that we'd be part of the empire forever. The works of men are sublunar things, subject to the measure of time, to change and decay – yet everyone always behaves as though they were ordained by heaven.'

There was nothing Anna could say to such a portentous statement. She began picking up the remains of the picnic and stowing them away. After a moment, Kallinikos grinned a bit shamefacedly and began to help her.

It took the crowd a long time to file out of the hippodrome, and when their party finally reached the street, it was to find it jammed solid. The carriages of the wealthy, which had come to take the more aristocratic race-goers home, were stranded, awash in a stream of slow-moving pedestrians.

The party from Philadelphion shuffled slowly into the Middle Street, and began to make their way past the carriages, which were themselves inching forward. Theodosia and her friends peered curiously at the windows, trying to see what the rich people were wearing, but most of the carriage occupants had their curtains drawn.

The crowd was beginning to thin a little and move faster when a voice suddenly called, 'Kallinikos!' and the whole party looked up to see that the curtain of one of the carriages had been swept aside. A man leaned out of the window and beckoned imperiously.

'It's Stephanos!' Kallinikos whispered in disgust.

Anna had gathered that, far from being 'shut up' by the alchemist's super-flammable distilled oil, the master of the Arsenal was more inclined than ever to sneer at his subordinate. The distilled oil was, apparently, too thin to be used in a conventional fire canister, and Stephanos ridiculed all Kallinikos' schemes to thicken it with pitch and pine resin. Kallinikos had been forced to work on the new incendiary in his own time, in the hot noon hours when the rest of the Arsenal's workforce was resting.

Kallinikos reluctantly obeyed the summons of his superior, and the others in the party followed him, the children ogling the fine horses and craning their necks to see the carriage's interior.

'Kallinikos,' Stephanos said again. He was a thin-faced man with eyes that bulged slightly and a brown beard trimmed to a point; he wore the white silk tunic of a courtier and a belt worked with gold. He glanced from his subordinate to the rest of the party. 'I'm surprised to see you here. I expected you to spend the day steaming your precious ambix.' He shot another curious look at the party from Philadelphion. His eyes paused on Anna, then rested on her with surprise and growing appreciation.

'My friends invited me to join them at the races instead,' Kallinikos replied mildly. 'I'm glad I did, too. What a spectacle!'

'Your *friends*,' repeated Stephanos, with another predatory glance at Anna.

Kallinikos politely introduced them: 'Mistress Anna; Master Johannes and Mistress Eudokia – Lord Stephanos Skyles, Magistros of the Arsenal.'

'Mistress Anna,' repeated Stephanos, with an ingratiating smile. 'I confess I am surprised to see Kallinikos in the company of such a beautiful woman. Normally he spends all his time distilling foul liquids he swears will be fatal to the enemy.' He arched his eyebrows in contemptuous dismissal of the notion. 'I hope you don't think *all* of us at the Arsenal are such bores. Some of us appreciate beauty when we see it.'

Anna decided that Kallinikos had not misrepresented Stephanos: the head of the Arsenal genuinely was a most unpleasant man. How rude, to ignore Johannes and Eudokia and instead try to sweet-talk the pretty woman who was obviously accompanying his subordinate! She was willing to bet, too, that he was married: he had the self-satisfied smirk of a cheat. 'I know about Kallinikos' distillation project,' she replied evenly. 'I gave him the ambix.'

Stephanos' smile faltered.

'Mistress Anna is the proprietor of a perfume manufactory,' Kallinikos explained. 'She used the ambix to extract the scents of sweet herbs, but was looking to buy a new one when I asked if I could have it.'

'A perfume-maker!' exclaimed Stephanos, renewing the oily smile. 'What other trade would be appropriate for one so lovely?'

Anna rolled her eyes in disgust. 'Garland-weaver?' she suggested. 'Gem-engraver? Artist? Musician . . . ?'

'Alchemist?' offered Kallinikos, smiling.

Anna raised her eyebrows at him.

'Because you transform base substances into noble ones,' he explained.

Theodosia giggled, and Kallinikos flashed her a grin.

Stephanos was now looking annoyed: his own flattery had been received with a contemptuous joke, but his subordinate's got a smile. 'Impudence!' he exclaimed, frowning at Theodosia. 'Did your parents never teach you not to laugh in the presence of your betters, girl?'

Theodosia stopped laughing. 'I was laughing because Kallinikos made a joke,' she said, with dignity.

'Silence!' commanded Stephanos. 'Street urchins shouldn't even *speak* in the presence of men of rank.' He glanced at Anna and at Kallinikos, daring them to respond, knowing that no matter how he offended them, there was nothing they could do. He was a man of rank in a fine carriage; they were a refugee and a shopkeeper on foot.

'I'm not a street urchin!' Theodosia protested indignantly. She pulled her cloak straight and drew herself up, her chin jutting and her eyes flashing. 'My father was noble!'

'Theodosia!' said Anna sharply.

Stephanos sneered. 'You should teach that girl to respect her betters, woman, or someone else may teach her – with a whip.'

'These people are respectable citizens!' Kallinikos protested angrily.

'Shopkeepers!' replied Stephanos, growing steadily angrier. 'One step up from the rabble and one step down from a nobleman's horse! Fit company for *you* maybe! "My father was noble", indeed! What was he then, girl? A soldier? A town councillor?'

'He was a prince,' replied Theodosia proudly.

Stephanos laughed, and her face went scarlet.

'It's true,' Johannes put in angrily. 'The girl is the daughter of Theodosius, the brother of Constans the Bearded. All the neighbourhood knows that.'

Stephanos stopped laughing at the matter-of-fact tone. He looked from Johannes, to Anna, to the others in the party. He looked back at Theodosia, who stood as straight and proud as any emperor.

'Theodosius had no offspring,' he said uncertainly.

Anna caught her daughter's arm. 'We're going home,' she said firmly. 'Come.'

Theodosia tossed her head, but allowed herself to be marched off. The carriage, still trapped by the traffic, was unable to follow.

When they were well down the road, Anna turned to her daughter and slapped her hard across the face. 'You *idiot*!' she whispered fiercely. 'You *fool*, saying that to an official! I pray God and his Mother that nothing comes of this!'

Theodosia cradled her face. 'He asked what my father was!' she protested sullenly. 'He called me an urchin!'

'And, God and his saints all know, you have the manners of one!'

The others were watching, the children indignant, Kallinikos bewildered, Zoe frightened, and Johannes and Eudokia worried. 'Shouldn't I have spoken, neighbour?' asked Johannes anxiously.

Anna drew a deep breath and let it out again. 'Probably nothing will come of it,' she said. 'The palace has paid no attention to us since Lord Theodosius died. I'd just prefer it, neighbour, if things stayed that way. It would be better to keep quiet about Theodosia in front of any court official.'

'I'm sorry,' said Johannes humbly. Anna nodded acknowledgement, then started to walk on, not trusting herself to say more. She was aware of Maria and Sophia hurrying to walk either side of Theodosia, and of their furious whispers about the unfairness of parents.

Kallinikos fell in beside her, still looking bewildered. 'Anna . . .' he began.

She gave him a furious glare.

'It . . . it isn't *true*, is it?'

She was so surprised she almost forgot to be angry. 'Yes, of course it is. Didn't you know?' People generally did know, if they knew more of her than her name.

'You *married* the son of an emperor?'

'No, of course not!' Anna exclaimed impatiently. 'Princes don't marry grocers' daughters. I was his concubine.' She tugged a fold of her cloak tighter and added, 'It was a legal arrangement. There was nothing disreputable about it.'

She was never quite sure how true that was. The position of acknowledged concubine to an unmarried nobleman was one most people regarded as respectable: it didn't involve adultery and it wasn't the same as casual fornication. The concubine of a member of the imperial house was even more respectable, touched as she was with the aura of a family chosen by God to govern the earth. On the other hand, it wasn't the same as being married. In the eyes of the Church, she had been living in sin, barred from taking communion until her lover's death restored her to grace as a penitent.

Kallinikos swallowed. He was silent for several paces, and then asked quietly, 'Why are you frightened?'

She looked round at him quickly.

'You *are* frightened,' he pointed out. 'Can I help?'

She sighed. 'No. Probably it's nothing. I just don't like . . . *calling attention* to us.' She was silent for a moment, then added, 'The Emperor Constans . . . wanted to forget that his brother Theodosius ever existed. No court official with any sense would have mentioned Theodosius' daughter to him. When he died – well, at first Our Lord Constantine had more important things to worry about, and then it was all long ago, and there was no reason for anybody to bring it up. I think the court has forgotten that we exist, and that's fine with me. If it were remembered . . . my Theodosia may be a bastard, but she *is* the Emperor's cousin. The Emperor might decide to take an interest in her, and if he did . . .'

Kallinikos glanced back at Theodosia, his face still stunned and bewildered. 'You can't believe he'd harm her!'

Anna grimaced. 'He had his own brothers' noses slit, didn't he? Just on *suspicion* of treason, to make sure they'd be unfit to hold public office! But . . . no, what I'm really afraid of is that he might take her away from me. Kings use their female relatives to seal their alliances, don't they? They say to barbarian kings, 'Be my ally, and I will give you ten thousand pounds in gold and my daughter's hand in marriage.' Our Lord Constantine doesn't have any daughters or sisters. Theodosia's illegitimate and the daughter of a shopkeeper, but she's the only female relative he has. He *might* want to use her. He could make her a princess easily enough if he decided that he wanted to.

Her throat tightened, as it always did when she imagined it: the palace functionaries tearing Theodosia weeping from her arms; herself left crying at the palace gates; her lively daughter transformed into a white-faced doll in silk brocade; herself isolated, perhaps even imprisoned in a convent, unable to help; Theodosia handed over to some savage barbarian, a king among the Slavs or the Khazars, who would rape and abuse her to her life's end. 'God forbid!' she cried passionately. 'God forbid! She would end up married to some foul barbarian at the other end of the sea!'

Theodosia had evidently been listening, because she suddenly tore away from her friends and ran forward to catch

59

her mother's hand. 'I'm sorry!' she exclaimed passionately. 'Mama, I'm sorry! I should have kept quiet.'

Anna hugged her fiercely.

'I'll tell Stephanos it was a joke,' offered Kallinikos abruptly, 'I'll ask him if he really believed it, and tell him we all laughed about it as soon as we were out of sight.'

Anna stared at him for a moment, then smiled warmly. 'Thank you.'

Stephanos, Kallinikos reported next day, was very annoyed to think that his subordinate's friends had played a trick on him, but apparently didn't doubt the story. 'I told him that I'd been fooled as well,' Kallinikos relayed. 'That I believed it myself, until you all started laughing. I think if I hadn't said that, he would have sacked me. He made all sorts of comments about city clowns who think they're funny, and told me I should be judged by the riff-raff I choose to associate myself with.'

Anna thanked him again.

'Stephanos is *horrible*!' exclaimed Theodosia, who'd been listening.

Kallinikos laughed. 'I won't quarrel with you there! They say even his wife hates him.'

Anna nodded to herself: she'd thought he was married, and she could easily guess why his wife might hate him.

'Today,' Kallinikos went on, 'he told me that if I wanted to "waste my time" experimenting with distilled oil, I'd have to pay for my own supplies.'

'Can you afford that?' Theodosia asked anxiously.

He shrugged. 'I can get round it.'

Anna frowned: that sounded as though he meant to keep on taking his supplies from the Arsenal, but use some trick of accounting to disguise the fact. 'You could get into trouble for that,' she warned him.

He waved that airily aside. 'I'm not going to *steal* things and sell them in the market! I don't see how I can get into trouble for *improving* the incendiaries, when I'm in charge of them.'

She was still uneasy about it.

'It's *stupid*!' Theodosia exclaimed. 'Stephanos ought to

be *eager* for you to succeed with your oil. After all, if you improve the incendiaries and he's in charge, he'll get most of the credit!'

Kallinikos snorted. 'That I doubt.' He grinned. 'He's a pen-pusher and an accountant: he knows nothing about fire. I, on the other hand, was hired specifically because I *do* know something about fire. He's afraid that if I succeed, I'll take his job – or at least the incendiaries part of it, and that would hit his purse and his pride. He's right to worry, too. I didn't come to this city to be poor. I mean to improve the incendiaries so much that nobody can refuse me the title and salary I deserve.' He gave them a defiant look, then grinned again. 'After all, I need to improve my position, don't I? It seems I'm consorting with the Emperor's cousin!'

Anna frowned.

'Sorry,' he said, abashed. 'You don't want me to mention it, do you?'

'I just don't like jokes about it,' she told him, still frowning.

'Sorry.'

There was a silence. Then Kallinikos said, with nervous determination, 'I tell you the truth, though: I thought you were a widow. You've always seemed so . . . so *respectable*.'

Anna gave him an offended look, and he put both hands up in surrender. 'I'm not saying you *aren't*! The son of an emperor isn't like a . . . an ordinary man. People don't say "no" to him, do they? And his concubine, well, that must be a . . . a very respectable position. I'm sure, um, even high officials respect imperial concubines, and treat them with honour. It's just that you don't . . . you're not the sort of woman I'd . . .' He stopped, floundering.

Expect, Anna finished for him, in sour silence. *In other words, you'd* expect *imperial concubines to be simpering courtesans in thin silk and a lot of face paint.*

'I just don't understand how . . .' He tried again, 'How a woman like you took up with the son of an emperor.'

'Tell him, Mama!' urged Theodosia. 'Tell him how you met my father!'

Anna sighed. Theodosia had heard the story hundreds of

61

times, and would probably tell it herself if Anna refused. 'Very well!' she exclaimed. 'When I was a girl I was very beautiful . . .'

'You still are,' put in Kallinikos quickly. Anna raised her eyebrows and looked at him, and he shrugged. 'Well, you know yourself it's true. I don't see why you need to look at me like that because I pointed it out.'

Anna suppressed a smile. 'I looked at you "like that" because you interrupted. *As I was saying*, I was a very beautiful girl. My father had a grocery shop near the Church of St Peter and St Paul, and from the time I was thirteen, young men would come in just to flirt with me. My father tolerated it if they bought things. He was always in need of money, poor man: my mother died when I was young, and then my brother died. My father spent most of his savings on doctors and on paying the rent when they were ill and he couldn't work because he had to look after them. Then he had to borrow money a year later when there was a fire in the neighbourhood and his shop was damaged. He got deep into debt. With just the two of us to run the shop, it was hard for him to manage the repayments, and there was no money at all for a dowry for me. My father used to worry about what would happen to me when he was gone. He was pleased when I turned out beautiful, because it meant there was a chance that someone would take me without a dowry.

'It was about the time I turned sixteen that Lord Theodosius started coming into the shop. He and some of his friends were in the habit of wandering about the city looking for amusements – nothing out of the ordinary, just cockfights and taverns and chasing pretty girls. He heard that the grocer by the Church of St Peter and St Paul had a pretty daughter, and he and his friends came to see. I didn't know who he was, of course: as far as I knew he was just another young nobleman. I sold him some spices and oil, and I laughed at his jokes, and I didn't think anything of it – though I did like him; he was a handsome man, and courteous and clever. Still, even as young as I was, I knew better than to take him seriously. There were many men who'd admired me by then, but none of them were offering marriage. Noblemen, of course, don't

marry shopkeepers' daughters, and the shopkeepers' sons all
wanted a dowry. Love, love, love they said, but I could guess
what would happen to me if I listened to them.'

Theodosia rolled her eyes heavenward.

'*You* should pay attention!' Anna told her severely. 'Go
down to the Amastrianon Market sometime and talk to the
whores. *They* didn't choose their trade, and most of them hate
it. Most of them are there because they believed some man
when he talked about love.'

Theodosia sighed in exaggerated boredom. '*Yes*, Mama! I
promise I'll never listen to any man who talks about love.
Tell Kallinikos about the man who wanted to marry you!'

Anna gave her a sharp look, but complied. 'My father
eventually succeeded in finding a man who was willing
to marry me without a dowry. He was a widower named
Eusebios, a coppersmith with a thriving business and two
children. I think now I was most unfair to him, for he was
a decent man, but at the time all I could think of was that he
had rotten teeth, and his breath stank. He was twice my age:
his children were nearly as old as I was, and I knew from a
friend that they were furious at the thought of having me as
a stepmother. I told my father I would rather die than marry
Eusebios. My father was exasperated. He was only trying to
provide for me, poor man, but I just couldn't see it that way.
We quarrelled for *days*: he used to lock me in my room as
soon as I finished work, and I cursed him, and we both lived
on dry bread and tears.

'One day Theodosius came into the shop just after I'd had
an argument with my father, and he asked me why I'd been
crying. I told him that my father wanted me to marry an
old man with stinking breath. At this the prince became
very indignant, and asked to see my father. He asked my
father if what I said was true, and then he offered to take
me in concubinage himself. He told us who he was. I was
thrilled.

'My father didn't know what to say. On the one hand, he
honoured our holy and Christ-loving emperors. On the other
hand, Theodosius wasn't offering marriage. At last my father
said honestly that his one desire was to see me secure and

well provided for, and that he feared that a prince would eventually be obliged to marry a woman of rank, and that I would be abandoned to poverty. At this Theodosius offered to settle some property on me, so that I would have a secure income of my own whatever happened.

'When I heard this, I cried out that there was a perfume workshop for sale near the Church of the Theotokos. I'd always wanted to work with perfume: I always loved sweet smells. Theodosius laughed and said what men always say – that it was a good trade for a beautiful girl – and at once agreed to buy it for me. I told him then that I would far, far prefer to be his concubine than Eusebios' wife. It seemed to me like *two* dreams come true together – to have a handsome prince in love with me, and a shop of my own to run!

'My father was still unhappy, poor man, but he didn't raise any more objections. Theodosius bought the perfume shop – this shop – together with the two slaves who had run it for its previous owner. Helena was one of them, and Zoe's mother the other – Elpis her name was, a skilled perfume-maker who taught me a lot; she died of a fever five years ago. Anyway, I moved in here, and he used to come to visit me.'

Anna was silent for a moment. Telling the story to Theodosia, she had always stressed how happy she and Theodosius had been, how much in love: she had, she realized suddenly, made it sound very much like a marriage. In fact, it had been nothing of the sort. They had never lived together. Theodosius had come to visit at most three times a week, usually arriving in the afternoon and leaving again by evening; when they spent a whole night together she'd treasured it. Her days had been spent learning how to run a workshop and a business. The challenges and satisfactions of that work had been more absorbing than the interludes of love – and had proved far more enduring.

She'd been in love with her prince, but she'd ended up marrying her work: that was the real truth. After Theodosius died, she'd thought at first that she would eventually settle down with a husband – but it hadn't happened, and she was now fairly certain that it never would. She'd had offers – naturally: any beautiful woman with money could expect them. None of the men who'd proposed to her had seemed worth the sacrifice of her independence, or the risk of seeing her household abused.

'My father loved Mama very much,' Theodosia said proudly. 'He was very happy when he found out that I was going to be born, too. He put some money aside to provide for me. Only, when he was killed his brother wouldn't let us have it.'

'I heard that he was executed,' said Kallinikos in a low voice. 'For treason, supposedly, only, no one seems to think there was any. We heard about that even in Baalbek.'

'Theodosius was born in the purple chamber of the palace,' Anna told him. 'He was the only man other than the Emperor who had the right to wear that colour. Constans was afraid of him because of it. He never gave him any responsibilities. Theodosius should have been made Caesar, or been given charge of the army or the fleet or at the very least a province. Instead he had nothing to do except wander about Constantinople looking for amusements among the common people. In the end, of course, Constans was afraid even to allow him that. He decided to have Theodosius ordained as a deacon, so that he couldn't hold secular power. They caught him in the Chapel of the Virgin in the palace, and they had the bishop all ready to perform the service. But Theodosius wouldn't agree to go along with it – he told them he had no vocation to the religious life. So they ordained him by force. He was furious. He called the Blessed Virgin to witness that he'd been ordained by violence, and begged her not to hold him responsible for the blasphemy his brother had committed before her face.

'That made Constans even more afraid and suspicious. He had Theodosius shut up in the Monastery of the Studion.' She swallowed, remembering it. He had simply disappeared: for weeks she had heard nothing but wild rumours about him. Theodosia had been born during that terrible time, and she had wept over the baby, wondering if her lover would ever see his daughter. It was only after a month that she received a letter. She had walked to the monastery gates every day after that, begging to be allowed to see her lover, and bringing

65

him small gifts of food or scented oils. She'd been allowed to speak to him twice, early in his incarceration. After that she was turned away.

'I've heard that the Studion is very strict,' said Kallinikos, when the silence dragged.

Anna nodded. 'They call the monks "the Unsleeping", because they keep vigil constantly, praying in shifts all through the night. I suppose that made them good guardians. Oh, they're holy men, I don't doubt it – but my Theodosius wasn't used to that kind of life. It wasn't that he was an enemy of orthodoxy: he wasn't, I swear it, he did his best to be a good Christian! But he didn't have any kind of vocation to the monastic life, and how can anyone endure such strict discipline without it? He hated the Studion.' She swallowed again, then continued heavily, 'In the end he was accused of plotting against his brother, and he was put to death. It's possible that he was plotting: he'd given up any hope of getting out while his brother was alive. He was never a traitor by nature, though. If Constans had given him power he would've had a loyal deputy who could've helped him preserve his own life. Instead all he got was the guilt of fratricide, and the hatred of the people.'

'Constans had nightmares about my father,' Theodosia put in, with satisfaction. 'Did you hear about that?' When Kallinikos shook his head, she continued, with relish, 'He used to dream that he saw my father dressed as a deacon, holding a chalice. My father would say, "Drink, brother, drink!" but when Constans looked into the cup it was full of blood. He used to wake up screaming. Everyone in the city heard about it. Everyone hated him because of what he'd done to my father. When he went to the hippodrome, everyone booed and jeered at him until he had to call out the army to make them be quiet. Eventually he ran away from Constantinople to escape. He went all the way to Sicily, and he was murdered in his bath, and it served him right.'

'I thought he went to Sicily because it was a better base for his naval campaign against Mu'awiya,' said Kallinikos.

'No, it was because of my father,' said Theodosia. 'It's true. You can ask anyone; they'll tell you.'

When Kallinikos had gone home, and Anna and her daughter were getting ready for bed, Theodosia was very thoughtful. She sat very still, frowning while her mother combed out her hair, then pulled her feet up on to the shared bed and studied her parent.

Anna began combing her own hair, aware of her daughter's eyes on her.

'Let me do that!' Theodosia offered. Anna smiled and sat down on the bed, handing Theodosia the comb.

For perhaps a minute Theodosia devoted herself to combing out the long tresses. 'Mama,' Theodosia said, finally, with false casualness, 'you *like* Kallinikos, don't you?'

So now it was going to come out into the open – and no, Theodosia *didn't* just want an uncle. 'He's a friend,' Anna said, in the same tone. 'I grant you, he's a very interesting man.'

Theodosia combed hair for another half minute. 'Don't you . . . ?' she began, then stopped.

'What are you thinking, darling?' Anna asked softly, turning her head to look round into her daughter's serious eyes.

Theodosia put the comb down. 'I was just wondering if you were ever going to get married. I was wondering if . . .'

'I am never going to get married,' Anna told her firmly. 'My love, if I married, my husband would become head of our household. I don't trust anyone else to love and care for my own people the way I do.'

The girl frowned. '*Other* households . . .'

'Theodosia, *other* households aren't the point. *Our* household isn't *like* other households. There's you. There's my business, which I'm *good* at. I'm not going to take the risk of handing over everything I've worked for and everyone I care about to someone else.'

The frown deepened. 'But if it was somebody you *liked*, somebody who really *loves* you, who wouldn't—'

'Did "somebody" ask you to say this?' Anna asked sharply.

Theodosia shook her head at once. 'No,' she said in a small voice. 'I just thought, well . . .'

'If I were going to marry,' Anna said deliberately, 'the best person would be Timotheos, who owns that perfume shop in the Milion. He's offered.'

Theodosia grimaced. 'Him! He's *old*! He's *boring*!'

'He's not *old*, darling! He's probably only ten years older than I am, and in good health. He's got that shop, and he knows enough to value my skill in the workshop. Marrying him would be profitable to both of us – but don't worry, I'm not going to. I don't trust him not to think he can run my business better than I do, and I don't trust him to play stepfather to *you*. If I can't trust him – a member of my own guild, whose family and reputation I know – why should I trust Kallinikos, whom we know next to nothing about? He *is* who you had in mind, isn't he?'

Theodosia said nothing.

'Why do you *want* me to marry? Are you unhappy with things as they are?'

'Nnooo . . . only sometimes people say things.'

Anna turned to sit beside her daughter and put an arm around the narrow shoulders. 'What sort of things?'

Theodosia shrugged. 'That they're sorry for me, because I haven't got a father. That you're proud. That you think you're too good for ordinary men.' She made a face. 'Maria said that Daniel the Charcoal-burner said you got the shop by whoring.'

Had he indeed? Well, *he* was a drunkard and a lecher, and the respectable people of the neighbourhood knew it and paid no attention to his opinion. 'People *do* say unkind things about women on their own,' Anna told her. 'I try not to give them an excuse. I think the neighbours know what I'm like, and what Daniel the Charcoal-burner's like.'

'The neighbours think we're odd,' said Theodosia unhappily.

Anna brushed back a lock of the thick gold hair and tucked it behind an ear. 'That's all right, so long as they think we're respectable. My love, we *are* odd. I'm an unmarried woman who's successfully running her own business, and you are the daughter of a prince: that *is* odd. It's not *bad*, though. I don't think the neighbours think it's bad, either.' She kissed

Theodosia's forehead. 'I want to keep us safe, my lamb; I want to keep you safe, if I can't do anything else. And that's why I'm not going to marry.'

'But I *like* Kallinikos,' Theodosia argued, 'and I'm *sure* he really likes you, and I'm *sure* he'd never do anything to hurt us . . .'

'I don't think he'd ever *intend* to,' Anna conceded, 'but I wouldn't trust him in charge of the household, either. He'd spend all our money on alchemy, that's what I think. No, darling: I don't *need* to marry, so I'm not *going* to marry. Not even Kallinikos.'

Four

Kallinikos continued to work on his distilled-oil incendiary throughout the summer. He would appear at the workshop in the early evening, smelling of bitumen, sulphur and pitch, and tell Anna and Theodosia all about the effect of adding dissolved nitre or Persian gum. He did not say where he was obtaining the supplies of these materials, but Anna doubted very much that he was paying for them.

She had other things to worry about, however. The war had cut off supplies of all the most common perfume ingredients. Myrrh and frankincense from Arabia; cinnamon and spikenard from India; cedar oil from Lebanon and balsam from Judaea – all were shipped from the entrepôts in Egypt and Syria up the Mediterranean coast, and now the Hellespont, gateway to the Mediterranean, was closed. The Arab fleet had moved into the Sea of Marmara. Late in July, Cyzicus on the southern shore, only fifty miles from Constantinople, fell and was occupied.

A few spice merchants re-routed their caravans north to Trebizond on the Black Sea, and shipped their goods from there to Constantinople – but the supply obtained by this means couldn't meet the demand. The churches wanted incense; the city's cooks wanted spices; the Great Palace wanted both. Prices doubled, then quadrupled. The Perfumers' Guild, acting for all the manufactories in the city, bought up as much as it could, and distributed the meager supplies among its members – but it did so, as usual, unequally. The richer and better-connected guild members, who owned shops in the plaza surrounding the Milion – the milestone that was the official centre of the city – took the lion's share. Smaller establishments, like Anna's, begged and bribed the guild for what was left. None of them got enough to allow them to make their standard blends of perfume. Customers grumbled about the quality of what they were sold, and grumbled even louder about the increasing price.

Anna worked hard trying to find substitutes for the imported spices among the seasonal and local materials which were still available. She had always made attar of roses, and when the rose season ended, attar of jasmine – a task which was less intensive because the season was longer and the flowers didn't have petals that needed to be stripped from the flower head. She had steamed marjoram and lavender and wild grape, and mixed them with the resins of juniper and pine, or with the ground root of the iris: all these common perfume ingredients were local, or came from the north and west, and were still available. She began experimenting with other aromatic herbs which she had used dried or in rinses, but not in perfumes: rue and rosemary, spearmint, rush and thyme and citron. She was glad she had her new ambix: perfumers who had disdained steam distillation could do little except complain.

'The Emperor should send out the fleet and drive the heretics back to Arabia!' declared one conservative member of the guild at one of the meetings. 'An orthodox fleet doesn't need to fear the enemies of God!'

The other members, however, were grimly silent. There were very few in the city who believed the imperial fleet had any chance against the enemies of God. After all, it had met the Arabs already, seventeen years before at the Battle of the Masts, and had been soundly defeated: the seas had been red with the empire's blood, and the Emperor himself had barely escaped with his life. Since then the Arabs had sailed up and down the Mediterranean as they pleased, confident that the empire no longer had the ability to oppose them in battle. No, the Emperor would do much better to conserve his fleet: the city would need it, if it was to survive.

All through the summer, there were men working on the city walls, checking for loose stonework and clearing out the dry moats which guarded them. Wagons rolled through the streets, carrying catapult shot and incendiaries to the

71

watchtowers. Troops arrived in the city, remained a few days, and were despatched again to strategic parts of the frontier where, it was hoped, they would be able to tie down the armies of the enemy. The military harbour of Kontoskalion was perpetually crowded with ships. The preparations should have been encouraging – but Anna couldn't help thinking that the enemy would be preparing, too.

'Does the Arsenal still have supplies of Median oil?' Anna anxiously asked Kallinikos once.

'Oh, yes!' Kallinikos agreed readily. 'Apparently there's a lot of it up the other end of the Black Sea, and we've been laying in quantities of it. The supply's safe as long as the city stands.'

When the harvest came in, at summer's end, fleets of merchant ships were despatched under military escort to the other end of the Black Sea to buy up supplies of grain. Despite this, prices in the city were high and became steadily higher. Then there were shortages: first of wheat, then of barley, spelt, chickpeas and lentils. Some blamed it on stockpiling, but most seemed to think it was a trick by the merchants and grain chandlers to drive up prices. Hungry beggars appeared in the streets, asking for a crust of bread; there were murmurs against some of the leading merchants, and stones were thrown at houses. At last an imperial edict was published: citizens could apply for a ration token and use it to buy grain from the granaries of the Great Palace. At once grain became available again, and the price went down. In the markets people nodded sagely: the Emperor had sorted out the merchants.

The churches of the city were crowded. Every Sunday, the priests prayed that God would preserve his people against the onslaught of the heretics, and with each passing week the 'Amen!' grew louder and more fervent. Anna made a donation of incense to their own parish church of the Theotokos. It was pine resin mixed with rosemary oil, rush and honey. On Sundays afterwards she would smell the fragrance she had blended, and silently beg the Virgin to protect her household.

Summer ended with the suddeness that was usual in the

city: one week the city basked in September sun; the next, the wind swung round to the north-east, the sky turned leaden, and the air filled with rain and wind-blown grit. Kallinikos began to appear dressed in a shabby woollen tunic over his linen one, wearing his cloak again. Anna was surprised that the last item wasn't immediately covered in oil.

'Oh, I put it aside when I reach the Arsenal,' he explained. 'It's hot work there.'

Early in October he asked Anna if she knew where to get a pump. 'A double-action force pump would be best,' he told her. 'The kind they call a siphon, that puts out a good jet of water. It doesn't have to work: I could repair it, if it's not too badly broken. I used to be able to make one in a few days, when I had the equipment.'

'I don't know anything about *pumps!*' she said in surprise. 'Ask Michael the Lead-worker down the road: he'd know. Is your street short of water?'

He looked crafty. 'No. I don't want it for water.'

She frowned at him. 'This is something to do with your distilled oil?'

He smiled, his eyes gleaming with suppressed excitement. 'Yes. I thought . . . no, it's probably better if I *show* you.'

Theodosia butted in eagerly. 'You'll show us the distilled oil? Will you set fire to it?'

'Yes!' exclaimed Kallinikos, and laughed.

Anna did not particularly want him to set fire to his distilled oil in her perfumery, but it was too late to say so: an argument with Theodosia would certainly be the result, and she couldn't face it. (*But* Mama*! How can you not want to see it? Aren't you even* curious*? Just because you don't like the smell?*)

Kallinikos duly arrived the following evening with a small white pottery flask, carefully stoppered and wrapped in an oil-stained rag. 'This is it!' he said, flourishing it. 'Liquid fire! It will burn better than any common incendiary and it's harder to put out. It has a couple of other properties, too, which I think are better demonstrated than described. Can I use your large water bath?'

Anna, surprised and confused, hesitated, but Theodosia at once ushered him into the workshop. The rose season was

73

long over, and it was quiet. Martina had gone home, and Zoe and Helena were in the kitchen preparing supper. The large water bath was a stone trough used to soak chopped herbs to make rinses; it sat, immovably, next to the kitchen door. That evening there was nothing in it but water, fetched from the fountain that morning to use in rinsing hands.

'You mind if I use this?' Kallinikos asked Anna. She grimaced, but shook her head: the water was already in need of changing.

'Good! First though, just for safety's sake, we ought to have something on hand to put it out. We need a couple of buckets of sand or earth.'

'We have a whole bathful of water,' Anna pointed out tartly.

The Syrian shook his head. 'Water won't put it out. It's not very good on most incendiaries, and it's useless against this one.'

Anna stared.

'Even an ordinary incendiary is more flammable than ordinary lamp oil,' explained Kallinikos. 'Nearly all the recipes contain pitch and sulphur. Throw water on them, and they spit and toss burning droplets everywhere. To put them out you need to smother them with earth or sand, or kill them with vinegar or, um . . .' he faltered slightly, 'urine.'

'You *piss* on them to put them out?' asked Anna incredulously.

'Theoretically, you could,' agreed Kallinikos, 'though I have to admit I've never seen it done. You'd have to be made of iron to hitch up your tunic in front of a spillage of burning incendiary! At the Arsenal we have buckets of sand everywhere, and when we get a spill it's smothered even before it has a chance to catch fire.'

'I'll get some dirt,' volunteered Theodosia eagerly. She picked up the buckets used to fetch water from the public fountain and ran out to the garden behind the house.

Anna looked at Kallinikos accusingly. 'My clean floor!'

'It's only *in case*,' he soothed. 'I don't think we'll need it.'

Theodosia returned in a few minutes with two full buckets,

her hands covered in muck. The dirt she'd collected was a stinking mulch: she appeared to have raided the compost heap. Anna rolled her eyes heavenward. '*You're* cleaning those buckets afterwards,' she warned her daughter.

Theodosia didn't even argue. She rinsed off her hands in the water tank, then looked eagerly at Kallinikos. Smiling, he unstoppered his flask. 'We need a match,' he said, 'or a coal from the fire.'

Again Theodosia dashed off, and returned this time with a coal from the kitchen fire, held in tongs. Helena and Zoe both followed her, their faces full of curiosity and apprehension: Theodosia had evidently told them what was about to happen.

Kallinikos obviously enjoyed having an audience. He bowed to the slaves, then held up the flask of 'liquid fire'. 'Here it is!' he told them. 'The best incendiary ever made! Soon to be used against the fleet of Mu'awiya, who calls himself Successor of the Prophet of God! Watch!' He unstoppered the flask and poured it into the tank of water.

While Anna was still blinking in surprise, Kallinikos snatched the coal from Theodosia and touched it to the surface of the water.

There was a *whoosh*, and then the water in the tank was burning, its surface covered with pale, blue-edged flames. There was a smell, acrid and bitter, and a gust of black smoke. Zoe cried out in fear.

'Holy Mary, Mother of God!' exclaimed Anna, and crossed herself.

Kallinikos laughed. He ripped the stained rag off the neck of his flask, and, holding it in the tongs, extended it into the fire.

It caught at once, producing a trail of harsh smoke. Kallinikos rested it on the surface of the water a moment, then thrust it under.

It continued to burn under the surface of the water.

Kallinikos pulled the rag up again, dropped it on the floor of the workshop, and stepped on it. The fire in the water tank was flickering now, and even as they watched, it ebbed, fluttered, and went out.

'Immortal God!' Anna whispered.

'You saw?' Kallinikos said happily. 'It floats. It floats on the surface of water and burns everything it touches, and it will even burn for a little while completely underwater.' He took his foot off the rag: it lay, scorched and sodden and dirty, on the workshop floor. 'You see why I want a pump?'

'No,' whispered Anna, still staring at her large water bath.

'With a force pump – a siphon – you could spray it from a ship. You could put a line of it across the sea, and move your own ships back to safety. Then when the enemy ships crossed the patch of oiled sea, all you'd have to do would be toss in a few fire canisters. Whoompf!' He gestured explosively. 'Up go the enemy ships!'

Like a painting of the Apocalypse, Anna saw the sea burning; saw ships, trapped in the fire, and men screaming as they were burned alive. 'My God!' she said, appalled. 'My God!' She looked at the Syrian's excited grin. 'How can you? How can you devise a weapon like this, plan to use it against *living men* – and *smile*?'

He stopped grinning. 'It's to defend Constantinople!' he exclaimed, hurt.

'But . . .' It was true, she dreaded the Arab attack with all her heart, she ought to be glad to think of the attackers dying – but still, the image of a burning sea seemed like something out of a vision of hell. It was a nightmare, a violation of nature that belonged to the ending of the world.

'You said the heretics are people like us!' Anna protested. 'That they love their wives and children, that they're not cruel or oppressive, that they're sincere in their worship of God! How . . . how can you . . .' She waved helplessly at the trough of dirty water, trying, and failing, to find words to communicate her sense that men should not use hellfire against their fellow men, even in self-defence. 'You couldn't put it *out*!' she cried in revulsion. 'If you got it on yourself, and it was burning, you couldn't put it out even if you jumped into the sea!'

'It would be a quick death, compared to some!' exclaimed Kallinikos, angry now. 'You think most soldiers die from

76

swords? That's the lucky few: most die from infected wounds, days or weeks after a battle. There was a man in the party I travelled with from Smyrna: he had a wound to his face, and it rotted. The maggots ate one of his eyes while he was still alive. There was nothing we could do. He died a day before we reached Pergamum. Fire's quick, and drowning's merciful.'

Anna stared at him and shuddered.

'Mother!' exclaimed Theodosia in outrage. 'Mother, how can you *scold* him! Can't you see that this is the salvation of the city?'

Anna looked at her daughter in surprise: Theodosia's face was flushed, her eyes brilliant. 'Don't you see?' she asked breathlessly. 'The enemy plan to take the city with their *fleet*. Now that we have *this*, they can't! They don't have liquid fire and they don't know how to make it. It will *destroy* their fleet, and they won't have any answer to it. It will save the city: can't you see that?' She bent over and picked up the dirty rag. She held it before her nose and inhaled deeply. 'It smells good!' she said, looking at her mother defiantly. 'It smells of victory!'

Even Kallinikos was surprised. Gently, he took the rag away from Theodosia. He stood holding it in his hand and looking at it as though he wasn't quite sure what it was.

Anna suddenly understood that for him the purpose of the fire had been something remote, something which, for all his inquiries about pumps, he had never really visualized. It was the fire itself he had worked for: his only real end had been the sight of it dancing upon the water.

'You did it for love, didn't you?' she asked wonderingly. 'For the love of fire.'

He looked up sharply, meeting her eyes. She felt she was seeing him for the first time. This was not the man she'd thought she knew – a rather puppy-like man, grinning, harmless, eager to be friends. This was someone lonely and desperate, tormented by a fire in the mind.

'Oh, yes,' he said. 'It's so beautiful. I know it kills people. I do know that, far too well. But I can't help finding it beautiful.' He looked back at the rag, then folded it over and tied it around the mouth of his empty flask.

Anna wondered if the salvation of the city was worth purchasing if it meant pouring hellfire upon the sea.

But it was, she saw. It was, because what would become of them all if the city fell? Cities which fought their conquerors were punished for it, everyone knew that, and Constantinople would fight against its attackers with all the strength of its pride and centuries-long history. The siege would be terrible, and if the enemy triumphed, they would be wounded and furious. There would be rapes, murders, looting; in the end, the entire population might well be led off into slavery. To save her world and her friends and her household and her daughter – yes, for them she would be glad of Kallinikos' fire. She could not love it, though.

'The salvation of the city,' Kallinikos repeated, looking at the flask. He looked up at Theodosia. 'You really think so?'

'Yes,' she replied breathlessly. 'I do.'

Kallinikos was, it seemed, sufficiently encouraged that he continued his quest for a pump. He managed to buy a broken one from a friend of Michael the Lead-worker, but it was missing many of its pieces, and he was very busy chasing round the city trying to buy the bits second-hand. The perfume workshop saw him only sporadically for a week. When they missed him altogether for three days, they assumed that it was because he was looking for another piece of the pump.

Then they received a letter.

It came in the middle of the morning, carried by a hulking black-bearded thug with bad teeth. Anna was alone in the shop: Zoe and Helena were busy tending the garden, and, since it was morning, Martina was in her own home. Theodosia was visiting her friends.

The thug leered. 'Got a letter fer Mistress Anna, the shop owner,' he said, waggling it between thumb and forefinger.

Anna identified herself and took it with a fastidious frown, then tried to ignore the man, though he stood ogling her while she examined it. The letter was written on a single thin strip of vellum which looked suspiciously like something cut from the margin of an official document; it was unsealed, and had simply been rolled up and tied with a few strands of hair. The writing was tiny: Anna, who had only a very basic knowledge of her letters, had some difficulty making it out. '*Kallinikos of Heliopolis to the perfume-maker Anna and her household,*' went the superscription on the back, and then, inside, *I have been arrested for stealing from the Arsenal. Please, for friendship, send food and money! Will repay when able.*' Anna finished stammering over the words and looked up at the black-bearded thug. She felt calm, strangely numb, and knew that she hadn't taken it in yet.

'Yer friend's in the Strategion Prison,' said the thug, with another leer. 'Where I work, see? He said you'd pay me fer deliverin' that.'

Anna swallowed. She went to the strongbox.

Unlocking it with her key, she found that her hands were shaking with rage. *She* had known Kallinikos would get into trouble for taking the supplies for his experiments, so why hadn't *he* been able to see that? Why hadn't he *borrowed* the money, and *paid* for his supplies?

She fumbled a half-day's wage out of the strongbox, then closed and locked it. She handed the coins to the jailer; apparently the amount was acceptable, because he leered again. 'I'd give it back fer a kiss, sweetheart,' he suggested.

She wanted to slap him; instead she merely shook her head. 'Your teeth,' she said, by way of explanation. 'My friend's asked for food and money . . .'

''Sright,' agreed the jailer. 'They don't get much by way of food witout they pay, see? An' he's goin' to be shipped. He'll need plenny of money to buy food along the way.'

'Shipped?' she repeated faintly.

'Sent to Cherson,' he explained.

She knew of Cherson, the remote settlement at the northern end of the Black Sea. Prisoners were often sent there, to work and die defending the city in its constant wars against the barbarians.

'But he can't even have been *tried* yet!' she protested. 'And he wasn't stealing, not really, not for himself! He was—'

'I don't know anythin' about that,' interrupted the jailer. 'I jus' know he's goin' to be shipped. I don't think you need a trial, not fer a foreigner. The Arsenal says he was stealing, that's good enough. Probably they're in a hurry anyway, 'cause it's late in the year already, and they'll want the prison empty before the weather turns nasty an' they can't ship nobody. You wanna make up a package for him now, I can take it.'

Take it, but not necessarily deliver it, thought Anna. The thought seemed remote, distant from the roar of anger, but she still had the sense to listen to it. 'I need to think what to put in it,' she said. 'Can I bring it to the prison later?'

'Yer,' agreed the jailer. 'Ask for Timon – that's me. I'll see yer friend gets it. Only, you better get it to me quick, 'cause, like I said, yer friend's goin' to be shipped in a few days.'

'Yes,' said Anna. 'Thank you.'

Timon the jailer left. Anna sank down on her stool and rested her hands on the counter. The scarred wood she had looked at every morning for years seemed totally unfamiliar, and her hands those of a stranger. She wished that Kallinikos would come in through the door with his stupid grin. She wanted to hit him. She wanted to grab him by the collar of his oil-stained tunic and shake him; she needed to scream into his face. How could he have expected to get away with stealing from the Arsenal, when he knew perfectly well that Stephanos was looking for an excuse to get rid of him? How, how could he have been so *stupid*?

She took a deep breath. Her chest hurt. 'Helena,' she called, faintly; then, more loudly, 'Helena!'

Helena didn't hear. Anna got up and blundered to the workshop door. 'Helena!' she screamed.

There was a silence, and then Helena appeared at the run, looking alarmed.

'Take the shop,' Anna ordered.

'Mistress?' asked Helena, surprised. 'What—?'

'That *idiot* Kallinikos has got himself *arrested*!' Anna shouted. 'The worthless *fool* is in the Strategion Prison and begging *me* to send him food and money! He's going to be shipped to Cherson for stealing from the Arsenal.'

80

'Oh, Mistress!' exclaimed Helena in horror.

'Quiet!' shouted Anna.

She went into the workshop, found everything there trivial and worthless, and went on upstairs to her bedroom. She sat down on the bed and began to cry. She hugged herself, rocking back and forth, trying to stop the sobs. It hurt to breathe, to be. She cursed Kallinikos for his stupidity and her pain.

Theodosia ran in about half an hour later. 'Mama!' she cried. 'Helena says Kallinikos has been arrested!'

Anna wiped her eyes angrily with her hands. 'Yes,' she said thickly.

'We have to *do* something!' exclaimed Theodosia. 'We have to get him out!'

'I don't know what to do,' said Anna, wiping her eyes again. Her nose was running too, but she didn't want to wipe it on the bedspread. 'He *was* taking supplies from the Arsenal. You know he was.'

'We . . . we have to tell someone about the liquid fire!' said Theodosia. 'That's *important*. We can't let Stephanos ruin that just because he's jealous. We have to tell someone!'

'Who'd listen to us?' asked Anna dully. 'Maybe we could make someone pay attention if we spent enough on bribes and persisted long enough – but we don't have long enough. They're going to ship him to Cherson before the weather gets too bad for sailing. He'll be gone within the week.'

'Oh, God!' Theodosia looked at her mother, her mouth working.

Anna held out her arms, and the girl ran into them. They sat on the bed, hugging each other in silence for a long time.

'What if I asked to see my cousin?' Theodosia said at last.

Anna looked up sharply. 'No!' she exclaimed fiercely. 'Don't even *think* it.'

The shock of that did at least clear her head. Theodosia was looking at her mulishly.

'Don't even think it,' Anna said again, and wiped her eyes once more. 'Do you think the Emperor would listen to a twelve-year-old girl? It wouldn't help Kallinikos, but it

81

could very well hurt *you*. I don't think it's necessary, anyway. I wasn't thinking. All we need to do is to raise a question. If there was even a small delay, he'd miss the next ship. Then they wouldn't be able to send him off until spring, and that gives us lots of time. You're right, the liquid fire ought to be enough to make *someone* pay attention. I hadn't thought of it. It ought to be worth a delay, at least.' She got to her feet.

'You just said nobody would listen,' said Theodosia.

'I wasn't thinking,' replied Anna. She hesitated, trying to think now. Who *would* listen?

'I'm going to go to Father Agapios,' she said finally. The priest at her local church was, she knew, well disposed towards her because of the gift of incense.

'Who'll listen to him?' asked Theodosia in disgust. 'He's a stupid old man.'

'His Bishop will listen,' Anna said sharply. 'And even the Emperor listens to the Bishop of Constantinople.'

'The Bishop won't listen to Father Agapios until *next year*!' exclaimed Theodosia. 'There must be a hundred priests in the Great Church alone: it will be weeks before Father Agapios could even get an appointment.'

'He'll be able to get an appointment with *somebody* who counts,' snapped Anna. 'I'll go to see him. Now.'

Theodosia stared at her. 'We have to get Kallinikos out!' she said fiercely. It sounded like an ultimatum. 'Not just because of us, because he's our friend and everything. We have to get him out because he's *important*.'

'We will do everything we can,' Anna promised.

She looked at her daughter for a moment. She needed to give Theodosia something to do, or the girl would return to that dangerous notion of asking her cousin the Emperor to help. 'Kallinikos wrote to ask us for food and money,' she said carefully. 'Can you make up a package for him while I speak to Father Agapios? Bread and cheese and dried fruit – things that will keep a few days. And a blanket – I bet the prison is cold. And maybe some parchment and ink, in case he needs to write again.'

Theodosia nodded vigorously. 'I'll put in a towel and some soap, too,' she said. 'Will they let us see him?'

'I don't know,' Anna admitted. 'We'll try.'

She washed her face, left Theodosia preparing the package, and set off for the church.

It was not far away, only a couple of blocks. Constantinople was full of churches: no one lived far from one, and citizens were legally required to attend regularly. Some churches were more popular than others. The Church of the Theotokos, dedicated to the Mother of God, was the most popular in Philadelphion, and was never locked, even now, on a Thursday morning. Anna slipped in and stood for a moment in the glittering dimness, letting her eyes adjust. The open space under the dome where the congregation normally stood to worship was empty, though one old woman had prostrated herself in prayer before the icon of the Virgin on the altar screen.

Anna walked silently over and joined her. The air here was scented with a lingering trace of incense: pine resin, rosemary and honey, the perfume Anna had blended in the Virgin's honour. Anna crossed herself and bowed her head. *Blessed Virgin*, she prayed silently, *help me. Help the one I love.*

She looked up at the icon: the solemn dark eyes of mother and child gazed serenely back. *Love.* The awareness of the word she had used in the privacy of her mind hung between them, and she felt suddenly that it was falling into an infinite space behind those painted eyes, spiralling out into an incomprehensible eternity of cherubim and seraphim where it was one of the few earthly words that retained any meaning. *Love.*

But I'm angry *with him,* she protested in astonishment. *He was such an* idiot*: what happened was his own fault!*

Those words, too, spiralled into the serene immensity of the Virgin's gaze, but they disintegrated in the long slow fall: *angry, idiot, fault . . .* fading away into meaningless echoes.

Do I love him? she asked, and even in asking it, knew that she did. It was nothing like the giddy intoxication she'd felt for Theodosius, her beautiful doomed prince. In many ways it had more in common with what she felt for her daughter: it was a sober love, that recognized faults with exasperation and forgave them with resignation. It was not, however, maternal or sisterly in the least.

She contemplated that fact in horrified wonder. How had *that* slipped up on her? Since the death of Theodosius, hundreds of men had admired her, and six had proposed marriage. Every one of those six had been richer and more reliable than Kallinikos, and four of them had been better looking. She had been perfectly indifferent to all of them. She had told herself that she, a free woman, had no need of a master; she had rejoiced in her independence, looked smugly at her perfume shop, and determined to share it with no one but her own child. How had this Syrian – this grinning, dog-like idiot who loved fire – stolen away her wits?

He has scattered the proud in the imagination of their hearts, the calm gaze of the Virgin reminded her.

I don't know anything about Kallinikos! she told the Virgin. *Only that he came to the city because he was ambitious to work on fire. For all I know he has an abandoned wife and children back in Heliopolis.*

The words fell away and disintegrated. What Kallinikos might have been or done in Heliopolis did not change what Anna felt, however it might affect what she could do about it.

She had no idea what she wanted to do. Marry the man? It still seemed far too much of a risk. She knew, though, that Kallinikos' arrest had struck her a crippling blow, and that if he were sent off to Cherson as a wretched prisoner it would torment her for the rest of her life.

Help me, she prayed at last, desperately. *Help me. He's been arrested, he's in prison. It's a long way to Cherson, and winter is coming. He might die. Help him. Save him.*

The Virgin and her son gazed back at her in silence. The Christ-child's hand rested on an orb and cross. *I am salvation*, said his solemn eyes. *That was the purpose of my birth.*

Anna was, however, bitterly aware that salvation and the preservation of *life* were not the same thing. She had prayed for Theodosius, too, when he was shut away under the guard of the Unsleeping; she had prayed and wept and felt certain that God heard her. She believed, still, that God had, and she believed that Theodosius was saved . . . but not on earth. The world was full of corruption and sorrow; whether a man lived or died depended on luck, and everyone's luck ran out in the end. There was no salvation on earth.

Help me, she prayed again. She crossed herself, rose, and went to look for the priest.

Father Agapios was working in his garden by the house behind the church. Theodosia's description of him as a 'stupid old man' was not quite fair: he was only old to the critical eyes of a twelve-year-old. A tall man in his forties, with a thick salt-and-pepper beard and a deep voice, he was married – as most orthodox priests were – and was the father of a loutish fourteen-year-old son whom Theodosia despised. He was loved by his congregation, however, for his good nature, and was much admired for his deep bass singing of the divine service. He was, however, very garrulous and not particularly intelligent.

He was pleased to see Anna, and thanked her again for the incense. It was some time before she could get him off the subject: he deplored the shortage of incense in the city, told her what other churches were doing about it, thanked her again, praised the appropriateness of the scents of rosemary and honey to the Blessed Virgin . . .

'Father,' Anna interrupted desperately, 'I need your help.'

'Of course, my child!' he agreed, at once looking solemn. 'I hadn't thought: this shortage of imported spices must be injuring your trade, too. A most calamitous business. When I was a child I would never have believed that our enemies could cut us off from the Mediterranean. A Roman lake, we called it, and thought it our very own possession, but—'

'No, no!' protested Anna sharply. 'My business is fine!' While Agapios blinked, she quickly told him of Kallinikos' arrest.

She exaggerated, of course. She said that the Syrian was a devout man who had fled the heretics because of his desire to help the capital of Christendom; that he had devised such an excellent new incendiary for the city's defence that his jealous superior had feared for his own job, and had falsely accused him of theft. However, even this simple version was hard for Father Agapios to grasp.

'Why haven't I seen him here?' he asked Anna in bewilderment. 'You say he's devout, but I've never seen him here.'

'He doesn't live in Philadelphion, Father,' explained Anna. 'He rents in a tenement over by the Platea Gate.'

'Oh. I thought you'd rented him a room.'

'No, Father. That wouldn't be appropriate, would it? I'm an unmarried woman. I can't take in strange men!'

'No, of course not! What was I thinking? But how do you know this man, then?'

Anna explained that he had helped her daughter when she was knocked down by a horse, and that she had befriended him afterwards, seeing that he knew no one in the city and was very poor. 'His superior has been taking most of his salary,' she said. 'I felt sorry for him. Theodosia regards him as an honorary uncle.'

Agapios was convinced, and swore that he would protest to the governor of the Strategion Prison . . .

'No, no Father!' said Anna, beginning to feel impatient. 'You must ask for help from the *Bishop*, or from someone near him. Kallinikos' superior, Stephanos Skyles, is an important man, and he's the one who's brought the accusation. The governor of the prison wouldn't listen to you if you contradicted the Magistros of the Arsenal.'

Agapios understood, but dithered about whom to approach. Anna suggested the Bishop's secretary. This was received with dismay. 'But he's a most *impatient*, abrupt, bad-tempered fellow!' the priest protested. 'He says, "Come to the point!", and shouts at me.'

Anna had some sympathy for the secretary. 'I can come with you, if you like,' she offered.

'That would be good,' said Agapios, with relief. 'We'll go tomorrow morning.'

'Can't we go now?' Anna asked unhappily.

'No, no!' said the priest, shocked. 'I have a vestry meeting this afternoon.'

Anna started home, unhappily wondering if Theodosia was right to have dismissed Father Agapios as useless. Who else, though, could she ask for help? The head of the Perfumers' Guild, perhaps?

No. He didn't have enough authority to raise a question against a decision by the Magistros of the Arsenal. Besides, the head this year was Anastasios, and he was the cousin of Timotheos, who was still angry with Anna because she'd rejected his offer of marriage. Could she appeal to a magistrate?

She arrived back at the workshop shortly after noon, and discovered that Theodosia had rendered the question completely irrelevant. The package for Kallinikos sat half-completed on the kitchen table, and Helena, who was putting her feet up beside it, said that Theodosia had left the house half an hour before. 'She said she was going to ask someone for help,' the slave informed Anna. 'She said she already told you who.'

Five

Anna stood in front of the Bronze Gate of the Great Palace, looking up at the cross mounted on the summit of the dome. The bronze cladding on the dome itself was dark from centuries of wind and rain, but the cross was gilded, and shone brightly against the grey October sky.

She had passed those gates before. On the last occasion, it had been in shackles, with a baby Theodosia crying in her arms.

She closed her eyes, trying to force away the fear-filled memories. Her arrest had been inevitable: Theodosius had just been executed for treason. The palace officials had been bound to question her. She should take comfort from the fact that they'd released her after a single night, and that they hadn't harmed Theodosia. There was no reason to feel such a horror of the place now. This time she was *not* under arrest. She was *not* going to the Noumera Prison. The Great Palace was a huge place, and most of the people in it probably didn't even know where that prison was.

In fact the Great Palace was almost a city in itself. As well as nearly a dozen imperial residences, it had its own harbour and warehouses. It controlled the trade in silk, which could be sold only in the palace's House of Lamps. Within its walls were barracks and banqueting halls, stables and churches, libraries and offices. Soldiers and servants, petitioners and priests, went back and forth through its gardens and grounds all day. Hundreds of people went to work through the Bronze Gate every morning, and came out again safely at the end of the day. There was nothing to be afraid of.

Unconvinced, Anna silently admitted to herself that there was everything to be afraid of. The palace was a devourer of lives. If Theodosia had entered it, how likely was it that she would be allowed to leave again unharmed? It would eat her. Perhaps it would wrap her in silk and suck away all her joy and freedom: that was the *lucky* outcome. It might send her back mutilated, her nose slit to discourage her from politics; it might lock her in the Noumera Prison. It might even kill her. As for Anna – the palace would spit out her indigestible plebeian bones, to limp home to the ashes of her life and hopes.

Anna took a deep breath and walked up to the monumental entrance way.

The great bronze doors stood open, though they were watched over by a pair of soldiers in the red and green uniform of the Scholarian Guard. Anna stopped between the men.

'Sirs,' she said respectfully. 'I am looking for my daughter, who I think may have come this way about half an hour ago.'

The guardsmen blinked at her from under their helmets. They were very young, she saw: novice soldiers set to keep the gates while more experienced men did the real work of preparing the city for a siege. 'Is your daughter called Theodosia?' asked the one on the right.

Anna felt a numbness settle over her heart. She'd hoped that the obvious conclusion had been mistaken, and that Theodosia had in fact gone somewhere else. She nodded.

'She was here,' the young man agreed.

'She said she was the daughter of Theodosius, the brother of the Emperor Constans,' said the guard on the left. 'Is it true?'

Anna swallowed and did not answer. 'What happened?' she asked instead. Her voice came out high and strained.

'She said she wanted to see the Emperor!' said the first guardsman. 'She said it was important to the city! We told her to go in and speak to the officer of the watch. Is she really the daughter of Theodosius?'

Anna fleetingly considered saying, *No, she's just touched in her wits, poor girl!* It was already too late for that, though. The officer of the watch would certainly have consulted his superiors by now. Theodosia's existence was a matter of record, and whatever she said or did now, the great bureaucracy would check. Nothing would serve now except the truth. 'Yes,' whispered Anna. 'I must speak to the officer of the watch.'

'In there on the right,' said the young soldier, indicating the entrance passage with a nod of the head. As Anna started down the passageway, he asked anxiously, 'Is there some treason?'

'No,' replied Anna in surprise. She took the door on the right.

The reception hall of the Bronze Gate was the first port of call for petitioners at the palace, and it had been designed to impress. The interior of the great dome was supported by eight arches set on four massive pillars; below it, the upper walls were decorated with mosaics of the campaigns of the Emperor Justinian, while the lower walls were variegated marble. All were faded now, though, their colours dimmed by years of grime from the smoke of the braziers used to heat the room through cold winters. The marble floor was stained and dirty. The officer of the watch, who was not much older than the guardsmen, sat hunched over a brazier at the far end of the room, along with two more of his men. A single tired petitioner huddled waiting on a bench nearby. Anna went over and asked her question.

'Your daughter?' said the young officer. 'Yes, of course! I sent her to the Octagon with an escort. Is she really . . . ?'

'Yes,' said Anna. 'Please, I should be with her. She's too young to be here alone.'

'Leontios will take you,' said the officer, snapping his fingers and indicating one of his men.

The subordinate, a pimply mail-clad youth with a prominent Adam's apple, leapt to his feet and saluted. 'Sir!' he exclaimed. 'Um – *where* in the Octagon?'

'Ask them where they sent the other one!' snapped the officer. Then he raised a hand, demanding a pause. He was staring at Anna with a worried expression. 'Is there treason?' he asked, as the gate guard had.

'No,' said Anna, as she had before.

'Your daughter said it was important to the city,' said the officer. 'And I thought, if she's really the daughter of Theodosius . . .'

Anna realized that the conclusion was the obvious one. A young girl claiming to be the daughter of a popular and murdered prince appeared at the palace gate asking to see the Emperor on a matter 'important to the city': what else could it mean but that someone had tried to use her in a treasonous plot? It was not a happy realization: it meant that the matter would be treated as serious and urgent.

'There's no treason,' Anna said wearily. 'A friend of ours who works in the Arsenal has made a discovery which my daughter thinks might help the city's defence, that's all.'

'Oh,' said the officer, and looked relieved.

The Scholarian called Leontios cleared his throat nervously and gestured at the doors that led on into the palace. Anna drew her cloak more tightly around her, nodded, and they set out.

The palace known as the Octagon lay near the Bronze Gate, just beyond the barracks of the Scholarians. It was a rambling building, begun by Constantine the Great, but added to by almost every emperor since. The emperor Heraclius had always favoured it, and his descendants used it as their principal residence. Anna had once asked Theodosius if she could see it, but he had grimaced and said he had no intention of taking her into 'that snake-pit'.

It didn't look like a snake-pit. It looked the way a palace ought to look: there were floors of marble or mosaic, curtains worked with purple and gold, exquisite statues standing on pedestals, silk carpets, dark paintings in heavy, gilded frames. The guards on the door directed young Leontius to go to the office of 'the Most Illustrious Andreas'.

'The *chamberlain*?' asked Leontius, looking alarmed.

'You know any other Most Illustrious Andreas?' asked the guard on the door.

Leontius swallowed and shook his head. Anna swallowed, too. The Grand Chamberlain was one of the most powerful officials in the empire, even though he was always a eunuch, and hence a freed slave. Andreas had held the title since the

Emperor's accession, and was famous throughout the empire for his cruel efficiency and his complete loyalty to his master. Theodosia had, indeed, managed to get her appeal treated as serious and urgent.

The young soldier gave Anna a look of nervous sympathy, which made her feel worse, and led her on into the palace. They made their way through a labyrinth of adjoining rooms, frequently stopping to ask a passing servant if they were going in the right direction. At last they came to a chamber on the north side of the building.

The only thing Anna noticed when she entered the room was Theodosia. She cried out in relief, and her daughter spun towards her.

Theodosia had obviously put on her best to meet her cousin: she was dressed in her good winter cloak of heavy red wool, and she'd put on her finest earrings and the garnet brooch Anna had given her for her birthday the year before. Her face was flushed, and her eyes were bright, though whether with anger or with fear, Anna couldn't say. Anna rushed across the space between them. She wanted to hug her errant child, but Theodosia's air of brittle dignity prevented her: instead she caught the girl's hands and pressed them.

Theodosia stood frozen a moment, then clasped her mother's hands with her own, pressing hard. She turned back to the man she'd been speaking to when Anna arrived. 'This is my mother,' she informed him.

That the man was a eunuch was plain from his smooth, beardless face; that he was a high-ranking courtier, from the broad purple stripe on his cloak of white silk: plainly, this was the notorious Andreas. He was slight and soft-featured, almost feminine in appearance, and his hands were adorned with numerous rings. 'So I see,' he remarked, in a fluting voice. 'Anna, the daughter of Kyrillos?' He glanced at the man beside him.

Anna glanced at the other as well, then froze, staring: the palace was a snake-pit after all, and here was a snake, one whose bite caused agony. She recognized the heavy face with its square-cut beard: this was the officer who'd been in charge of questioning her after her arrest.

He did not seem to want to meet her eyes. He nodded at the eunuch, who nodded back with an air of satisfaction. The officer was much less satisfied: he fidgeted unhappily and stared at the floor.

'We were about to send for you,' the chamberlain informed Anna.

For a horrible moment she was sure they would send her back to the Noumera Prison. Then she told herself fiercely that they merely wanted to confirm Theodosia's identity before they troubled the Emperor. The officer from the prison was here only because he could identify Theodosia's mother.

'I followed my daughter as soon as I knew she'd gone, my lord,' Anna replied quietly. She was relieved that she managed to keep her voice even.

'Indeed, she said she'd come without your permission,' remarked Andreas significantly. 'Would you have prevented her?'

'Yes,' agreed Anna at once. 'I saw no reason to trouble Our Lord the Emperor because a friend of ours has been arrested. Sir, my daughter is young and excitable. She is worried about our friend. If she has imposed on you with something that doesn't merit your attention, please forgive her.'

Theodosia's head snapped up. 'It's for the city!' she declared loudly. 'The city can't afford to throw away any weapon, let alone this one!'

The eunuch surveyed her with amusement. 'And how much experience do you have of weapons, little one? Never mind. I will inform His Sacred Majesty that you're here and asking to speak with him. Whatever he thinks of your errand, I am sure that he will be . . . *intrigued* . . . by *you*.' He waved a languid hand at the bearded officer. 'You may go back to your duties,' he said.

The officer saluted and left. Anna felt as though the room suddenly contained more air, and drew a deep breath in relief.

Leontios the guard shuffled his feet uncomfortably. 'Sir?' he asked nervously. 'Should I go back to the gate?'

Andreas gave him a look of displeasure. 'No. You are to stay with these women until I dismiss you.'

The young man's Adam's apple leapt as he swallowed, and he bowed humbly. Anna wondered if the fact that Andreas hadn't summoned a more senior man to guard them meant that he was favourably disposed to them, or whether it only meant he didn't think they were worth taking seriously.

The chamberlain went out, leaving Anna alone with Theodosia and their guard. Anna guessed that they were standing in Andreas' office. It was certainly an office of some sort: it held a writing table, with a seal stamp and a document rack, and it was luxuriously appointed. There was a carpet of pure silk, and the lampstand was made of gold.

Theodosia looked at her mother. The girl's face was still flushed, and her eyes were brilliant. She looked so lovely that Anna's throat hurt. *My child*, she thought wretchedly, *what have you done?*

'I had to, Mama,' Theodosia said, as though she'd heard the thought. 'It isn't because I'm worried about Kallinikos. I am, but that's not why I had to come. It's for the city!'

'You've wanted to do this for a long time,' replied Anna quietly. That had somehow become very clear to her.

Theodosia hesitated, then nodded. Her lower lip trembled. 'I want to know about my father.'

Anna rested a hand on the girl's thin shoulders. *No, you don't*, she thought – but she couldn't say it. She had, she saw now, lied to Theodosia – or perhaps not lied, but omitted uncomfortable truths. She had known that to a great noble like Theodosius a beautiful concubine was an item much like a fine horse: something to impress friends with and to enjoy in hours of leisure. Concubines were not *important*. A nobleman might love his concubine – but he might well love his favourite horse, too. She had never really mattered to Theodosius – not the way the people who inhabited the snake-pit of the palace mattered. She had, however, painted for her daughter a picture of a kind father who would have loved and protected his daughter as though she were legitimate. She had done it, she saw, because she hadn't wanted her precious child to feel she was nothing but a shopkeeper's bastard. Theodosia, however, had believed her, and now was trying to claim a heritage which was largely imaginary.

Anna remembered how the officer who had just left had questioned her in the Noumera prison. 'I think you're lying,' he had said, 'I think he did confide in you.'

'No,' she had replied, 'No, I was just his mistress. He never confided in me at all.'

They had put her on the rack and beaten her on the soles of the feet until she screamed and wept. She remembered the officer twisting his hand in her hair to pull her head up. 'I think you're lying,' he'd said again, stroking the tears of pain from her face with calloused fingers. 'Any man would pour out all his secrets to a face like this.'

'He never told me anything!' she had sobbed. 'You had him watched for months; you *know* I'm telling the truth. Please, please let me have my baby back! She's only a bastard: you know she doesn't matter to anyone but me!'

That had been the worst part of the whole nightmare: that they'd taken Theodosia away from her as soon as she reached the prison. She still didn't know what they'd done with her. The baby was returned to her the following morning, hungry, dirty, crying, but unharmed, and Anna had been allowed to hobble home. She had never told anyone about that night in the Noumera Prison. It was a place and time which she'd never wanted to visit again.

If they took Theodosia away now, Anna would never get her back.

'What will happen, will happen,' she said sadly. 'We are all in the hands of God.'

The chamberlain returned a few minutes later, smiling to himself. 'As I thought,' he told Theodosia. 'His Sacred Majesty is intrigued, and wishes to see you at once. Your mother may accompany you.' He waved at young Leontios as though he were brushing away a fly. 'You are dismissed.'

The young man smiled with relief, then nodded nervously to Anna and Theodosia. 'Good luck,' he whispered – then cleared his throat, saluted smartly, and jingled out.

Andreas curled his lip in distaste. '*Where* are they recruiting the Guard these days?' he asked nobody in particular. 'Come along!'

He led through another series of rooms, each grander and

more beautiful than the one before it. 'I don't suppose you've had an audience before?' he asked. 'Very well: you approach His Sacred Majesty until you are about three paces away, and then you prostrate yourself. When he acknowledges you, you may rise. You may stand or kneel in his presence, but not sit. You should not speak unless he invites you to do so. You should address him as "Master", like a slave, or as "Your Majesty": he is God's viceroy, and to address him as though he were just another nobleman would be presumptuous.'

Theodosia nodded, as though she were taking it all in. Anna just felt numb. They came to a gilded door where another pair of guards stood watch, and were admitted into a great hall under a high dome. It had eight sides, and at one end was an apse decorated with a mosaic of Christ in majesty. Beneath it stood a throne, and on the throne sat the Emperor. The purple of his cloak echoed the purple robe of Christ above his head, and his fair hair was bound with the jewelled circlet of the imperial diadem. A handful of guards and attendants stood, statue-still, along the sides of the room, like images in a church.

Anna was surprised by two things as they approached across the vast hall. The first was that Constantine, fourth monarch of that name, was not much older than the young men who guarded his gate. She should have known that, of course: she'd known he was only a child when Theodosia was born. Somehow, though, she had never thought it through. How could he be so young when he was God's viceroy on Earth?

The second surprise was how much he looked like his uncle Theodosius. He had the same thick, fair, slightly curly hair and the same wide forehead; his eyes were the same dark, changeable hazel. As they approached he leaned forward, resting an elbow on his knee and gazing at Theodosia with eager interest.

At three paces from the throne, the eunuch stopped and prostrated himself on the carpeted floor. At once Anna copied him, hearing the rustle of clothing as Theodosia did the same.

'You may rise,' said the Emperor. He had a strong, deep

96

voice. Anna got to her feet, pulled her cloak tight again. She found that Constantine was gazing at her.

'So,' he said. 'This is the beautiful concubine who left my uncle convinced that he had no vocation to the religious life. I'm disappointed, Andreas.'

'Disappointed, Master?' asked the eunuch, smiling.

'She looks utterly respectable,' said Constantine. 'When I used to imagine having a beautiful concubine, they were always dressed in something more interesting!' He waved a contemptuous hand at the black cloak. 'What's the point of this, Woman? Widow's weeds, when you were never a wife? A pretense of modesty, when you stand there with your bastard at your side? Is it intended to persuade me of your virtue, and make me willing to part with a stipend for the upkeep of my traitorous uncle's only offspring?'

'No, Master,' Anna murmured. Sick with shame, she glanced at her daughter.

Theodosia had gone crimson. 'My mother *is* modest and respectable!' she exclaimed angrily. 'Everybody knows that!'

The was a rustle as some of the attendants by the wall whispered to each other. Anna, alarmed, tried to shush her daughter with a warning hand: this was, after all, a man who'd had the noses of his own brothers slit. The Emperor, however, merely looked at Theodosia with raised eyebrows.

'My mother never even wanted to come here!' Theodosia went on, oblivious to her danger. 'She told *me* not to come, but I disobeyed her, and she came after me. *I* came because I thought you'd want to know about a weapon which could destroy the Caliph's fleet – but I guess you'd rather just sneer at us . . . Your Majesty!'

Fortunately, the Emperor simply seemed to be amused by so much boldness in such a young girl. He laughed. 'Go on, then!' he exclaimed. 'What's this weapon that can destroy a fleet? Your temper, perhaps, little girl? Your insolent tongue?'

Theodosia drew a deep breath. The edges of her nostrils were white. 'You have no reason to insult me like that!' she declared. 'I haven't asked you for anything, and I haven't even finished saying why I came!' She gestured imperiously

97

at the mosaic of Christ behind the Emperor's head. '*He* didn't insult people who appealed to him, even if they were poor and sinful.'

Constantine straightened on his throne. 'Oh, clever! Did someone tell you to say that?'

'Don't you even care about destroying the Caliph's fleet?' demanded Theodosia furiously.

'Of course I care about that!' exclaimed the Emperor impatiently. 'But if the thing were so simple that a young girl knew how to do it, I do think my generals might be able to work it out.'

'We have a friend,' Theodosia announced. Her voice was clear and strong, unafraid, though Anna stood near enough to see that she was trembling. 'An engineer who works at the Arsenal, an expert in fire. He's invented a kind of liquid fire. It floats on water. He thinks it could be pumped out in front of the enemy fleet, and then you could set fire to it and burn their ships.' She drew another deep breath and continued, 'He showed it to us. It works.'

There was a silence. Then Constantine shook his head. 'If this were true, it would have been reported to me.'

'No, it wouldn't,' Theodosia replied at once, 'because Stephanos Skyles, your Magistros of the Arsenal, is afraid for his job. First he told our friend he had to work on the liquid fire in his own time, and then he forbade him to use the Arsenal's supplies for it. Our friend did all the work anyway, but he did it on his own, and he was planning to go behind Stephanos' back when he had enough of the new fire ready to demonstrate. He was getting a pump so he could pump some out on to the sea and show everyone how well it works. Only, Stephanos has charged him with stealing from the Arsenal, and he's been thrown into prison. He's going to be sent to Cherson. Nobody else knows about the fire.'

There was another silence. The Emperor stared at Theodosia, frowning. 'Why is it that you know about it, then?' he asked.

'Kallinikos bought an ambix from my mother,' Theodosia replied. 'We're the only friends he has in the city. He told us all about it.'

Constantine was puzzled. 'An ambix?'

'You use it to distil things, Your Majesty,' Theodosia said knowledgeably. 'My mother uses one to make perfume. Kallinikos used his to distil Median rock oil and make it more flammable.'

Constantine's eyes narrowed. 'This Kallinikos is the engineer? And he was employed by the Arsenal? This liquid fire – you say you've actually *seen* that it works?'

'Yes,' agreed Theodosia. She was trembling more violently now. 'He showed it to us. Mama?'

'He did,' agreed Anna. 'He poured it into a water bath and set fire to it. It burned like the fires of hell, on top of the water.'

The emperor sat silently on his throne for a long moment. One finger tapped the armrest, moving without pattern or rhythm. Then he turned to his chamberlain. 'Andreas,' he said.

The eunuch bowed.

'This merits investigation. Summon Stephanos Skyles, and this engineer Kallinikos . . .' He glanced at Theodosia.

'Kallinikos of Heliopolis,' supplied Theodosia.

The Emperor frowned again. 'Of *Heliopolis*? He isn't from the city?'

Anna felt a weakness at the knees. She realized belatedly that Theodosia's judgement had been true, and keener than her own: the liquid fire *was* important. The Emperor had admitted Theodosia out of simple curiosity, but the fire was potentially something that mattered to him.

'He's from Heliopolis in S–Syria, M–Master,' Anna stammered eagerly. 'He's a refugee from the heretics. He arrived in the city only this spring. He told me that he wanted to work on fire, and that he wanted to stop the Mohammedans from ruling the world.' She found herself looking into those misleadingly familiar hazel eyes. 'I think,' she went on, 'that the guards who admitted him to the city sent him to the Arsenal because they were convinced he could help to defend us. I think Lord Stephanos saw him as a threat from the start, but didn't dare do anything openly because then he'd have to explain himself to the city guards. He's been

trying to make Kallinikos give up and go somewhere else.'
She hadn't, in fact, thought about it at all before, but now it
seemed to make sense.

The Emperor looked at his chamberlain. 'See what we
have on this Syrian,' he commanded. 'And on Stephanos
Skyles.'

Andreas bowed. 'Master, if I may . . .' he fluted. The
Emperor looked permission at him, and he went on, 'We
should send for Sissinios as well. If there's a question of
misconduct by Stephanos, he ought to be present.'

'Well thought of,' conceded Constantine. 'See to it.'

Andreas prostrated himself, then rose to go.

'Kallinikos is in the Strategion Prison,' Theodosia told
him.

The eunuch gave her an indecipherable look. 'Thank you,'
he said drily.

He left. The Emperor leaned back in his throne and looked
at Theodosia.

'So,' he said, after a silence. 'That was why you decided
to come to see me?'

'Yes, Your Majesty,' she agreed. 'It was important.'

'If your report is accurate, it is,' he admitted. He looked
her up and down. 'How old are you?'

She flushed slightly. 'Thirteen in December.'

'Twelve! I confess, until this afternoon I had no idea I
had a bastard cousin. The concubine I'd heard of, but not
the bastard daughter. Yet there you stand, twelve years old,
a very pretty girl – and, so it seems, interested in affairs of
state! Did my uncle make any provision for you?'

There was a silence. 'My mother told me that he *tried* to,
Your Majesty,' Theodosia declared defiantly. 'But when he
was killed, the Emperor gave the money to the Monastery of
the Studion instead.'

Constantine looked at Anna. 'And you never tried to get
it back? Or claim a stipend for her?'

Anna bowed very low. 'No, Master. I have never claimed
anything on my daughter's behalf. I do not claim it now.
Your Majesty, my daughter and I are humble people. In
Philadelphion, however, our own neighbourhood, we are

100

considered well-to-do, even wealthy. My business provides us with a good livelihood, and we are perfectly content with what we have.'

'Your business?'

'I am a perfume-maker, Master.'

'Indeed, so your daughter said. A respectable trade for an almost-widow.'

She no longer found that sarcastic accusation so paralysing. 'Yes, Master,' she said neutrally. 'My trade *is* respectable, and I practise it honestly. Your Majesty, I beg you not to take offence at the way I am dressed. A woman managing a business on her own must struggle for respect in the best of circumstances. A woman such as myself, who has never been a wife, must struggle harder. I wear black, not to deceive men, but to make it clear to them that the goods for sale in my shop do not include the proprietor.'

Another moment of silence, and the cold assessment of those familiar eyes. 'You say, then, that you have had nothing to do with men since the death of my uncle?'

Anna bowed. 'I have had neither the need nor the wish to become any man's dependant.'

He thought about that. His eyes drifted to Theodosia, and back again. 'So, you have brought up my little cousin in modest respectability, as the heiress to a perfume shop?'

'Yes, Master.'

'And you, cousin?' said the Emperor, turning his attention back to Theodosia. 'Are you as "perfectly content" as is your mother with this humble, respectable way of life?'

Theodosia hesitated. Anna saw the Emperor notice the hesitation, saw the smile, and felt chilled to the heart.

'I love my mother,' Theodosia replied at last. 'I know she loves me. I trust her to choose what's best for me.' She paused again, then straightened her narrow shoulders and added, 'I would never have come here just to *ask* for something. It wouldn't be right for me to *ask* for things.'

'Your father was a traitor,' said Constantine, leaning forward on his throne. 'My father was right to have him put to death. There can be only one emperor. Anything else is anarchy, and the whole state would suffer for it.'

101

Theodosia met him stare for stare. 'My father would have been your father's loyal servant, if he'd been given the chance!'

Constantine smiled. 'And would you be *my* loyal servant, little cousin, if I gave *you* the chance?'

She dropped her eyes and was silent a moment. Then she looked up again. 'Yes,' she agreed, with an open, unmistakable sincerity. 'I'm your loyal servant already. I wouldn't have come here today if I weren't. You're emperor, you're in charge of the war. Everyone in the city should obey you and support you, or we're all lost.'

Constantine struck the arm of his throne and gave a crow of delight. 'Well spoken, child! Before Christ, I wish my generals had heard that!' He snapped his fingers and turned to one of his attendants. 'Take these ladies out and present them to the Empress. Say that I ask her to accept them as ladies in waiting, or to find some other rank suitable for them, as she wishes. Explain that I recognize the girl as my cousin.'

The attendant he'd spoken to, a young eunuch, at once prostrated himself. Theodosia copied him. She got up again and looked at her cousin. 'May I come back when Kallinikos gets here, Your Majesty?'

The Emperor smiled again. 'I will have you summoned at once.'

The young eunuch led them out of the Octagon audience chamber. They walked through two grand and empty rooms, and then Anna stopped. Now, it seemed, there was an *empress* to face, and she didn't see how she could. All the events of the day seemed to crash down upon her at once, and she could not go on. *Only this morning*, she thought wonderingly, *only this morning I was working in the shop*. The ordinary beginning of the day now seemed like a happy memory from childhood, recollected with longing in the middle of adult turmoil.

'Mama?' asked Theodosia anxiously.

Anna seized her roughly. 'Oh, my girl!' she exclaimed, half-hugging, half-shaking her. 'What have you done to us?'

Theodosia pushed her away, then stood looking at her reproachfully. 'Don't!' she pleaded. 'It isn't over yet!'

102

'I don't think it will *ever* be over,' Anna told her bitterly. 'Not until we're dead.'

Theodosia's face worked. 'Don't!' she said again. '*Please*, don't. Not right now!'

She was almost on the point of bursting into tears, and that somehow gave Anna strength. She reached out and gently tucked a stray lock of hair up under her daughter's scarf. 'I won't, then,' she said. 'We will both just have to be brave.'

Theodosia took several deep breaths, then turned and nodded to the attendant, who had stood watching this in silence. He was a complete palace functionary – smooth-faced, silk-clad, black hair oiled and curled into innumerable ringlets, unfathomable thoughts going on behind dark eyes that gave nothing away. He smiled placidly and led them on into the palace.

The Empress Anastasia was choosing silk when the guests were presented to her. She reclined gracefully on a golden couch in her own audience chamber, surrounded by a crowd of her ladies. She was a spectacularly beautiful girl, with full red lips and huge brown eyes, and she wore her purple drapery with negligent assurance. One of the palace eunuchs held up samples of material for her to examine while the merchants competing to sell to her hovered respectfully in the background.

The imperial guide went up to her and whispered something. The Empress looked at Anna and Theodosia. 'What, now?' she asked, pouting.

The young eunuch whispered some more.

'A *bastard*?' asked the Empress, wrinkling her nose in disgust. 'I didn't know Theodosius had any!' She looked at her guests another moment with distaste, then grimaced as though she'd smelled something revolting and beckoned them to approach.

She was, Anna realized, going to comply with the Emperor's request, but only because she had to. She was a well-brought-up aristocrat, and she clearly hated the thought of accepting a pair of dubious commoners into her retinue. She had no power, however, except what her husband allowed her,

103

and she would not oppose him – though she might vent some of her displeasure on the women who had just been foisted upon her.

Anna and Theodosia moved forward, then – at a nod from the eunuch – prostrated themselves to the woman who wore the purple. The Empress sat up, casually extended a purple slipper to be kissed, then gestured for them to rise.

'I gather you're a bastard cousin of my husband,' she said, looking down her nose at Theodosia. 'And that this is your mother—' another disdainful look, at Anna – 'the discarded mistress of his uncle the traitor!'

The court ladies whispered among themselves, staring.

Anna bowed low. 'Not a discarded mistress, Your Majesty.' The young woman's contempt stung, and her self-control had been shaken to breaking point over the course of the day. 'I was the concubine of the lord Theodosius, and he didn't discard me: he died. I know that it offends you to have to deal with me, but there's no need to make the thing worse than it actually is.'

The eunuch who'd guided them smiled. The court ladies looked shocked. The empress flushed slightly. 'Insolent woman!' she exclaimed. 'You come here asking for favours . . .'

Anna at once prostrated herself. 'Forgive me,' she said, climbing back to her feet. 'I didn't come here asking for anything. I was perfectly contented with my perfume manufactory and my shop in the city, and I never asked anything from the sacred palace. I have no more wish to be here than you to have me. My daughter, however, discovered some information important to the security of the city, and insisted on bringing it to her cousin the Emperor. Now we've delivered it, all I want is to take my daughter and go back to my shop. If your Majesty wishes to dismiss us, I will be very glad to go.'

The Empress looked at the attendant eunuch. He folded his hands together and looked pious. 'His Sacred Majesty asks you, in the loftiness of your noble nature, to look on these women favourably,' he began, in well-rounded fluting tones. 'It is true that his cousin came to him, not to ask favours, but to bring him some information concerning a weapon invented by a friend, which may be important to the defence of the city. Our gracious master was, however, pleased to learn of the existence of a cousin he had known nothing about, and delighted to find her so virtuous and loyal. Her mother was, it is true, a concubine, but since the death of her patron she has conducted herself with a modesty and piety that would put many wives to shame. She has kept strictly from the society of men, and has devoted herself to prayer for her patron's soul and to bringing up his daughter in virtue and holiness. His Sacred Majesty, knowing how you rejoice in goodness, is sure that you will reward these two with the serene light of your celestial favour.'

Anna blinked in astonishment; Theodosia was dumbstruck. The Empress grimaced. 'I *do* rejoice in goodness!' she protested petulantly, with a look at Anna and Theodosia which said plainly she didn't see any in them.

However, she surveyed them one more time, then said, 'Well, since my husband asks it, I must agree to number you among my attendants. At least you *look* presentable enough. I warn you, though: I have the power to dismiss you for misconduct, and if you misconduct yourselves, I will use it! Sophronia!'

One of the court ladies bowed.

'Get them some proper clothes, will you?' The Empress lay down on her couch again and snapped her fingers to summon back the eunuch with the silk.

Sophronia, a horse-faced matron in a cloak of flowered silk, beckoned them back the way they'd come. Their guide came with them, looking pleased with himself.

'I don't suppose any of that was true?' Sophronia asked him, when they were in the next room.

The eunuch bowed and smiled. 'It's what they were saying in the Octagon, Lady Sophronia. I just coloured it a bit. I thought it sounded good, myself. You didn't like it?'

'Overdone,' said Sophronia judiciously. 'She isn't stupid. She suspected you were making fun of her.'

The eunuch's eyes opened wide. 'I wouldn't do that! You know me, you know that I just like elevated language.'

105

'Ha!' exclaimed Sophronia, in the voice of one who knows better.

'You didn't even like "the serene light of your celestial favour"?' the eunuch asked winningly.

'That was pretty,' Sophronia conceded.

The eunuch smiled in satisfaction. 'I thought so.' He bowed, and headed back towards the Octagon.

Sophronia turned to Anna and Theodosia. '*Was* it true?'

'My mother has always been modest and respectable,' said Theodosia belligerently. 'That's true.'

'Hardly,' sniffed Sophronia. 'Since there you stand, and she without a husband.'

'My lady,' said Anna, with acid politeness, 'if you think my morals are so lax that they make me unfitted for the court, you are welcome to appoint some devout churchman to inquire into them. I hope, though, that in fairness you would allow him to inquire into the conduct of the other ladies of the court as well.' Although Anastasia was reputed virtuous, if half the rumours that reached the city were true there were several ladies in her retinue who would emerge from such an inquiry rather badly.

Sophronia arched her eyebrows and looked down her long nose. 'Been listening to gossip, have you?'

'Not by intention,' replied Anna pleasantly, 'but when there is a great deal of it about, it is hard to hear none of it.'

Sophronia sniffed. She and Anna gazed at one another for a moment like cats vying for places on a disputed wall. Anna found that she was hoping the other woman would say something offensive. She knew how to deal with prim, superior matrons who sneered at her. She'd met enough of them, after all.

Sophronia, however, seemed to sense this: she backed down. 'Well,' she said, turning away with a dismissive air, 'I suppose I'd better find you some court dress.'

The palace had a storeroom full of 'court dress': the clothing was distributed to the courtiers every Easter, a gift from the Emperor or Empress. Sophronia, it seemed, held the rank of 'Chartoularia of the Vestiarion of the Serene

Augusta', and was in charge not only of the Empress's wardrobe itself, but of the clothing reserved for gifts. She swished about among the racks and chests full of fine silks, bullying an inventory clerk, until clothing was found to fit Anna and Theodosia.

The first layer of court dress was a long tunic with sleeves, made of fine white silk; over this went a stola, a long sleeveless overtunic, richly brocaded and fastened with the distinguishing mark of an imperial lady-in-waiting: a girdle of gold links. A cloak was normally draped over the top of the whole assembly, but court ladies were supposed to provide this for themselves.

'Do you need to change now?' Sophronia asked, eyeing Anna's black wrap with disdain.

Anna was saved from having to reply by the return of the young eunuch who'd guided them before. 'His Sacred Majesty has sent for his cousin,' he announced. 'The engineer you told him about has arrived.'

Six

They were led back to the Octagon with the new court
dresses bundled in their arms. At the entrance to the
audience chamber, their guide took pity on them and detailed
a servant to take charge of the new clothes.

When they entered the great hall, Anna looked about hungrily for Kallinikos. He was not there. Apart from the attendants, the only people with the Emperor were the chamberlain
Andreas and a tall, lean man with a pointed black beard, who
wore the scarlet cloak of a general over a gilded breastplate.
He stood to the Emperor's left, and he looked annoyed about
something.

'Here are my little cousin Theodosia and her mother,' the
Emperor said, as Anna and Theodosia made the prostration.

The tall man looked at them in irritation. 'This *child* is
accusing Stephanos?' he asked. 'You summoned me for *that*,
Master?'

The Emperor smiled. 'Cousin, here is Lord Sissinios the
Drungarios.'

Both Anna and Theodosia stared. They had heard of
Sissinios, appointed Drungarios of the Karabisianoi, or Lord
Admiral, three years before after the turbulence of a prede-
cessor's execution. He was reputed to be an able and energetic
admiral and a devout churchman. He had been given charge
of the imperial fleet, the first line of the city's defence. He
was also Stephanos Skyles' superior.

The Emperor was now sitting back in his throne, watching
Theodosia with pleased anticipation. *He thinks she's funny*,
Anna thought, with a stab of resentment. *He's amused by
this bastard girl who dares to talk back to him.*

Theodosia bowed to the imperial drungarios, hesitantly and

rather clumsily. 'Lord Sissinios,' she said respectfully. 'All I've done has been to tell His Sacred Majesty what I know about the liquid fire.'

'What *you* know about fire, little girl?' asked Sissinios in disgust. 'That's a lot, is it?'

'I know that it works,' said Theodosia.

Sissinios snorted in contempt, but Constantine smiled. 'That is indeed what we most need to know about it,' he remarked.

'The engineer undoubtedly knows more,' the Emperor continued, still smiling. He snapped his fingers. 'Bring him in.'

The attendants had obviously had Kallinikos waiting outside, because at this there was a ripple down the sides of the room, and then the door at the far end was thrown open, and the Syrian was marched in between two guards.

He looked very much the worse for his three days in prison. His tunic was stained with worse than oil and torn near the hem, so that a great strip of it flapped around his calves as he walked; his cloak was missing altogether. His hair and beard were matted and dishevelled and he had a black eye. His hands were shackled in front of him, and his bruised face had an expression of hopeless disbelief. He stared at the floor in front of himself, not looking round. When his guards stopped him before the throne he glanced up at the Emperor, then dropped down on to his face on the marble floor, looking more overwhelmed than humble.

'Kallinikos of Heliopolis,' said the Emperor.

Kallinikos sat back on his heels without getting to his feet or raising his head. 'My lord,' he said, in a hoarse voice. 'I can explain . . .'

'I have been told that you have invented a new kind of incendiary, one that floats on water. Is this so?'

The Syrian's head came up at that, his eyes wide in surprise. He looked directly at the Emperor for the first time, then glanced round. He saw Anna and Theodosia. For a moment dismay and shame flashed across his face. He looked down again. His lips moved, but Anna could not hear what he was saying.

'Is this so?' repeated the Emperor, impatiently.

Kallinikos looked up at him again. 'Yes, my lord.'

Andreas cleared his throat. '*Master*,' he corrected gently.

Kallinikos flinched. 'Master.'

'I have been told,' Constantine went on deliberately, watching the prisoner carefully, 'that you are an expert in incendiaries.' He held out his hand, and an attendant placed in it a sheet of parchment. 'I have here,' the Emperor continued, 'a letter from the commander of my garrison in Cyzicus, dated this spring, saying that you greatly assisted them there in the preparation of fire canisters. He recommends you to the defenders of the city with some passion.'

'They were short of bitumen,' said Kallinikos. 'They were substituting olive oil, but it doesn't work very well. I told them they should add a mix of resin, oil, and coal dust and . . .' He trailed off, then said, 'Uh – yes, Master, I helped them with their fire canisters.'

'I also have a letter from a Captain Nikomachos, formerly commander of the garrison in Smyrna, which describes you as a learned man, well versed in military engineering, especially in the making of fires. He says he believes you to be sincere in your desire to defend the city against the onslaught of her enemies, and he urges the authorities here to make use of you.'

'We travelled together to Cyzicus,' said Kallinikos. 'We got to know each other.'

'We also have a report concerning you from one of our agents,' the Emperor continued. He looked at Andreas.

The chamberlain studied a paper in his hands. 'Yes. Compiled after the fellow was given work at the Arsenal, in the usual way, by questioning traders familiar with the news of Heliopolis. It seems,' he looked up again, 'that one Kallinikos, a member of one of the town's leading families, was recently obliged to flee Heliopolis after burning down a mosque. The city's Mohammedan priest accused him of sorcery.'

Kallinikos said nothing. He stared at the floor.

'*Did* you burn down a mosque?' asked the Emperor.

'It was an accident,' replied Kallinikos unhappily. 'And it wasn't burned down, it was just damaged a bit on the north side. But it's true that the imam blamed me for it. The sorcery charge . . . that's nonsense. Khalid ibn Yasir, the imam – he only put that in because he was so angry about his mosque, and because . . . well, Heliopolis, it's always been a pagan city, there *is* a lot of sorcery around, and Khalid's devout, he gets worked up about it and starts seeing it everywhere. I'm not a sorcerer, though, I swear it on the holy sacrament. I'm an orthodox Christian, like all my family. But I knew . . . I knew nobody was going to listen to me, not with Khalid foaming at the mouth about the damage to his mosque. I had to flee.'

'What actually happened?' asked the Emperor, leaning forward slightly, his elbows on his knees.

'It was an accident, Master,' Kallinikos repeated, meeting his eyes. He looked down again and drew a deep breath. 'I had a house near the mosque, and a fire started in it and spread to some of the neighbouring buildings. My house . . . my house burned to the ground, with my wife and my daughter and my nephew inside it. How could anyone believe I *meant* that to happen? What sane man would murder his own family in order to singe the bricks on the north side of some worthless mosque? I . . .' He stopped again, drew another breath, this one ragged. 'I thought I'd come here. I thought, if I'm to be damned for making fire, I'll make one that counts. I did invent the liquid fire you've been told of, Lord. Master. Yes. And it works, too. I was going to demonstrate it as soon as I had a pump.'

'A pump?' interjected Sissinios, after a silence. He was frowning. 'Why do you need a pump to demonstrate an incendiary?'

Kallinikos turned towards him. It was evident that he knew who Sissinios was: presumably he'd seen him at the Arsenal. 'To pump it out on to the sea, my lord. Through a hose. I mean, you wouldn't want to get it on your own ships. It's deadly stuff, as flammable as naphtha and harder to get off.' He gestured with his manacled hands. 'It floats, you see. My idea was that you could pump it out on to the sea, then set fire to it when the enemy ships reached it. I was planning to apply for an appointment to tell you about it, My Lord, as soon as I had the pump working.'

'It burns *on top of the water*?' asked Sissinios, still frowning.

'Yes,' agreed Kallinikos. 'Obviously, you'd have to use it in *calm* water. On a rough sea it would be churned about and mixed with water, and it probably wouldn't work then. I'd have to do some experiments to see. But on calm water it will blaze like the sun, and it will stick to anything that touches it and set that on fire, too. I've tested it.'

'Does Stephanos *know* you've made this stuff?' asked the drungarios.

Kallinikos' face darkened. 'No, My Lord. My Lord, he . . . I couldn't trust him. He's been out to get rid of me from the moment I arrived. The harbour authorities sent me to him with the recommendation that I be placed in charge of incendiaries, but he's set me to work making fire canisters with the slaves. He takes half my salary every month and tells me I should be grateful to be allowed to remain in the city at all. When I started working on the fire he told me that I couldn't use workshop time, and he only stopped short of banning me from doing the work at all when I offered to apply to Captain Sosthenes of the harbour guard for space. I had to buy my own distilling equipment, and once the work was under way, he told me that I couldn't use workshop supplies. He knew I couldn't afford to *buy* supplies, not on what I get as pay! But, My Lord, it isn't true that I was stealing. I made a full account of everything I borrowed, and I was going to present it to you once I'd done my demonstration. I would have repaid the value of it then, if you'd insisted, but I thought . . .' he hesitated, looking at Sissinios' forbidding face, then went on, 'I thought that after you'd seen the fire, I'd be rewarded, not punished.'

There was a moment's silence. 'Do you understand,' the Emperor asked quietly, 'that you are making a serious accusation against your superior, Stephanos Skyles, Magistros of the Arsenal? You are saying that he has deliberately tried to suppress the development of a weapon which might be of benefit to the city, at a time when the city is threatened with a most dangerous assault and siege.'

Kallinikos hesitated again, blinking. 'I'm not trying to

112

accuse him of *treason*! he exclaimed. 'It's just that the man is . . . is a pen-pushing *fool*! He's good at inventories and moving supplies around, but he wouldn't recognize a new incendiary if you burned him with it. He can't tell the difference between asphalt and bitumen. He thinks all incendiaries are the same, that you can easily substitute one for another, and that messing with stinking oils and sulphur is no job for a gentleman! But in spite of that, he wants the whole Arsenal in his hands, all the titles and all the money and all the power, with no challenge from anybody and everybody else just a slave. He's willing to cheat and lie to get rid of anyone who might become his rival. That's my accusation – not treason!'

'He's been a very effective Magistros of the Arsenal!' Sissinios replied angrily. He turned to the Emperor. 'Master, he's a good man, and I would find it very difficult to replace him. At the moment we have a surplus of material for the war. *All* the materials, not just this engineer's precious incendiaries! We have plenty of timber and rope for ships, we have more catapults than we can man, along with a vast supply of ammunition for them. We have an abundance of arrows, bowstrings, spears and swords, as well as everything we need to make more of them. We are in a good position to defend the city, and for that we owe some thanks to Stephanos Skyles. I do not want him disgraced.'

Kallinikos jerked his hands impatiently, making the manacles clank. 'My Lord, if the weapons you have could win this war, why is Mu'awiya's fleet sitting in the harbour at Cyzicus? I've brought you a new weapon – a gift you could never even have hoped for. Are you going to throw it away, because you don't want to disgrace Stephanos Skyles?'

'Admit Stephanos Skyles,' ordered the Emperor.

There was another ripple around the hall, and then the double doors were opened again, and Stephanos Skyles came in.

He was sleek and gleaming in full court dress, but he had an expression of nervous belligerence. Anna guessed that he'd seen Kallinikos before the other man was admitted, and that he knew why he'd been summoned. She saw him notice Sissinios the Drungarios and relax a little.

He stopped beside Kallinikos, then moved fastidiously aside before making the prostration to the Emperor. Unlike the Syrian he got to his feet afterwards. At this Kallinikos got up as well.

Constantine leaned back on his throne and rested his chin on a fist, gazing with critical pleasure at the two men who stood side by side before him, one of them resplendent in brocaded silk, the other manacled and in rags. 'Stephanos Skyles,' he began, 'I gather you have accused this man, Kallinikos of Heliopolis, of stealing from the Arsenal, which is in your charge.'

Stephanos bowed. 'Indeed, Master. It is, unfortunately, quite clear that he has done so. I am—'

'That's a lie!' exclaimed Kallinikos. 'I *borrowed* supplies. I kept full accounts. You never even *asked* me about them!'

Stephanos raised his eyebrows and looked at the Emperor with an air of exasperated appeal.

'You must not interrupt,' Constantine told Kallinikos mildly.

He ducked his head in apology, rattling the chains, and the Emperor nodded to Stephanos to go on.

'I am surprised that such a trival matter ever came to Your Majesty's august attention,' finished Stephanos. 'I discovered a theft and dealt with the culprit in the way I deemed appropriate. If I have displeased Your Majesty by it, I am very sorry, but I did not believe that Your Majesty would want me to connive in the misappropriation of goods intended for the defence of the empire.'

'I have my young cousin here to thank for bringing the matter to my attention,' said the emperor, smiling again. He gestured at Theodosia.

Stephanos noticed her for the first time. He stiffened in surprise and alarm, then shot a look at Kallinikos which mingled hatred and reproach.

'My cousin,' Constantine continued, 'asserts that her friend was not stealing, but using supplies from the Arsenal to develop a new type of incendiary which might be of value

114

to the city. I have questioned him, and he affirms this, and accuses you of trying to obstruct him in order to maintain your own supremacy and privileges.'

'I put an end to his thieving!' replied Stephanos vehemently. 'The child merely wishes to believe her friend guiltless.'

The chamberlain coughed. The Emperor nodded to him, and the eunuch asked mildly, 'Then you deny that this engineer has made a new incendiary?'

Stephanos hesitated. He glanced nervously at Theodosia, then at his patron Sissinios. 'He may have brewed up some new variation on one of the compounds we employ,' he conceded. 'He is knowledgeable about fire: that was why he was hired. However, we employ several varieties of incendiary already, and I did not see any benefit in diverting workshop time and effort into devising a new one. I told him that if he insisted on wasting his time on this enterprise, he should do it in his leisure hours, and at his own expense.'

Andreas raised his eyebrows. 'You are not claiming, then, that he has stolen goods for his own use, or to sell in the market?'

Stephanos bit his lip. 'No,' he admitted.

'It seems to me,' said Constantine, 'that a diversion of workshop materials by a worker who is seeking to improve their effectiveness should merit, at most, a reprimand and an order to repay their value. Arrest and deportation would appear excessive.'

Stephanos swallowed. 'Master, goods were missing. I'd told the man he couldn't have them, but he took them anyway. I have always taken great care over the funds and goods you have entrusted to my charge, and I was offended. If I overreacted, I am sorry.'

'Do you know anything about this new incendiary?' asked the Emperor.

Stephanos shrugged. 'It's complicated to make. Kallinikos was distilling Median oil for it: he showed me the result. It's thin and watery stuff, and it gives off nasty fumes. To be any use it has to be thickened with gum and resin, which make it expensive.'

'The man claims that it will float on the sea!' broke in Sissinios impatiently. 'That it will *burn* on the sea, and consume the ships of the heretics like the vengeance of God!'

Stephanos was now looking very uneasy. 'I don't know anything about that,' he protested. '*I* never saw it floating!'

Andreas coughed again; again the Emperor nodded for him to speak.

'It seems to me, Master,' said the eunuch smoothly, 'that this whole fracas is the result of a misunderstanding. Stephanos the Magistros clearly had no idea that the engineer's discovery might be valuable. He was, perhaps, unduly hasty in dismissing it as useless and punishing the engineer for persisting with it, but that he did so is not entirely his fault. The engineer seems to have lost patience with a superior whose knowledge of fires was so much less than his own, and to have made no effort to keep him informed.'

'Well put,' said Constantine, with some satisfaction. 'An unfortunate misunderstanding. It is clear that the engineer Kallinikos is not guilty of theft, but his superior is also innocent – except, perhaps, of excessive zeal in the defence of military supplies, which is no bad thing in a master of the Arsenal.'

Stephanos bowed, looking relieved. Sissinios also bowed. The drungarios was smiling with satisfaction: he could get the new incendiary and still keep his Magistros of the Arsenal.

'However,' the Emperor continued, 'it seems to me that this new incendiary does have the potential to be very valuable, and that Stephanos Skyles was wrong to dismiss it so hastily. Kallinikos of Heliopolis, I want to see this fire of yours. If it works as well as you promise, I will set you in charge of producing more of it, and give you the rank and privileges of a magistros, with an authority in the Arsenal equal to that of Stephanos.'

'I could show you the fire tomorrow, Master,' said Kallinikos, taking the offered opportunity at once, despite his stunned expression. 'If nothing's happened to the batch of it I made before, and if I can get the pump working.'

Constantine looked inquiry at Stephanos.

Stephanos bit his lip. 'I had the pump thrown out,' he

admitted. 'I don't know what happened to the batch of incendiary. My people may have disposed of it.'

'The pump will be replaced at your own expense,' decreed the Emperor. There was ice in his voice, and for the first time, he sounded really dangerous. 'And if the incendiary is lost, you will supply the engineer with everything he needs to make more of it, at your own cost. You will also repay the engineer the half of his salary you have been taking from him since he came to Constantinople.' He leaned forward, fixing Stephanos with his eyes. 'Understand me,' he said softly. 'If this discovery works, it will be a valuable weapon against the enemies of God. You very nearly succeeded in ensuring that it was lost to us. Your superior praises you and tells me that you would be difficult to replace, so I choose to believe you were guilty of nothing more than ignorance and misplaced zeal. Do not prove to us that we were mistaken.'

'Yes, Master,' said Stephanos, visibly shaken.

'Excellent!' Constantine leaned back again. 'Kallinikos of Heliopolis: the charges against you are dismissed. Prepare your incendiary, and notify Lord Sissinios when you are ready to demonstrate it. Cousin Theodosia!'

Theodosia bowed, a little less clumsily than before. The Emperor smiled at her. 'I am indebted to you for bringing this matter to my attention. You may help your friend to his house, but I ask that you return tomorrow to attend on my wife and to be instructed in the protocol of the sacred palace.' He smiled again. 'It would be a shame to allow my only female relative to languish in the modest respectability of a perfume shop in Philadelphion.'

Theodosia bowed again, her face alight with excitement. 'Thank you, Master,' she said.

The Emperor waved a hand in dismissal, and the assembly prostrated itself and filed out.

The antechamber of the audience hall was crowded with men in armour: Scholarians in red and green; several marines of Sissinios' Karabisianoi fleet in blue tunics; and two nervous and subdued toughs in leather jerkins. Anna recognized one of them as Timon, who'd visited her shop that morning.

117

All the soldiers edged back respectfully as those who had had an audience with Christ's viceroy re-emerged into the common world.

Theodosia stopped beside the door and stood very straight, trembling a little. Her face was fierce and elated.

Sissinios snapped his fingers, and his men stood to attention.

'I'm sorry, my lord,' Stephanos Skyles told him humbly.

The drungarios rounded on him. 'And so you should be! You must have been *blind* to let a thing like that slip past you. What use is the Arsenal, if the city falls? I spoke up for you, Stephanos, but if it happens again I'll keep silent.'

'Yes, my lord,' said Stephanos, cringing.

Sissinios gave him a look of disgust and strode out, followed by his guards. Stephanos winced, then noticed Anna watching him. He grimaced angrily and left the room in a hurry.

The young eunuch guide had accompanied them from the hall, and was now giving instructions to the pair of jailers; they were nodding respectfully. Timon brought out a ring of keys and went over to Kallinikos, who stood by himself in the middle of the antechamber, gazing at the floor. The jailer tapped him on the shoulder, then fumbled through his keys until he found the one that fitted the manacles.

'They say yer free,' he told Kallinikos, unlocking the shackles. 'Did you leave anythin' in the cell? I can bring it along to yer lodgin' if you like.'

'No,' said Kallinikos. 'There's nothing in the cell.' He rubbed his wrists, then looked up and saw Anna watching him.

It was the first time their eyes had met since she realized she loved him. A shock went through her, as though she'd seen her own name on some list of awful significance; as though the Syrian were someone from her past, someone she had always loved, who had now returned from the dead.

'I'm sorry,' Kallinikos said hoarsely. 'I know . . .' he gestured helplessly.

Anna glanced at her daughter. Theodosia seemed to come to herself. She smiled widely and went over to Kallinikos.

'Don't be sorry!' she told him. 'Didn't you hear? My cousin acknowledged me! He *likes* me! He's told the Empress to make us ladies-in-waiting!' She hugged him, then stood back, bouncing on her toes. 'It's *wonderful*!'

Kallinikos looked at Anna. There was no response she knew how to make, so she shrugged.

'Let's go home,' she said. She studied Kallinikos a moment, more critically this time, once more taking in the black eye and the dirt and the torn tunic. The manacles, she noticed, had left rings of raw skin around his wrists. 'Where's your cloak?' she asked him.

'I think it's still at the Arsenal,' he told her. 'I was at work when I was arrested.'

Anna doubted very much that it was still at the Arsenal. It was a good cloak, and the other workers wouldn't be expecting Kallinikos to come back for it: by now somebody else would have taken it home, and wouldn't want to identify himself as a thief by bringing it back again. She turned to the palace eunuch. 'Sir,' she said respectfully, 'Do you think someone here could lend him a cloak? It's a cold day, and he has a long walk home.'

The eunuch smiled. 'Your Distinction's kindness is indeed praiseworthy! If you will wait here, I will arrange a carriage for Your Distinction's party and a cloak for Magistros Kallinikos.'

'A carriage?' Anna repeated in surprise.

'Of course!' the eunuch said again. 'It wouldn't be appropriate for His Sacred Majesty's cousin to *walk* home from the palace.'

Theodosia laughed excitedly.

They waited in the anteroom. Anna still had no idea what to say, so she stood in silence. In an improbably short time, the eunuch returned. He brought with him the servant with the court dress – which Anna had forgotten about completely – and he was carrying a cloak. It was a guardsman's cloak, shorter than a civilian one, and made of a heavy dark green wool.

'Here you are, sir!' said the eunuch, draping it around Kallinikos' shoulders. 'If you'd return it to me when you

119

have your own, I'd be obliged. My name is Basiliskos, sir, of the Office of the Vestiarion. Now I'll show you to your carriage.'

He led them out of the Octagon, into the yard before the barracks of the Scholarians. Sure enough, a carriage was waiting there – a light four-wheeled one drawn by four fine bays. It was painted in green and gold, covered with a curtained awning, and driven by a servant in the livery of the palace. Basiliskos opened the door for them, and helped Theodosia in.

'Thank you,' she said, smiling at him.

'It is a pleasure to be of assistance,' he replied, smiling back. 'If there is anything you need from the sacred palace, Lady Theodosia, I hope you will turn to me at once.'

Theodosia laughed again.

Anna climbed into the carriage and sat down next to her daughter, feeling that she scarcely knew the radiant, excited creature beside her. Kallinikos, after a moment's hesitation, climbed in and sat opposite. Basiliskos gave some instructions to the driver, and the carriage rattled across the barracks yard and rumbled through the tunnel-like entrance of the Bronze Gate.

'Did you hear that?' asked Theodosia happily. 'He called me "Lady Theodosia"!' She smiled at Kallinikos. 'And he called *you* "Magistros".'

'He's trying to attach himself to us,' said Kallinikos flatly. 'He's decided that we're worth making friends of.'

'Because my cousin was so nice to me,' she replied, contentedly. 'He was. When we first came, I thought he was going to be horrible, but then he decided that I was all right, and everything was *wonderful*. He was so gracious and . . . and *lordly*, and kind, and handsome, too. Mama, does he look anything like my father?'

'Yes,' Anna admitted. 'He looks a lot like your father.'

Theodosia sighed happily. 'I was so scared. I hoped he would listen to me, but I never thought that . . . that it would be so *wonderful*. I was scared, right up until when we came back in and he introduced me as his "little cousin" and smiled at me. Then I knew it would be all right.'

She continued to chatter as the carriage rattled on down the Middle Street, recounting everything that had happened: how quickly the Emperor had understood the importance of the liquid fire, how he'd seen right through Stephanos, but spared him to please Sissinios; how beautiful the Empress was; how helpful the eunuch Basiliskos had been. She picked up the bundle of court clothing and stroked the silk. 'I can't wait to put it on!' she exclaimed. Anna said nothing.

When they passed the mechanical clock in the Forum of Constantine, the figure that represented the tenth hour was just sliding back into its little kennel: there were still two hours to nightfall. Anna had received Kallinikos' note during the third hour that morning. So quickly the world could change!

They arrived back in Philadelphion, and the driver of the carriage dropped them off at the perfume shop. The door was locked. Anna unlocked and opened it, and Theodosia ran through, holding up her new silk tunic and stola and eagerly shouting to Zoe and Helena.

Anna turned back to Kallinikos, who was still standing in exactly the spot where he'd descended from the carriage.

'I . . . I think I should go home,' he said.

She leaned against the door frame. 'I think you should wash first, and put some ointment on your wrists, and have something to eat, and let me mend that tunic.'

'I'm sorry,' he told her.

'Come on!' she ordered.

He shook his head. 'I should go home. I never had any right to come here in the first place. I certainly don't have one now.'

'You stink,' Anna told him savagely. 'Your clothes stink. You're crawling with lice: I noticed. You've made yourself my friend, Kallinikos: should I let you go back to your filthy cold den at the Platea Gate in that state? You can't even heat water there!'

'I've cost you your only child,' Kallinikos said in a strained voice.

She leaned back, feeling the door frame against her spine. In the house behind her she heard Theodosia's high excited voice telling the two slaves about the Emperor. 'You never

121

took anything from me which I wasn't going to lose anyway,' she said at last. 'If it hadn't been you and now, it would have been someone or something else in a year or two. You heard her: she's *happy*. She's overjoyed! I was always going to lose my daughter, Kallinikos. Let me at least keep my friends.'

He came forward finally and took her hands. He looked into her face for a long moment, trying to say something. Then he gave up and kissed her. It was like coming awake after a bewildering dream, hearing the house-noises in the dark and knowing where you were. She kissed him back, knotting her hands in his hair, holding him. Breaking off at last, they stood looking at one another. His eyes were dark and fathomless and sad. 'You are the most beautiful woman I have ever known,' he told her.

She shook him angrily and pushed him away. 'You can come in and wash,' she told him. 'I'll give you an oil against the lice.'

She had the two slaves heat water and fill the large water bath, then left him alone in the workshop to wash. He eventually came into the kitchen, well scrubbed and wrapped in the cloak from the palace. 'I left my tunic soaking in the water,' he said humbly. 'I hope . . .' He stopped, staring at Theodosia, who had changed into her court silks.

She beamed and pirouetted, a vision in white and gold. 'Isn't it beautiful?' she asked, stroking the brocade of the stola. 'I've been waiting to show you. Mama, now I'm going to go show Sophia and Maria!'

Anna shook her head. 'Not dressed like that, you aren't,' she said firmly. 'Do you think imperial ladies-in-waiting go running through the muddy streets – in white silk?'

Theodosia bit her lip. 'I'll change,' she said, 'and *then* I'll go and tell them what's happened. I have to tell them about my cousin!'

Do you think imperial ladies-in-waiting go running across the road to their friend the baker's daughter for a gossip? thought Anna. She didn't say it, though. Theodosia would lose her friends soon enough: let her enjoy them while she could. She nodded, and Theodosia dashed upstairs to change.

122

Kallinikos sat down at the kitchen table and ran his hands through his wet hair. He had draped the cloak to cover his torso, and it left his left shoulder bare. His skin was darker than that of most city natives, and the oil of gentian she'd given him to kill the lice shone on it. Anna found herself wanting to run her hands over the warm bronze gleam. The memory of the kiss in the doorway had settled itself into her mouth and her breasts, a physical thing, solidly sweet in the bewilderment and fear.

'There's bread and soup,' Anna told him, and gestured for Helena to bring him some.

He ate it ravenously, dipping the bread in the soup with a trembling hand and swallowing it without chewing. Anna watched him from the other side of the table. 'Didn't you get any food in that prison?' she asked, when he was wiping out the bowl.

'Very little,' he admitted. 'Gruel, once a day.'

Anna *tsk*ed unhappily. 'Who gave you the black eye?'

'What? Oh. Is it?'

'Yes.'

'Oh. A couple of the other prisoners didn't like Syrians.'

'I thought maybe it was the guards.'

'No. In fact, they stopped the Syrian-haters before they did worse. The jailers were decent men, considering their work. One of them offered to take a letter to my friends, and then he came back and told me that you were going to send food and money.'

'I meant to. And I went to our priest here: I thought we could get the Bishop to help you. It was Theodosia's idea to go to her cousin.' She was silent a moment, then met his eyes and added, 'She left here without my permission, while I was talking to the priest. I didn't sacrifice her for you. I intended to beg and bribe for you, but I wouldn't sacrifice her.'

'Good.' Kallinikos nodded to himself. 'That's something, anyway.' He rubbed at a stain on the table, then looked up and met her eyes again. 'I should say thank you,' he told her in a low voice. 'I . . . I didn't think I was going to get out.'

'You were *stupid* to take things from the Arsenal when you *knew* Stephanos was trying to get rid of you!' Anna

123

exclaimed – the thing she'd been longing to tell him since the jailer first visited.

He winced. 'Yes. I can see that – now.' He sighed. 'I *thought* I'd have a chance to defend myself, though. I had a complete record of everything I borrowed, and I could prove I wasn't a thief. Even when I was first arrested, I wasn't too frightened. I thought there would be a couple of bad days, and then I'd present my case to a tribunal and be freed.'

'But there wasn't any tribunal?' asked Anna. 'Was that legal?'

'Apparently, yes,' admitted Kallinikos bitterly. 'Technically, I wasn't convicted of theft in a court: I was disciplined for it by my superior at work. Because I'm not a citizen of Constantinople, and have no legal right to remain here, I can be deported without actually being convicted of a crime.' He rubbed at the stain on the table again. 'What it comes down to is that I'm still not used to being poor. In the back of my mind I still think of myself as a man of good family who doesn't need to be afraid of things like that.'

There was a silence, and then Anna remarked neutrally, 'They were saying that your family was powerful.'

He grimaced and shook his head. 'Not *powerful*. Not like . . . like the drungarios or even Stephanos Skyles. We're just an old family and respected in Baalbek. But nobody there would ever dream of shipping one of us off without even a trial!' He paused, then added earnestly, 'I tell you the truth: the fact that you *aren't* from an important family may mean that you can keep your daughter. Illegitimate *isn't* legitimate, either, no matter how noble the father. Theodosia may just cling to the edges of the court for a little while, and then come back because the Emperor's lost interest in her and she's tired of being sneered at.' He grinned apologetically. 'My mother always treated a shopkeeper in silk like a wormy apple she'd found in a basket from the greengrocer. There must be plenty like her here. Your daughter may find it impossible to make a life at court.'

Anna was encouraged: the likes of Sophronia would certainly sneer at Theodosia. Remembering the Emperor's smile, she did not believe that she'd keep her daughter – but it might, nonetheless, be true.

There was another silence, and then he asked, 'Didn't you have court dress, too?'

Anna nodded. 'They gave me some.'

'Well, that's a good sign, isn't it? They aren't intending to take her and leave you here.'

Anna chewed her lip. 'Maybe. Maybe they just haven't yet decided what to do about me. We surprised them.'

She wondered what would happen if the palace admitted both her and her daughter as courtiers. The thought of spending her days in the snake-pit being sneered at by the court ladies appalled her. Would it be better than losing her only child?

She didn't want to talk about it any more. She changed the subject. 'Did you have to leave a lot of family behind in Heliopolis?' she asked.

He looked down. 'My mother. My brother and sister. Two nephews, not counting the one who died in the fire, and a niece.' He looked up. 'I miss them all.'

'And your wife and daughter?'

'I try not to think of them. I can't think of them without thinking of the fire, and I try never to think of that. But I'll tell you, if you want me to. More than I told the Emperor.'

She was quiet for a moment. 'In the Octagon,' she said at last, 'you never mentioned alchemy.'

He nodded. 'You don't want to mention it, not in connection with an accusation of sorcery. But yes. That was part of it. I had an alchemical workshop in my house, and Khalid ibn Yasir, the imam, was convinced that it was sorcerous. He was always complaining about the smell of my "unholy arts" polluting his mosque. I tried to explain to him that alchemy only uses the natural changes in sublunar things, but he was sure it was some kind of wicked Greek magic. It's true what I told the Emperor – Heliopolis *is* a pagan city and there *are* a lot of magicians there, and Khalid *was* always getting worked up about it. He's a real Arab, a desert Arab of the Quraysh: he wasn't used to cities. He couldn't do anything about me, though, because the governor wouldn't support him. Safwan – the governor – is a city Arab, and more reasonable. Alchemy is perfectly legal and isn't even un-Islamic. The Prophet never said anything against it, and there are plenty of Muslims who're interested in it.

'My brother's eldest son, my nephew Aristarchos, used to help me sometimes. He liked fire, too, and mixing things together and watching them change colour. He was about a year older than Theodosia when . . . when he died. He was a fine boy, and we were all proud of him. He was full of life and jokes, very clever, curious about everything . . .' Kallinikos drew a deep breath and stopped.

'What happened?' asked Anna.

'I went out and left Aristarchos in charge of the workshop,' Kallinikos admitted miserably. 'I shouldn't have. I know that; I think I knew it even at the time – but I told myself he was nearly grown up and he wouldn't do anything stupid. In alchemy you often have to let something simmer in a water bath for days. Normally I just told one of the slaves to check on the fire and top up the water occasionally, but that time we had a substance at a critical stage. I'd planned to be there to take it off the fire when it changed colour, but there was a problem with the city's water.' He grimaced. 'My brother and I were in charge of the water supply for the city, you see. There was a breach in an aqueduct, and I was needed to go out of town with pumps and pipes and men to dig, to get the thing fixed. Aristarchos swore that he'd look after the metal we had cooking, that when it turned he'd take it off the fire and put the fire out. So I went off to fix the aqueduct. When I got back, the house was smouldering ash.' He ran a hand over his face. 'I was frantic. I grabbed people in the street and asked them to tell me where my family was. I ran to my brother's and my sister's, screaming, "Are they here, are they here?" But of course, they weren't. They were in the house.'

Anna didn't know what to say. She set her hand on top of his.

'We found the remains of my daughter,' he went on. 'I know it was her, because the bead necklace I gave her for her birthday was scattered in . . . in the bones of her ribcage.

She was only five, such a sweet, lovely little thing, all smiles. The other remains, we couldn't be sure.' He pulled his hand away, covered his face.

'We must all die.' Anna said, after a silence. 'The grass withers, the flowers fade. Only God endures forever.'

'Sublunar things,' agreed Kallinikos. He wiped his face with his hands, then rubbed his hands against his thighs. 'Above the moon the heavens are perfect and unchanging, but all things below the circle of the moon are subject to change, decay and death. I tell myself that, I ask myself why I should expect my own flesh to be exempt from that law – but she was only five!'

'My brother was nine when he died of a fever,' Anna told him.

'Oh, I know!' exclaimed Kallinikos. 'Probably the only people in this whole city who haven't suffered loss are those who are too young to understand it. I'm lucky, compared to that poor farmer's wife I saw in the hills above Smyrna.' He wiped his eyes again. 'What I found . . . hard . . . was to be accused of murdering them. To have Khalid ibn Yasir screaming that I was an evil magician, and that I would burn forever in the fires of hell – because of his *mosque*! How could anyone think I gave a damn about bricks and mortar, when I had to bury the ashes of my little girl? I'm sorry. You see why I try not to think about it.'

'Then . . . then why do you still want to work on fire?' asked Anna. 'Surely, if you want to forget . . .'

'I want to master fire,' said Kallinikos, and lifted his burn-scarred right hand, curving the fingers as though they held a flame. 'It took away everything I loved, and now I'm going to make it yield to me and obey.'

Seven

It was dark by the time the supper things were put away. Theodosia returned, flushed with the admiration of her friends, and hung up her court dress in the workshop, draped over a basket of saffron crocuses, so that it could absorb the scent.

Anna gave Kallinikos' tunic a scrubbing and hung it up by the kitchen fire, but it was still soaking wet. She did not have the heart to send him home to the Platea Gate dressed only in a borrowed cloak. She made up a bed for him in a storeroom upstairs and told him he could go home in the morning.

'Why can't we rent him that room?' Theodosia asked, as she and her mother prepared for bed. 'All we use it for is imported aromatics, and we don't have hardly any of them right now. I know you say you can't have a man staying in the house, but *other* women take lodgers.'

'Other women are wives or widows,' said Anna bitterly. 'I am neither. At your cousin's court they will describe me as a whore. Don't look like that: you'll hear it from them, so you might as well get used to it.'

'But you're not!' protested Theodosia.

'I slept with your father, and he rewarded me with a perfumery,' Anna stated flatly. 'To the world, the only difference between me and the girls in the Amastrianon Market is that I was paid more.'

'But . . . but you never slept with anyone else, and you *loved* him, didn't you? So you're like a *wife*. You can't say that anyone who gets something from sleeping with someone is automatically a whore! People *marry* for money all the time!'

'Don't ask me to explain the world's reasoning! I'm telling

128

you what they'll say, Theodosia. The Great Palace isn't like Philadelphion. Here people know me, they see me as successful and respectable. There I'm nobody and I *will* be treated with contempt, you can be sure of it.'

'I won't let them say things like that about you!'

'How are you going to stop them?'

Theodosia frowned at her. The frown deepened steadily, and then she burst out, 'You're still really angry and upset about it! It *worked*, and he was really nice to us, but you're still angry with me about it!'

'Angry?' repeated Anna. 'My darling, I love you very much. If I'm angry, it's because I'm afraid of losing you.'

Theodosia's face cleared a little, and she said, 'You think he'll make me marry some barbarian, and you won't see me again?'

Anna sighed. She sat down on the bed. 'Theodosia – love – do you really think that nothing important is going to change?'

The frown deepened again. 'What do you mean?'

Anna shook her head. 'My love, do you think an imperial lady-in-waiting is supposed to trot down the Middle Street with her court dress over her arm, and change when she gets to the palace? The Emperor acknowledged you as his cousin and a member of the house of Heraclius. Princesses of the imperial house don't live above a shop on the unfashionable end of the Middle Street. The Emperor's already said you won't be allowed to "languish" here in Philadelphion. They'll take you to live in the palace. Maybe they'll take me as well, and maybe they won't.'

'But . . .' Theodosia was worried now. 'But . . . what about the shop?'

'If they want me at the palace I'll have to sell it.'

Theodosia bit her lip. She came over to her mother and sat down beside her on the bed. Anna put her arms around her and kissed the top of her head.

'I don't . . . I don't want that,' said the girl, fighting tears. 'I never thought of that. I want to be a princess, but I don't want you to lose . . . I know you love the—'

'Shhhh,' Anna told her, comforted by the solidity of the

body in her arms. 'I could be completely wrong. Kallinikos was saying I might be wrong, and he made a lot of sense. I was wrong about the liquid fire, wasn't I? So maybe I'm wrong about this as well.'

Theodosia began to cry. 'What if they *don't* want to take you as well?'

'Shhh,' said Anna again, rocking gently back and forth. 'Shh, my lamb. It will be all right. Whatever happens, we are in God's hands.'

Theodosia fell asleep quickly: the long and desperate day had taken its toll. Anna lay awake, wondering if this would be the last time she ever held her sleeping child in her arms. She thought of the thousand times she had cradled her daughter. She imagined the warm, soft limbs encased in white and gold; imagined all the rebellious liveliness stilled into a statue-like calm, giggles forever smothered by imperial dignity. She ached at the thought of Theodosia married to age or cold money or barbarism, injured and alone in a great house. Her mind ran endlessly over the blank darkness of the future.

Trying to wrench her thoughts from what might happen to Theodosia, she found herself thinking about Kallinikos. She remembered again what she had felt when they looked at one another at the palace, and what she had felt when he kissed her.

She could get up, walk along the landing to the storeroom and wake him. She could have that sweet comfort again. He'd be pleased enough to give it.

She pressed her face into her daughter's soft hair. Did she want to marry the man? She was not at all sure of that: she still didn't want a master. Besides, he was complicated, in many ways still a mystery to her: he might well prove a good friend but a very bad husband. Did he want to marry her? She wasn't sure of that, either. It seemed that he came from an old and distinguished family. A man whose mother treated jumped-up shopkeepers like wormy apples might not want to marry a grocer's daughter. She was not going to be a concubine again – probably wouldn't be *allowed* to be one again, with Theodosia an accepted member of the house of Heraclius. So, what was the comfort of love

130

but a path to heartbreak at best, and at worst to disgrace and ruin?

She would not indulge herself with deceitful comfort or false hope. At this moment she was alive, in her own house, with her child in her arms; if she lost Theodosia, at least it would be to honour and wealth. A beloved friend who had been locked in the Strategion Prison that morning was now free, and sleeping peacefully nearby. These things were true comfort, and she would be grateful for them.

She remembered her night in the Noumera Prison, and the man she'd seen that afternoon in the chamberlain's office. Yes, she would give thanks to God that tonight they were safe! However much she was afraid of the future, things could have turned out much, much worse.

The carriage arrived to take them to the palace early next morning, while they were still eating breakfast. There was a jingle of the shop bell at first light, and Zoe opened it to find the young eunuch Basiliskos on the doorstep.

'Good morning, and good health!' he greeted Anna, when she came to see what the commotion was. 'I realized that no one had made any arrangements to bring you to the palace this morning, so I've been so bold as to remedy that defect.' He gestured behind him at the carriage waiting in the street. It was the same carriage as before, and it was provoking consternation among the early risers of the neighbourhood.

'We weren't expecting you,' said Anna stupidly. Like the carriage he'd arrived in, Basiliskos looked totally out of place in Philadelphion. His court silks and oiled black ringlets gleamed incongruously against a background of charcoal-carts, water-carriers, and children leading goats.

'No, of course not,' agreed Basiliskos with a smile. 'I can see that you haven't changed into court dress – which, indeed, shows your wisdom, because it would be almost sacrilegious to *walk* across the city in it! But it would be more fitting if you changed here, rather than in some borrowed room at the palace. That was why I brought you the carriage. The driver and I will wait while you get ready.'

He turned and went back to the carriage. Anna gaped

131

after him for a moment, then closed the door and shouted for Theodosia.

Kallinikos had still been asleep, but the bustle eventually woke him up. He arrived downstairs, draped in his borrowed cloak and yawning prodigiously, to find Anna, in her court dress, in the workshop blending perfumes. 'What are you doing?' he asked; then added, 'You look like golden Aphrodite.'

'Huh!' exclaimed Anna, in fierce contempt of pagan goddesses. 'The carriage for the palace is outside. I'm preparing some bribes.'

'Bribes?' he asked, coming closer.

She waved him back impatiently and measured out a spoonful of attar of roses into a fine glass flask full of almond oil. 'Gifts for a few of the people at the palace, to make them well disposed to us,' she elaborated, stoppering the attar of roses. She got up and fetched two boxes of the precious imported aromatics: frankincense resin and Judean balsam. She added a few grains of each to the oil, stopped the flask with her thumb, and shook it vigorously. 'Expensive perfume,' she explained, and held it out to him to sniff. 'Most people like to get some.'

'It smells mostly of the stuff you put in last,' he commented.

'Yes. The last-added scent always dominates.' She stopped the glass flask and put it in a small leather bag with some others.

'Why?' asked Kallinikos, scratching his beard.

She laughed and leaned forward to kiss him. It seemed such a natural thing to do that she didn't even think about it, until afterwards. 'I don't know why,' she said. 'We must be off. Good luck at the Arsenal.'

'Good luck at the palace,' he replied.

Theodosia rushed in, her hair braided but her head uncovered. 'Oh!' she said, seeing Kallinikos. 'I forgot you were here! We're off to the palace! Mama, did you make something for Basiliskos?'

Anna indicated the bag. 'Come and see us this evening,' she told Kallinikos. 'Tell us how things are at the Arsenal.'

132

He nodded. She headed out, tossing her black cloak about her and calling back to Helena to mind the shop.

'It was nice of you to come and fetch us,' Theodosia told Basiliskos, when the carriage was once again rattling along the Middle Street.

'It was my pleasure,' he declared, and laid one plump white hand over his heart. He licked his lips, and Anna at once suspected that he was nerving himself to ask for something.

'You were very nice to us yesterday, too,' Theodosia went on, before he could. 'My mother's got you a present to say thank you.'

The eunuch's eyes widened and he smiled in what seemed to be genuine surprise and pleasure. 'A present? For me?'

Anna dug it out of the bag. Basiliskos was not getting the glass flask with the scent compounded of roses and frankincense: that was for the Empress. For the eunuch she had prepared a small ceramic pot of pomade.

'For my hair!' he exclaimed in delight. He lifted the lid of the pot and dipped a finger in, then closed his eyes, inhaled deeply. 'Sandalwood?' He opened his eyes again. 'How very generous! It's been impossible to get sandalwood all year. How did you know I liked it?'

Because you smelled of it yesterday, thought Anna, *and if you really couldn't get any of your own, I wonder why?* She did not utter the thought, however; instead she smiled modestly and murmured that she was pleased he liked the gift.

'You are indeed very kind,' said the eunuch, pressing the lid back onto the pot of unguent and tucking it away into a fold of his clothing. He licked his lips and nerved himself again. 'Has Your Grace given any thought to her household at the palace?'

He was addressing Theodosia. The girl swallowed, eyes wide.

'I would be very glad to take charge of it for you, Lady Theodosia,' said Basiliskos, in a rush. 'I would like to work for you, Your Grace, truly I would! If His Sacred Majesty says anything about it, perhaps you could mention my name . . . ?'

133

'We don't know that she'll have a household at the palace!' protested Anna. 'The Emperor hasn't said anything about it.'

'No,' agreed Basiliskos. 'But it does seem likely that she will, doesn't it? And then she'll need someone to look after it for her, won't she? And I would be good. I know I'm praising myself, but I would be. I've been at the palace since I was seven years old, I know all the people and all the protocols, I can keep accounts and there's nobody better at writing in a beautiful elevated style . . .'

'Aren't you happy at the office of the . . . it was the Vestiarion, you said, wasn't it?' asked Anna. 'Under Lady Sophronia?'

'Not Sophronia,' said Basiliskos. 'She's Chartoularia for the Empress; I'm under the Illustrious Loukios, who does the same job for the Emperor. And no, I'm not happy there: I'm bored.' He grimaced ruefully. 'It's not that I don't like clothes. Some of them are beautiful. It's just that working in the Vestiarion is almost *all* clothes and inventories, and it's *dull*.'

Anna had grave misgivings. It seemed probable that there was some problem between Basiliskos and this Loukios, his superior. She wondered if it concerned missing sandalwood unguents, and whether the eunuch's real ambition was to have control of a comparatively unsupervised establishment to pilfer. 'If all you do is look after clothes, why were you in the Octagon yesterday?' she asked suspiciously.

'I did all the inventories on Monday,' he replied at once. 'Then I did all the Thursday maintenance work in the morning. That meant that I was free, so Loukios assigned me to attend on His Sacred Majesty. I was very glad of it, gracious ladies! You were the most interesting thing I've seen all year.'

Theodosia laughed. 'Us?'

'Who else? The whole palace is buzzing with talk about the brave and beautiful daughter of the Lord Theodosius, who never appealed to her cousin on her own behalf, but dared it for the good of the city!'

Theodosia laughed again. 'Are they really saying that?'

134

He spread his hands in concession. 'Some of them are.'

'Theodosia!' said Anna sharply.

Theodosia looked at her mulishly.

'He's flattering you quite shamelessly,' Anna told her, abandoning discretion. 'You shouldn't make any promises to him until you know more about him!'

'I do flatter,' admitted Basiliskos, suddenly and unexpectedly. 'I'm sorry, though, if you think I was trying to mislead you or deceive you. It's just that I like to make things sound grand and beautiful.'

'I like you,' Theodosia said, looking at him directly, 'I'm glad you *want* to come to work for me. I *will* ask, if I can.'

'Thank you, My Lady!' said Basiliskos warmly. 'Thank you very much.'

Anna abruptly realized that he had addressed himself almost entirely to Theodosia, and that when he had spoken to Anna herself, it had been without using any of the titles and honorifics he'd lavished on her daughter. The fear she'd managed to set aside that morning came back, redoubled.

On arriving at the palace, Basiliskos escorted them not to the audience chamber but to the office of chamberlain Andreas. The eunuch was sitting at his desk reading a set of wax tablets when they were admitted, but as they came in he set the tablets down and – an act of extraordinary courtesy from such a high official – got to his feet to welcome them. He shook hands with Theodosia, his face wreathed in smiles, and proclaimed himself glad to welcome His Sacred Majesty's long-lost cousin to the palace. Theodosia, he informed them, was to have an audience with His Sacred Majesty immediately.

'I had hoped, however,' he went on, 'that Mistress Anna might remain here with me for a little, to discuss the practicalities of your new situation. I trust that is acceptable to you both?'

There was, of course, no possibility of saying that it wasn't. Theodosia was led off into the Octagon by Basiliskos. She paused once to look back, her face pale with anxiety and excitement. Anna forced a reassuring smile, then watched her daughter's straight back disappearing through the next door.

Andreas reseated himself at his desk and picked up the tablets again. Anna stirred uncomfortably, then forced herself to stand still and face what was to come.

'Mistress Anna,' began the chamberlain, looking through the tablets. 'I was pleased – though not actually surprised – to discover that your report of yourself yesterday was nothing but the truth.' He glanced up with a smile, then looked down at the tablets again. 'The head of the Perfumers' Guild reports that you are a member in good standing, well reputed and successful. He did, it is true, imply that you sometimes flirt in an unseemly way – but a Mistress Danielis, also of the guild, dismissed this as the result of his resentment that you had refused a cousin's proposal of marriage.' The eunuch turned to the next page. 'Your parish priest reports you as a devout and modest woman, and praises your generosity to the Holy Church. One of your neighbours describes you as "a very respectable" woman, and says that, although men have approached you with offers of marriage or . . . less *proper* liaisons, you never encouraged them, and have refused them all. It would seem that you are indeed a worthy mother even for a member of the imperial house.'

Anna bit her lip, feeling a bit sick. To have such a full report on his desk this morning, the chamberlain must have sent some of his agents out to make enquiries about her the moment she left the palace the previous day. Why was he *announcing* that he'd set his spies on her? Was she supposed to be afraid of the extent of his knowledge, or was she just meant to be pleased and grateful that he approved her qualities as a mother? As though a court eunuch knew anything about motherhood!

'It must be a source of pride to you,' Andreas continued, smiling at her complacently, 'that the daughter you have reared with such devotion has now been accepted by her father's sacred house!'

Anna bowed slightly, not trusting herself to reply.

'I fear, though, that a slight problem has arisen in regard to your own position,' the chamberlain continued, resting his elbows on his desk and twining his fine beringed fingers together. 'It seems that Her Sacred Majesty, the Serene

136

Augusta, was offended yesterday by what she termed your "insolent attitude".'

Anna swallowed. 'I—'

Andreas lifted a forefinger, cutting her off. 'I cannot say that I see any insolence in what you are reported to have said. I can understand that a humble woman such as yourself would be overwhelmed by finding herself in such exalted company, and would sincerely wish herself safely back home . . . and of course a woman of your background could have no idea how to express this *tactfully*. I have explained this to the Sacred Augusta, who graciously condescends to excuse you. There is no danger of your being dismissed and stripped of the golden girdle for misconduct. However, I am—' the fingers spread slightly – '*concerned* at this inauspicious beginning. I am also concerned that your very humility makes you unfitted for a lofty station. Do you even *want* to join your daughter here?'

Anna swallowed again. 'Sir,' she said, unsteadily, 'my daughter . . .' She realized that she didn't know what to say next, and drew a deep breath, trying to compose herself. 'Sir, I have only my daughter. My parents and my brother and my patron are all dead. I do not want to lose her.'

The eunuch regarded her a moment in silence. 'She is of an age when she would soon be lost to you anyway,' he pointed out. 'Any tradesman apprentices his sons by the time they're twelve, and marries off his daughters not much later.'

'Sir, she had already begun her apprenticeship, with me,' Anna replied. 'As for marriage, I had hoped to find her some worthy young man of our own trade, or, if there were none suitable, one who practised another respectable trade nearby, so that she could continue to work beside me. I had hoped never to part from her.'

'The position is changed now,' said Andreas.

'Sir, I am well aware of it,' Anna acknowledged bitterly. 'Forgive me, though, if I seem slow to grasp all the consequences. It is hard to give up a lifetime's dreams overnight.'

The chamberlain bowed his head gracefully. 'I understand. However, you must set your humble dreams aside. Your daughter is destined for higher things. She is old enough to seek them on her own, and indeed, seems ambitious for them. It does not seem to me that you share her ambitions, and I very much doubt that you would find the court a comfortable or congenial place.'

They were going to take Theodosia in, and leave Anna outside the gate. Anna bit her lip, trying to think of a good reply.

'It seems to me,' Andreas went on smoothly, 'that a virtuous woman who has successfully raised a child for the imperial house might well take advantage of her new liberty by devoting herself to the service of God. If you wished to enter a convent, my good woman, the sacred palace would be happy to assist you.'

Anna stared at him sickly. So. That was the story they had in mind. The virtuous concubine of the murdered prince brings up his daughter decently and devoutly in obscurity, then relinquishes her to her 'higher destiny' and retires discreetly into a convent: that was how the tale was intended to go. It provided the final seal on her respectability, giving Theodosia a status almost as good as legitimacy. It also disposed of a woman who might become an embarrassment.

'No,' she whispered; then, with sudden ferocity repeated, 'No!'

'No? You are a devout woman, or so, at least, my reports suggest . . .'

'I am a devout *laywoman*,' Anna said firmly. 'Like my patron Theodosius, I have no vocation to the religious life.'

The statement hung there, potent and dangerous. Theodosius had been ordained by force. The result of that sacrilege had been public hatred and private nightmares for the brother who ordered it.

'Are you sure?' asked Andreas, after a moment. 'Are you hoping to marry, after all? This man Kallinikos . . .'

Anna had no intention of opening *that* subject with this ruthless courtier. 'Sir,' she said, '*you* can never marry, and I hope that you, too, are devout, for God help us if such a trusted advisor of His Sacred Majesty holds God in contempt! Would *you* have no objection to becoming a monk?'

138

The chamberlain was startled. Piety and otherworldliness were not what he was famous for.

'I run a business,' Anna went on. 'Your spies told you that I was good at it. What use would my skill as a perfume-maker do me in a convent?'

The eunuch gazed at her for a long moment, his brow slightly creased. Anna stared defiantly back.

'Well,' said Andreas at last. He looked down at his tablets, then up again. 'Well, there is no need to decide your fate immediately. As you pointed out, your daughter's situation has altered overnight: one must grant you some time to accustom yourself to it. However, I do feel that it would be better if—' he hesitated delicately, then went on – 'if you did not join your daughter's household immediately. She will, after all, be a lady of high rank now: she will need skills you cannot give her, and she must learn to look to others for advice.' He hesitated again, then added condescendingly, 'I am sure that you need time to set your own business in order, as well.'

He did not volunteer what she was supposed to be setting her business in order *for*, if she wasn't preparing to enter a convent. She was bitterly certain that this was because he hadn't bothered to think of another reason. Probably he still thought she could be pressured into renouncing the world: the power of the palace over the city was almost limitless, and if they were really committed to their plan there was no way she could withstand them.

Whether or not they forced her into a convent, they were not going to take her into the palace: that decision had been made. Perhaps the Empress had complained, said that she would take the daughter, but not the mother; perhaps the Emperor and his advisors had discussed Theodosia and come to the conclusion that she would be more malleable if they could cut her off from her mother and her past. Whatever the reason, Anna was not wanted at the court. She would have to leave Theodosia in the snake-pit, alone.

'Please,' said Anna, her voice soft now with anguish. 'I love my daughter.'

Andreas closed his tablets. 'Of course you do! So, naturally you want what is best for her! Your presence in court would be a hindrance to her. If you love her, it is time to let her go.'

I would let her go more easily if I thought she'd be happy, Anna thought. *But this is not a happy place, and you who inhabit it are not kind people.*

It was not a thought she could utter. She pulled her black cloak more tightly around her and bowed her head.

'No doubt she will be grieved to part with you,' Andreas continued relentlessly. 'You must do your best to comfort her.'

Anna looked up when she heard the cold edge to his tone. For a moment their eyes met and held. 'I imagine,' she said harshly, 'that if I fail to comfort her, you will ban her from seeing me – "because it would distress her".'

The eunuch regarded her a moment with slightly narrowed eyes. 'You're a clever woman, aren't you?' he said after a moment of silence. 'An unexpected quality in such a beauty, but a convenient one. Indeed we would. Come, you know that we mean your daughter nothing but good. If you are reasonable about this, you will see her frequently. You are no more *losing* her than any other loving mother *loses* the son she proudly apprentices to a trade.'

There was no mention of what would happen if she were *unreasonable*, but he knew she had inferred it already: she would be banned from seeing Theodosia at all. There would be no appeal. Andreas and his fellows ruled the court, and it was only the shadow of the Emperor's goodwill to Theodosia that granted Anna any access at all. Anna bowed very low. 'I want what is best for my daughter,' she murmured. 'I will comfort her as well as I can, and then return to Philadelphion to set my business in order.'

Theodosia returned from her audience with the Emperor excited and worried. 'Basiliskos was right!' she exclaimed, hugging Anna. 'We *will* get our own household here in the palace, with our own slaves and everything! I asked my cousin about Basiliskos, and he thought it was funny that the staff were "courting me already" and said that "such

140

industry deserves its reward". Mama, I know you don't trust Basiliskos, but I think we ought to have somebody who *wants* to be with us, not somebody who was just sent to us and maybe doesn't want to be there at all.'

'Probably you're right,' Anna replied. 'My lamb, I've been talking to Andreas. He thinks it would be better if I didn't join you here – not immediately, anyway.'

Theodosia went very still. She looked at her mother, then at Andreas. She opened her mouth to protest. Anna stopped her, gently catching a stray wisp of hair and tucking it in behind a braid. 'You know that I love you,' she said. 'I'm not abandoning you, so don't think it! Andreas says that we should regard this as an apprenticeship: you need to learn a trade that I can't teach you, and if I stayed here I would just get in the way. He doesn't think I could fit into the court, and probably he's right. He thinks I would just confuse you and make things more difficult for you. So I'm going to go back to Philadelphion and keep things in order there, and you'll stay here in the palace and learn how to be a lady. I'll come to visit you as often as I can, and bring you all the news of home, and you can tell me all about the court.'

Theodosia looked at Andreas again, and did not protest. Instead she put her arms around her mother and hugged tightly. 'You'll come see me every day?'

'Unless you're too busy.'

'I'll never be too busy! Never!' The girl hugged her even harder, to the point of pain.

'I'll never be too busy to come,' Anna told her, fighting the tears. 'My love, I will always be here if you want me.'

Andreas nodded to Basiliskos, and the younger eunuch murmured some excuse to Theodosia, detached her, and led her out. Again Anna watched her straight silk-clad back retreating into the labyrinth of rooms; again the girl paused in the next doorway, and looked back. In white and gold, crowned with the deeper gold of her hair, she seemed like a girl from an old, old story – a virgin sacrifice, bound for the darkness at the labyrinth's heart. Anna shivered. The monsters in this labyrinth were real enough: she had met one once in the Noumera Prison. *O God, keep my daughter!* she prayed passionately.

Basiliskos touched Theodosia's elbow, and she turned, with a whisper of silk, and disappeared from sight.

'Excellent,' said the chamberlain, with some satisfaction. 'You can visit her tomorrow morning. I will see that they send a carriage for you.'

They also provided a carriage to take Anna home. She realized, as she climbed into it, that she had come away with the flasks of perfume intended as bribes still untouched in her satchel. *I shall have to give them to Theodosia tomorrow*, she thought. She would bring a few things from home, too: the little scent bottle in the shape of a dove, which Theodosia had loved since she was tiny; the tortoiseshell comb, the cup painted with a chariot and horses . . . all the things that Theodosia loved best, that might comfort her in the cold grandeur of the palace.

The clock in the Forum of Constantine said that it was still an hour before noon. For more than twelve years she had cared for a child, and in only three hours, had lost her.

She arrived home to find her shop and workshop crowded. Martina was there, although she wasn't supposed to come until the afternoon, and with her were a horde of neighbours, including Theodosia's friends and their parents. Of course, Anna realized dully: they all knew what had happened, either from Theodosia herself the previous night, or from the enquiries of the chamberlain's agents.

The small crowd all greeted her with cries of excitement when she stepped down from the carriage in her court silks, and Father Agapios pushed through from the back, looking worried. She abruptly remembered that she was supposed to have accompanied him to the bishop that same morning.

'Daughter!' exclaimed the priest. 'Are you well?'

She didn't know how to answer that, so she bowed respectfully and apologized for having missed their appointment.

'Where's Theodosia?' asked Theodosia's friend Maria, staring as the carriage rattled away again down the Middle Street.

Anna bit her lip, struggling with herself.

'Have they kept her at the palace?' asked Father Agapios, in awe.

'They took her, but not Anna!' exclaimed Martina indignantly.

Anna pulled her black cloak forward to cover her face. 'Please,' she choked, with all the dignity she could. 'I thank you all, neighbours, for your concern. Yes, the Emperor recognized my daughter as his cousin, and they have taken her to stay in the palace. I will be staying here, for the time being at least. I am . . . I am much . . .' She could not go on, and realized with horror that she was about to break down in tears at her own front door.

'Let her be!' exclaimed Maria's mother Eudokia, coming forward to take Anna's arm. 'Anna, come inside and sit down.'

Anna went in, sat down, allowed herself to be fetched wine. She gave a brief account of events to Eudokia, Father Agapios, and to Martina, who could not be kept out. The priest viewed Theodosia's sudden elevation as providential, and gave thanks to God for it; Martina was indignant that Anna had been rejected. Eudokia understood, however, that to Anna this was loss, pure and simple, and her silent sympathy was a great comfort. Nonetheless, Anna sent all her supporters away as soon as she could, shut up the shop, and did her best to endure the rest of the day.

She expected Kallinikos to stop by on his way home from the Arsenal, and was not sure whether she was looking forward to his visit or dreading it. However, the only person who came by that evening was a ragged errand boy with a note.

Kallinikos to the perfume-maker Anna and her household, it read. *Cannot visit this evening; am staying at the Arsenal until the fire is ready. Sorry. God keep you!*

Anna told herself that she was glad he hadn't come. She might, in her grief, have done something she would later regret.

That night, though, lying alone in the bed she had shared with her daughter, she wished that he were lying beside her, and wept bitterly.

Eight

O ver the next few days Anna was allowed to visit the palace every morning. She never met any official more important than Basiliskos or the officer on duty at the gate, but when she left, the carriage driver would announce that he would pick her up again the next day. On the one occasion when she asked him who had told him to come, he seemed confused, and asked her if she didn't want him.

'No, no!' she said hastily. 'I was just wondering who I had to thank for this.'

'Ah,' said the man, with understanding. 'Well, I belong to the household. I take my orders from Gregorios, the head groom. I don't know who authorized him to assign me, though. Do you want me to ask?'

Anna shook her head quickly, afraid that the very act of asking might cause the authorization to be withdrawn. 'I won't question a blessing,' she said, and the driver grinned.

The suite of rooms allotted to Theodosia were not situated in the Octagon, like those of the Emperor and the Empress, but in the Palace of Boukoleon, which lay to the south-west, overlooking the sea. They formed a section of the north wing. They were beautiful, spacious rooms, with carpets of silk and furniture of citronwood and ivory, and they included a private bathhouse, and a small garden with a marble fish pond. A dozen slaves, under the direction of Basiliskos, looked after the rooms and saw to it that Theodosia had everything a princess might require. Tutors had been assigned to instruct her in literature, religion and music.

'I told my cousin that I know how to play the lute,' she told Anna, on the first visit, 'and look!'

A beautiful lute, its body inlaid with a pattern of birds in

144

tortoiseshell, mother-of-pearl, ivory and gold, and its strings made of silver, lay on one of the silken cushions.

'He had that sent over within an hour!' exclaimed Theodosia, touching it reverently. 'Isn't it beautiful?'

'Very beautiful,' Anna agreed. 'What does it sound like?'

Theodosia hesitated. 'Well, *I* sounded better on the old one. But maybe that's just because I haven't learned to play this one properly yet.'

'Maybe,' said Anna. She'd suspected at once that no instrument so obviously made for its looks would actually sound very good.

Anna was relieved to find that, although Theodosia missed her mother and her friends ('I didn't sleep *at all* last night; I just lay awake and missed you!') she was not crushed and disorientated. Instead she was full of resolution – and plans.

'Basiliskos says I ought to have attendants,' she told Anna. 'Free attendants, he means, not slaves. So I thought maybe Sophia and Maria could come here. If *they* were here this would be *fun*! And they could learn literature and music with me, and when we grow up we can all marry lords, and stay best friends forever!'

Anna doubted very much that any lord would marry the daughter of a baker or charcoal vendor, no matter how well versed she might be in literature and music. 'What does your cousin say about that?' she asked.

'I haven't asked him yet.' Theodosia made a face, and added, 'He probably won't let me have any attendants right now. I'm officially an attendant on the Empress myself, and I'm still supposed to be settling in. But I thought, maybe in a month or so . . . maybe they'll let you come to stay, too, when I've settled in! Will you tell Sophia and Maria I want them to come here?'

Anna did tell Sophia and Maria about it – she felt the girls would be glad to know that their friend missed them and still wanted to see them – but she made it clear to Sophia's and Maria's parents that she did not expect anything to come of the plan.

'Good,' said Eudokia, and Anna nodded. Eudokia, too, understood that residence in the Great Palace was unlikely to be either comfortable or profitable for a commoner, and Eudokia was no more eager to lose a daughter than Anna had been.

In the afternoons Anna tried to continue with her work. Theodosia's absence from house and workshop, however, pressed on her, a weight that seemed to grow with every hour. What was the point in building up a business if there was no one to inherit it? Why struggle for prosperity and respect, when you knew that you could never escape derision where it counted most? There was silence, too, where once there had been lute music, sulks and giggles. It seemed to grow with each day that passed. It lay down beside her at night, and she would curl up in it, listening to it and staring into the dark.

There was no further message from Kallinikos. Anna expected him every evening, and every evening was disappointed. She continued to tell herself that it was just as well, but the pretence was wearing a bit thin. He had occasioned the bitter loss she struggled to come to terms with; was he now leaving her to face it alone? She had befriended him against her better judgement when he was a penniless refugee; Theodosia had saved him from prison. Now, it seemed, he couldn't even be bothered to let them know how he was, or to find out what had happened to them! If his business at the Arsenal was so important that it left him no time at all, then surely he could at least send another message?

By the fourth day, she was so hurt and angry that she decided that if he ever did turn up again, she'd slam the door in his face. The only reason that he was admitted to the house that afternoon was that it was Zoe who opened the door.

Anna was in the workshop, filtering an oil of saffron. She heard the bell jingle, then heard Zoe talking to someone in the shop. The slave girl's shrill exclamations were much louder than the brief, low replies, and Anna didn't realize at first that the other speaker was Kallinikos. When at last she recognized the voice and got up, it was too late: he was already coming into the workshop.

She gave him a look of such bitterness that he stopped dead

in the doorway, and Zoe, behind him, retreated hastily into the shop.

'I'm sorry,' he said.

He was wearing a long cloak of white silk, banded with a single narrow purple stripe: the privileged cloak of an imperial magistros. Beneath it, his tunic was as dirty as ever, and his face was haggard with exhaustion.

'Get out!' Anna ordered, low-voiced and furious.

He swallowed and nodded. 'I will. Only . . . only first could you just tell me? Zoe said Theodosia's at the palace. Is she all right?'

Anna snorted in angry contempt. 'She misses me. She misses her friends. How long that will last, I don't know: probably she'll eventually learn to despise us. She's a princess now – and it seems that you're a magistros! I'm surprised you came back *here* at all, when you could've visited *her* at the palace!'

He made a dismissive gesture. 'I didn't know. But, Anna, surely you know I'd much rather come here than anywhere in the city?'

'Then why *didn't* you come?' demanded Anna in anguish. 'Why didn't you even send a message?'

'I wanted to,' he replied helplessly. 'I wanted to, but, I tell you the truth, I've been afraid to leave my equipment long enough to find a messenger.'

Anna wasn't sure whether to run to him or hit him. She crossed her arms, glaring.

'Are *you* all right?' asked Kallinikos.

She said nothing.

'I'm sorry,' he said again. 'I'll go.' He turned and went back through the shop.

She followed him, realizing as she did that she didn't want him to go, but still too angry to ask him to stay. 'At least tell *me*,' she said, as he reached the door. 'Did you do your demonstration of the fire?'

He turned back, eagerly. 'Yes. This afternoon. That's why I have the cloak.'

'Oh,' she said. After a moment she added grudgingly, 'Congratulations.'

147

'I wanted to celebrate with you and Theodosia,' he said. 'I thought . . .' He shook his head. 'I thought we could go out to dinner.'

Reason and curiosity were beginning to make headway against the tide of rage. 'What did you mean, you were afraid to leave your equipment?' Anna asked cautiously.

'I was afraid that Stephanos would do something to it, to make sure the fire didn't work,' Kallinikos replied matter-of-factly. 'Not *in person*, obviously, but all the other workers are his, even the free ones. They all know that he tried to get rid of me, and that he was shown up and embarrassed for it in front of his patron and the Emperor. They all know that he hates me worse than ever, and that he'd be grateful to anyone who harmed me. They all knew that if the fire didn't work when I demonstrated it, I'd be nobody again. So – I didn't dare leave my equipment where they could tamper with it. I was afraid that if I even slipped out to find a boy to take a message, somebody else would slip in and put water in the mix or crack one of the seals on the pump.' He shrugged again. 'I tell you the truth: I locked myself into the room with it.'

'Where did you sleep?' asked Anna in bewilderment.

'Locked into the room with it,' he repeated. He hesitated, then added, 'It was more comfortable than the prison, at least. Warmer.'

'Oh,' she said blankly. 'What about food?'

'I didn't worry about that at first,' he said carefully. 'I just ate the rations they give you at the Arsenal. Yesterday, though, I came back from the latrine and found one of Stephanos' favourites trying to pick the lock on the door. Then I worried that maybe they were stupid enough to try anything, and . . . and I didn't eat, or leave the room again, until it was time to do the demonstration. Anna, I couldn't let that demonstration fail. I've endured so much for it already – and *you've* endured so much, too! It was the thing that drove your daughter to the Emperor.'

'Oh,' said Anna, after a moment. 'No, you couldn't let it fail. I . . . didn't realize.'

'I thought we could go out and celebrate,' Kallinikos said sadly. 'The Emperor gave me a purse full of gold.'

'The Emperor was there?'

'Yes. Him and Sissinios and Stephanos and the head of the naval docks. I did the demonstration in a stone docking slip. Pumped the fire out onto the sea, and then tossed in a handful of burning tow.' He flung his hands out with a ghost of his usual enthusiasm. 'It went up with a whoosh, of course, and they were all delighted. Oh – oh, God, I nearly forgot! Listen: this is very important! They want it to be a state secret. I reminded them that you know about it already, and they told me to warn you that it's now a state secret and that it's treason to talk about it. Make sure your household know that.'

'It's treason to talk about the fire?' squeaked Zoe, who'd been listening round-eyed from behind the shop counter. Anna shot her a look, and the young slave ducked her head apologetically.

'Yes,' Kallinikos said seriously. 'Punishable by death.'

'Oh!' wailed Zoe in dismay. 'Oh, oh nooo! I told all my friends about how you set fire to our water bath!'

Anna looked at Kallinikos in exasperation and alarm.

'Well, tell them you exaggerated!' Kallinikos ordered the girl. 'And tell them that when I tried it on salt water it wouldn't burn at all. Better yet, don't mention it again unless someone asks, and then say that it isn't working properly now and I'm still tinkering with it.'

Zoe swallowed and nodded. 'I'll go and tell Helena,' she said, and ran out of the room.

'Go and tell Martina, too!' Anna called after her. Martina was at her own home that afternoon: Anna, unable to bear the other woman's avid interest in how Theodosia was coping at the palace, had given her the week off on half pay. 'Immortal God!' she exclaimed, turning back to Kallinikos with another look of exasperation. 'And you were going to go off again without bothering to *tell* us about that?'

He ran a hand through his dishevelled hair. 'I . . . wasn't thinking clearly. I haven't slept well the last three nights, and I haven't eaten since yesterday. Today has been . . .

has been . . .' He stopped, then resumed, 'I showed them the fire, and it blazed up like the sun, and the Emperor and all the court shouted in delight. The Emperor gave me the cloak and a bag full of gold, and all I was thinking about was you. I came straight here from the docks. All the way over I was thinking about what I'd say, how we'd celebrate. Then Zoe told me that Theodosia was gone, and I knew . . . she was the light of the sun to you, wasn't she? I'd thought that if I could get myself a position and some money you'd like me better. I wanted so much to . . . to *please* you, and instead I've done nothing but harm.'

Anna knew, abruptly and without any doubts, what was going to happen now. Probably it wasn't wise. In all her experience, love led to grief. She wanted it anyway.

'It wasn't your fault,' she said gently. 'She was, yes, the light of the sun to me, but *she* was the one who went to the Emperor. It's true, what I said before: if it hadn't been now, on your behalf, it would have been later, for some other reason. She wanted to know what her father was like and she wanted to be a princess. I suppose any girl would.' After a moment she added softly, 'I don't blame you, Kallinikos. And I never despised you for being poor. Whether or not you have money doesn't make any difference to me.' She wanted him to be very clear on that point. What he would obtain would be given, not bought.

He was quiet a moment, surprised. 'You're always making comments about how poor I am,' he pointed out. 'How poor I *was*, I mean.'

She nodded. 'I know. On purpose. I could tell that you were embarrassed about it, and I wanted to discourage you – to make you content yourself with friendship.'

'With *friendship*?' he exclaimed fiercely. 'I *wasn't* content with it, and I think you know that!'

'Do you think you're the only one who ever wanted me?' she demanded, suddenly angry. 'I've been *hunted* all my life! Do you think I like wearing black all the time, and never laughing in public, and never speaking freely to anyone with a beard? I hate it, but I *have* to do it, or every adventurer who passes by will be after me like a . . . a tomcat after a pretty

150

little mouse! I have a house, I have a business, I have – had – a child. If I'm not respectable, I'll be *destroyed*. I *liked* you from the day we met – but I never agreed to fall in love with you! You were lonely and you wanted friends. You helped Theodosia and *she* liked you, so I thought, very well, I'll be his friend. Does the fact that I never agreed to more make me cruel and deceitful and uncaring? Should I simply have sent you away?'

'You tried to.'

'Yes, I did! And maybe I should have tried harder!'

He raised a hand defensively. 'I wouldn't have gone. I'm sorry. I know I . . . forced my way into your house. But I was used to having a *home*, and I'd lost it. Ever since the fire, I hadn't had anything except hardship and grief. I *endured* and endured and then . . .' He lowered his hand, looking at her with longing. 'I came here. The first day I came here, when I watched you put Theodosia to bed, it was like looking through a window into Paradise. A beautiful woman and a beautiful girl, living in a house where everything is prosperous and warm, where even the workshop is fragrant. How could I just turn my back and go away? But I'm sorry, I shouldn't have reproached you. You were never cruel or uncaring, and you were certainly never deceitful: you made it plain from the start that I couldn't have you. Only . . .' He shrugged. 'Well, a man always hopes that he can persuade a woman to change her mind.' He shook his head. 'Even if he knows he has nothing to offer her.'

Anna, alert to any approach, abruptly realized that he wasn't going to make one. He was too ashamed. If anything was to happen, she would have to make it happen herself. She had never done that, never, and she had no idea how to begin. Move closer to him? She couldn't: it was too forward, too brazen. Respectable women *never* approached a man!

'You have plenty to offer,' she said, in a thin voice that even to her own ears sounded insincere.

He snorted. 'A white silk cloak – but your lover was entitled to a purple one, and you have the gold girdle in your own right. A purse full of gold – which you don't need, and which you now say you never cared about anyway. The

151

status of a magistros and the freedom of a bachelor – the first obtained by your daughter's sacrifice, and the second by the death of a wife. Oh yes, I have a lot to offer – but nothing, I think, of any value to you.'

He would go, Anna realized in horror: he would walk out the door, believing that he'd never win her, and maybe he'd even be so convinced of it that he wouldn't come back. '*You're* of value to me!' she blurted out in a panic. 'You don't need the cloak, or the gold, or the title. You're of value all by yourself.'

He caught his breath, his eyes wide.

'I realized when I got your letter about the arrest,' she told him. 'I would have given all the wealth of my house to set you free.' She stretched out her hand towards him. 'I realized then that I *love* you. Don't go. Please!'

He took the three steps away from the half-open shop door, caught the hand, then dropped it and pulled her into his arms. Holding him for the second time, kissing him, she found herself thinking, with fierce defiance, that this was worth whatever grief might follow.

For his part, he was utterly desperate: she understood that as soon as he touched her. Arrested, imprisoned, beaten; dragged before the Emperor and set free; locked into a room with his creation of fire, and finally rewarded with wealth and authority that almost at once had seemed worthless – he had endured too many strains and reversals to be able to bear any more. He wanted to be certain of her.

She thought of putting him off – but why should she? Having made up her mind that she wanted him, and thrown convention aside to let him know it, what was the point of delay? What use was *respectability* now? It was dust, nothing but dust, to be brushed off the solid hard-angled things beneath. All earthly considerations were dust: rank and status; money and property; contract and the legalities of matrimony – they were all sublunar things. What she felt for Kallinikos belonged to the world beyond the circle of the moon.

She led him upstairs to her room, tossed off her black cloak, sat down on the bed she had shared with her daughter

152

for so many years and held out her arms. Kallinikos came into them, and she unfastened his cloak, ran her hands along his arms, breathing in the scent of Median oil, resin, and sweat. He groaned, began to fumble with the pins on her tunic, then gave up and pulled her skirts up.

Later they would laugh about how they were too desperate even to undress. At the time they were embarrassed, each uncertain what the other would make of such frantic urgency. After the first passionate relief, however, there was space for words, for reassurances and declarations. He apologized, and she kissed him. Lying side by side on the bed, still half-dressed, he traced the line of her cheek with a gentle finger.

'What can I say now?' he asked. 'You don't like to be told how beautiful you are.'

She lay back on the pillow, looking up at him. Not really a handsome face, even when that mop of hair was tidy: the nose was too big and the teeth were crooked. Why was it so dear to her? Why did that ridiculous grin set her very bones alight? 'You don't have to say anything,' she murmured.

'Why don't you like to be told that you're beautiful?' he asked, still tracing the lines of her face. 'Too many men have said it?'

She thought about that. 'I suppose so,' she admitted. 'I used to like it. When I was a girl it made me feel happy and important. After Theodosius died, though . . . I got tired of it.' She caught his hand and kissed the scarred fingers. 'It wasn't as though it could do me any good. I didn't even like most of the men who praised me, and when I did like one, I started wishing that he wouldn't talk like all the idiots. It isn't who I am, anyway. Illness or an accident in the workshop could ruin all my fine looks, but I'd still be the same inside. So, I started feeling, what's the point? It isn't really *me* they're praising at all. It's a statue, an image. They don't really know *me* at all.'

'You sound like a Muslim,' he told her. 'They don't approve of images, either.' He kissed her. 'Me, I think all we know is images. Maybe they aren't reality, but we can only get at reality by going through them. Angels in heaven

153

may know the true forms of things through pure reason, but here on earth we learn only through the impressions made upon our senses. So maybe I love the Anna inside, but I only learned that she was there because the Anna outside made such an impression on me.'

She laughed. 'You're too clever for your own good.'

'I kept thinking about you when I was in prison,' he told her, smiling. 'I always imagined you in your workshop, smiling to yourself as you worked, the way you do. It's hard to imagine sweet scents in prison, but I'd hold my breath and think of you, and it was like smelling jasmine.' He ran his thumb along her lips. 'I thought that even if they sent me to Cherson, I could keep that, the way your ambix kept the scent of marjoram even after it was empty.'

'I was very angry with you,' she told him. She tried to bite the thumb, and he took it away, so she stroked his beard. The old puckered burn scar was *there*, a smooth patch in the coarse black hair. The tip of her middle finger just fitted it. 'You *knew* Stephanos wanted to get rid of you. You ran right into his net.'

'True,' he said, and kissed her. 'And that made you angry?'

'Furious.'

'Downstairs you said that it made you realize you loved me.'

'That too.'

He laughed. 'So, all I had to do was make you angry?'

She knotted her fingers into his hair and held his head. 'Lots of people make me angry, Kallinikos. I don't love them. I was angry because you'd been stupid, and left me to hurt for you for the rest of my life. Don't be stupid again.'

'I am stupid sometimes, though,' he said, looking back at her with sad eyes. 'I killed my family through being stupid, and I got myself tangled in Stephanos' net. Being stupid isn't something one decides to do, so I can't promise I won't do it again.'

'Be more careful, then.'

'I promise.' After a moment, he added, 'I'll build my alchemical workshop outside the house. There are some

154

ruined houses behind your garden, aren't there? I could fix one up, put the workshop there. Then even if there was a fire, it couldn't damage anything other than the workshop itself.'

That took her breath away. They had just made love for the first time, and he was planning where to site his alchemical workshop?

'It would keep the smells out of your perfumery, too,' he pointed out.

'Just what sort of plans are you making here?' she demanded.

He'd started work on the pins of her tunic again, but he stopped. 'Aren't you planning to keep the perfumery?'

That was a different question altogether. 'The chamberlain made it very clear that he'd like me to enter a convent,' she informed him bitterly.

He was shocked. 'God forbid!' He set to work on the pins with more haste. 'You don't want to enter a convent, do you? Here, if I do that, does it make you want to enter a convent? If I—'

'Stop it!' she squeaked, laughing. 'Oh . . . oh . . . no, stop, it tickles! No, I do not want to enter a convent!'

'Good! You can marry me, and keep the perfumery, and I'll build an alchemical workshop and—'

'Marry you?'

He stopped what he was doing. 'You just . . . I *assumed* that you expected us to . . .'

'How can I *assume* anything?'

He frowned anxiously. 'You think they'd *force* you to enter a convent?'

'I don't know,' she told him, wearily now. 'I don't know what they'll do. I only know it's what they want. I told Andreas I have no more vocation for the religious life than Theodosius did, and he . . . took the point. But they may decide they can make me change my mind.' She put her arms around him and lowered her head against his chest. It was a hard, strong chest, and she could feel his heart beating against her cheek. 'There are all sorts of things they could do,' she whispered, admitting the fear for the first time. 'They could ruin my business – easily! All they'd have to do would

155

be tell the guild to find some fault with me, and then I couldn't get supplies. I'd have to do what they want or starve. Or they could threaten to ban me from seeing Theodosia. They've already made it plain that I can only see her if I don't make a fuss about what they want to do with her.'

'Poor Anna!' He stroked her hair, then began kissing her head and ears. 'I think we should get married *quickly*. Then there'd be no point in trying to force you into a convent. They'd have to make the best of it. They can't object to me too much, anyway, not after giving me the cloak.'

The kisses as well as the words were beginning to give her hope where before she'd felt nothing but dread. 'I wasn't sure you'd want to marry me,' she confessed.

'How could you not be sure? You knew I wanted to do *this* . . .'

'Stop it!' she gasped, laughing again. 'There have been lots of men who wanted to do *that*, who didn't want to marry me. You said your mother treated shopkeepers in silk like wormy apples.'

'She's in Baalbek,' he pointed out. 'And even she wouldn't treat an imperial lady-in-waiting like a wormy apple. Anna, surely you know that I want a home, not a whore?'

Put like that, she did know it. 'Maybe,' she conceded. Then she added, in a rush, 'I don't want a master. I've refused offers of marriage because of that. I like you better than any man I know, but, still, I don't want you as a master. You're too wrapped up in your alchemy and your fires, you'd neglect everything else. If I agree to marry you, you must agree to allow me to govern my own household and run my own business.'

'Of course,' he agreed, seeming surprised that she even mentioned it.

'All I want,' she continued breathlessly, as though he hadn't spoken, 'is to stay in charge of the perfumery. Zoe and Helena, too: they're part of my household, and I've brought Zoe up ever since her mother died. I don't want anyone to sell them, or send them off somewhere else, or change their duties. And I don't want to have to give up working and become a proper lady. I *like* my workshop. I *like* my independence.'

'Yes, all right!' exclaimed Kallinikos, starting to grin.

'Maybe I'll have to change things to satisfy the palace,' she went on, 'but if things do change, *I* want to be the one to change them.'

'Anna!' he protested. 'I've already *agreed*.'

She glared at him. 'I'm serious.'

'So am I! I know I get too wrapped up in alchemy. My wife was always telling me so. If you want to govern the household yourself, I'm delighted to be rid of the burden of it. And if you decided to become a proper lady and stopped making perfume, I'd be very disappointed. I've been imagining us working together in your workshop, puzzling over the nature of scents. My wife . . .' He stopped.

His wife, she thought, with a sense of dread. He had never mentioned the woman before that audience in the Octagon, and had not talked about her since, though he had wept for his daughter. Anna didn't even know the woman's name.

She wasn't sure which would be worse: that Kallinikos had adored his wife, or that he'd despised and neglected her. If the first, then she would be in perpetual competition with a woman whose death – and Kallinikos' sense of guilt for it – had made a saint; if the second, then what could she expect for herself? 'Your wife,' she repeated flatly.

'Eukleia hated alchemy,' he told her honestly. 'Like Stephanos, she thought gentlemen shouldn't mess with stinking oils and sulphur. She tolerated it the first couple of years of our marriage, but then she got more and more exasperated with it.' He grimaced unhappily. 'She complained about all the money I was spending on supplies; she complained about what the neighbours said. Every time I came into the house smelling of sulphur she wrinkled her nose and walked out of the room. I started avoiding her unless I'd just bathed. She told me that alchemy would be our ruin, and that if I loved her at all I'd give it up.'

'But you didn't.'

He nodded. 'I know I should have, given what came of it, but—'

'You don't intend to.'

'No,' he agreed, looking into her face.

157

Well, she thought, *I can live with that*. She stroked his beard again, then kissed him. She could still smell the Median oil. 'You can do alchemy as much as you want,' she told him. 'My only condition is that you use your own money for it: I'm not spending *my* earnings on mercury and sulphur! I think building a workshop at the bottom of the garden is a wonderful idea, though. The smell would be very bad for my trade otherwise.'

He sighed deeply and put his arms around her. 'Anna,' he said contentedly, 'I've been looking for you all my life.'

PART II

AD 674

Nine

Anna knew, even before her husband came into the room, that he'd had another quarrel with Stephanos. The shop door banged open and slammed shut, and there was a snarled curse. She set down the essencier she'd been working with, wiped her hands on her apron, and met him in the workshop doorway.

'You're early!' she said, and kissed him.

Kallinikos stood stiffly a moment, then relaxed, kissed her back, and gave her a squeeze round the middle. 'That son of a *whore* again!' he exclaimed bitterly.

'What's he done now?' she asked.

In the year and a half since Kallinikos had earned the title of magistros, it had been a rare week when Stephanos hadn't done *something*. Usually it was something small – a snide comment meant to be overheard, a petty hindrance over supplies, a minor harrassment of one of the workers subordinate to his rival. Occasionally it was more serious, like the attempt to take control of his rival's budget, or the worker flogged for carrying out an order Kallinikos had given him. Sissinios the Drungarios had, despite his earlier warning, continued to support Stephanos for nearly a year, but in the end had given up on him.

'Fitting of the siphons again,' Kallinikos announced, with a grimace of disgust. He stamped on through the workshop into the kitchen, and sat down heavily at the table.

'I thought that was settled,' said Anna, following him.

'So did I!' Kallinikos ran both hands through his hair. 'But he's told Demetrios that our men must obey his orders whenever we're working on board a ship. When Demetrios wouldn't agree to it, he told him it was a rule and he was going to apply it anyway.'

Anna made a sympathetic noise. Demetrios was the foreman of the gang of incendiary workers who'd been assembled for the secret preparation of the liquid fire. The fire and the 'siphons' for pumping it had grown to be quite a complicated assemblage, and the team producing them now numbered sixteen. Three prototypes had been developed, and now the most successful of them – a reinforced lead-lined holding tank, a double-action force pump, and a leather hose sealed by a clamp – was due to be fitted into selected warships. There had, however, been disputes over who was to do the work. Stephanos had claimed that it was the Arsenal's job to install weapons on ships; Kallinikos, that anything to do with fire was the responsibility of his own group. The quarrel had eventually racketed to the Emperor, who had assigned the work to Kallinikos, though only after issuing an exasperated warning to all parties to stop wasting time.

'If he's blocking you from going on the ships,' said Anna hopefully, 'then he's disobeying the Emperor.'

'He's not that stupid,' said Kallinikos in disgust. 'He's not actually stopping us from going on the ships: he's just let it be known that he expects the men to obey his orders when they do go aboard. They, of course, are well aware that if there's any conflict between his orders and mine they could end up being flogged, and they're refusing to set a foot on deck until the matter's settled. This lets Stephanos say that it's not him blocking the work, it's our people refusing to do it!'

Anna frowned. Like her husband, she was aware that the Emperor would not be happy to have to adjudicate the matter again. It was early March now. The Arabs had consolidated their hold on Cyzicus over the previous summer. Sissinios had led a naval expedition to Egypt, to prevent the Egyptian fleet from reinforcing the Syrian one, but he'd been too late. He had fought a fierce and successful campaign in the Egyptian Delta, only to learn that the fleet had sailed for Cyzicus the week before he arrived. The huge Syrian and Egyptian armada had spent the winter safely harboured only fifty miles across the Sea of Marmara from Constantinople. An

162

equally huge army, commanded by the Caliph's son Yazid, had marched to Cyzicus and encamped around it. When the weather improved, before the end of April, the fleet would sail to Constantinople and try to establish a beachhead; if it succeeded, it would ferry in the troops to prosecute the siege. The liquid fire was planned as the centrepiece of the imperial resistance, and the Emperor had expected it to be ready months ago. He would certainly be angry with Stephanos if there was another delay – but he'd be angry with Kallinikos as well.

Kallinikos was not good at defending himself, either. He forgot court protocols, neglected to pay bribes or lip service to officials who might have helped him, and had a lamentable tendency to try to explain technical problems instead of just blaming them on his adversary.

It was, Anna thought wistfully, much more complicated than she'd expected when Kallinikos got his cloak.

'I'll go talk to Basiliskos,' she decided.

She had come to rely on Theodosia's head of staff for political advice. Basiliskos understood the court as only someone who'd been brought up among its intrigues could. 'He'll find somebody who can reason with Stephanos,' Anna continued, hoping it was true. 'After all, Stephanos can't want it to go back to the Emperor any more than we do. However it turned out, he'd be in trouble again, and Sissinios won't protect him any more.'

Kallinikos groaned. 'The wretch probably believes I'm not *willing* to take it back to the Emperor. Yes, talk to Basiliskos! Do you want me to come?'

She went round behind him, put her arms around him and kissed the top of his head. He smelled of metal and soot today, not Median oil: he must have been supervising the work on the pumps in the forge. He still looked like a workman: the magisterial white silk garment only emerged from the cupboard on special occasions. Today he was wearing a plain woollen cloak over the usual dirty tunic and leather apron, and there was soot on his hands and ash on his boots. She smiled at the thought of Theodosia's delicate attendants scrambling along behind him trying to clean up.

'Go have a bath,' she told him. 'I'll do it. Oh, but you can send Sergios for the carriage.' She went upstairs to change into court clothes.

The carriage was one of the more useful features of their position as members of the court. Kallinikos had decided that they needed one, even though they had nowhere to put it, and he'd purchased it – and the horses to draw it – with some of the Emperor's bounty. Anna had been horrified at first, but had quickly grown to appreciate the convenience, and now used it more than Kallinikos did. It was a light, two-wheeled carriage, open, but with an awning to protect against rain, and it could carry two in comfort or three if they squashed. It was drawn by a pair of mares, which Anna had named Honey and Nutmeg for their light-brown colouring. There was no separate space in such a small vehicle for a driver, but Kallinikos had shown Anna how to handle a team, and the mares were elderly, placid, and well trained.

The carriage and horses were kept at livery stables half a mile up the road, but Anna rarely had to fetch them herself. Another advantage of increased wealth and power was more servants. Fourteen-year-old Sergios, an orphan, had worked at the Arsenal, running errands and doing odd jobs in return for scraps of food and a place to sleep: he had been deeply grateful for Kallinikos' offer of a servant's place and a salary. There were others, too: old Paul, who was helping Kallinikos with his workshop; Berenike, who helped Anna with hers, Georgos, who tended the expanded garden, and Chloe, who did the cooking and laundry for the enlarged household.

Anna descended to the shop again, dressed in her court silks, and stood waiting in the doorway to the street. It was a grey, blustery day, and cold enough to make her go back for a good warm woollen cloak to put over her finery. She'd just returned to the doorway, draped in it, when the carriage came rattling down the Middle Street with Sergios driving it. *Too fast*, Anna thought, disapprovingly: the mares were jingling along at their fastest trot! They pulled up smartly by the shop door, and Sergios knotted the reins and jumped down.

'You were going much too fast!' she told him severely, coming forward to climb in.

'Yes, Mistress,' he said humbly, dropping his eyes and holding out his hand to help her up. He was small for his age, but strong and wiry.

'No, I mean it!' she said irritably, taking the hand and holding up her skirts to make the step. 'You were going much too fast for the Middle Street! People live here. *Children* go running out into the road, to say nothing of the dogs and chickens!'

'Yes, Mistress,' said Sergios.

Anna knew he wouldn't go any slower next time: he'd just rein in before he reached the house. The boy adored driving the carriage, and the faster he went, the better he liked it. 'If I think you're going to hit someone,' she told him, unknotting the reins from the post, 'I'll have to start sending Paul to fetch the carriage!'

Sergios looked alarmed. 'Yes, Mistress!' he exclaimed, this time with some fervor. 'I won't go too fast on the Middle Street! I promise!'

'Good!' She took the reins in hand, shook them, and set off at an easy walk.

Through the markets, past the Tower of the Winds and the Forum of Constantine, she guided the little mares. In the round plaza of the Milion, just before the Bronze Gate, the horses slowed down. She hesitated, then allowed them to pull the carriage aside and stop where they usually did, in front of a perfume shop – *her* perfume shop, the second outlet for the products of her workshop.

The money that paid for it had been the Emperor's wedding gift. All her apprehension about being forced into a convent had been misplaced. The palace would undoubtedly have preferred it if she became a nun, but marriage to a titled member of the court was the next best thing, and the chamberlain had been smoothly supportive of the plan the moment he learned of it. Just as well, because it had proved impossible to carry out quickly and quietly, the way she and Kallinikos had intended. They hadn't taken into account the fact that it was Kallinikos' second marriage. The Church always regarded second marriages with suspicion, and contracting one was a lengthy process. Without the support of the Emperor it would have taken the better part of a year to get approval, but a single note from the Octagon had meant that permission was obtained overnight. The Emperor had attended the ceremony in person, and had afterwards presented the newly-weds with ten pounds of gold. Half of that sum had built an alchemy workshop for Kallinikos, and the other half had gone on this outlet.

By Anna's reckoning, her investment would have repaid itself in another year. The slaves who ran the shop – a married couple who'd worked for the previous owner – told her that it had never been so busy or made such a profit. She knew that this was partly because Theodosia had made it fashionable, but she was confident that her own skills had something to do with it as well. Imported aromatics were still scarce, and Anna's improvised blends of local materials had become popular. She sold the cheaper ones at her old shop in Philadelphion and the more expensive ones here. She no longer waited on customers herself – the palace had made it clear that they considered that beneath the dignity of the mother of a member of the house of Heraclius – but she didn't mind leaving the slaves to do the selling as long as she could manage the workshop. Business was booming in both locations, though the expensive goods made more money. She gazed at her new shop – closed now for the evening, its glossy black shutters bolted and locked – and gloated.

She could go in. She could ask Irene and Jakobos how the day had gone and whether they wanted to make any changes to the list of goods they'd requested for the next delivery – but then she'd have to find someone to hold the horses while she was busy. No – she had no real reason to visit her shop tonight. Her business was at the palace. She shook the reins, clicked her tongue, and started the mares on towards the Bronze Gate.

Most of the guards were aware of who she was by now: the carriage rattled through into the grounds of the palace after only the briefest of halts. Anna skirted the Scholarians' barracks and drove down the hill along a narrow, white-paved lane flanked by a hedge of myrtle; beyond it the sea showed grey and white-capped under an overcast and windy sky. Just before the palace of Boukoleon there was a stable block. She pulled in, planning to leave the carriage in the care of familiar grooms.

No one was in the stableyard, but she heard raised voices in the carriage house. She climbed down from her carriage, secured the reins to a hook on the wall, and went to ask someone to see to the horses.

'Intolerable!' exclaimed a man's voice – a deep, indignant voice with a distinctive hissing whistle to it. Anna stopped short, recognizing it.

'My Lord, it's the twelfth hour!' protested someone else – a groom, by the pleading tone. 'How can I let you go out after dark without an escort?'

'Very easily!' snarled a third voice, very similar to the first. 'You hitch our horses to our carriage and get out of our way!'

Anna began to creep silently back to her carriage. With luck she could manage to move it out of the way, and the men in the carriage house wouldn't notice her.

'My Lords, His Majesty—'

'Gave orders that we cannot be allowed out without a guard, did he?'

'No, My Lords, but the late hour . . . Your Excellencies might be robbed, or—'

'We are dining with a friend in the New Town!' snarled the first voice. 'I hardly think an armed guard is required for *that*!'

'Yes, My Lord,' faltered the groom. 'No, My Lord.'

'Good! Prepare our carriage!' The door to the carriage house was flung open.

Anna was just climbing back into her carriage. She had no option but to get down again and bow.

Heraclius, second son of the Emperor Constans the Bearded and named after his great-grandfather, gave her a startled glare. He was only a few years younger than his brother the Emperor, and would have been good-looking if he'd still had a nose. The split, porcine scar that was all he had left, however, instantly drew the eyes, reducing the rest of his face to a blur and a beard.

167

Breath whistled in his mutilated nostrils as he drew it in sharply.

His younger brother, eighteen-year-old Tiberius, pushed impatiently past him and regarded Anna with fierce contempt from an equally disfigured face. 'Uncle's old whore!' he remarked, curling his lip. 'What are you doing here?'

Anna bowed again. 'I've come to visit my daughter, My Lord.'

'To teach her a few more whorish tricks, eh?' sneered Tiberius. 'Every day this place becomes more of a brothel.'

'Your Excellency is joking,' Anna said woodenly.

'I wish I were!' Tiberius spat. 'Music teachers, dancing masters, a perpetual reek of cheap perfume, and you and that little slut simpering through the middle of it! This was *our* palace once!'

It was true: the Boukoleon had belonged entirely to the two princes before the Emperor sent Theodosia to live there. They had never used the north wing, however, nor had any interest in it: Theodosia's rooms had been standing empty when she moved in. It hadn't stopped them from bitterly resenting what they saw as a slight from their brother, or from venting their anger on Anna whenever they met her. With Theodosia herself they were, apparently, unpleasant but more circumspect.

Anna had learned that responding to Tiberius only encouraged him. She bowed again, keeping her face expressionless. He would get bored quickly if he failed to provoke a reaction.

'How's your husband?' asked Heraclius unexpectedly.

He was never crudely abusive like Tiberius: his barbs were always subtle and carefully placed. 'My Lord, he's well,' Anna said warily. 'As I hope Your Excellencies are well.'

'You'd think all those fumes would poison him,' jeered Tiberius, 'but I suppose they're sweeter than the stink from his own smelly rags!'

Heraclius held up a hand, warning his brother to stop. 'I heard,' he said casually, 'that he's had another argument with his colleague.'

168

Now how did you hear that? Anna wondered uneasily. 'No, My Lord,' she said blandly.

'No?' repeated Heraclius disbelievingly. 'I am relieved to hear it. Our brother sets great store by your husband's invention.' He surveyed her a moment. His eyes, when one managed to notice them, were darker than those of his brother Constantine, brown rather than hazel. 'One gathers, however, that our brother is less enthusiastic about Magistros Kallinikos himself. These continual squabbles with Lord Stephanos would exasperate anyone. Myself, I'd put an end to them. I'm sure there are slaves at the Arsenal who could do your husband's job – and be grateful, too, for their elevation, rather than discontented and perpetually ambitious for more.'

'My husband is not ambitious, My Lord,' Anna said, knowing that she was wasting her breath.

'No? Two years ago he arrived in Constantinople, a ragged beggar exiled from his own city for sorcery. Now he's Magistros of Fire, dressed in silk, married to the mother of a member of the imperial house . . . an illegitimate member, perhaps, but a favoured one. He is permanently in contention with Lord Stephanos Skyles, who was his superior, is now his colleague, and who fears to become his subordinate. That looks like ambition to me.'

'You're mistaken, Your Excellency.' No point in saying more.

'And do you think my brother believes that?' asked Heraclius, with malicious pleasure. 'If you do, the mistake is yours.' He snapped his fingers, glanced back at the anxious groom in the door of the carriage house behind him. 'Our carriage!'

Anna chose to take that as her own dismissal. She bowed again and hurried off towards the palace. She hadn't managed to ask the grooms to look after her horses, but she hoped they'd take care of them anyway – and if they didn't, well, the mares were tethered, unable to stray, and she'd see they got especially pampered once they were back in their own stable.

Damn Heraclius. He was probably right. Probably the Emperor did believe that Kallinikos was ambitious, and

169

consider the running battle with Stephanos to be the result of a new immigrant's hunger for power. Certainly he had been increasingly unsympathetic to Kallinikos' complaints. It was entirely possible that he might decide that the best way to resolve the problem would be to dismiss Kallinikos and appoint one of the workers in his place.

Demetrios, the foreman, was certainly familiar with every stage of the fire's production. He was not actually a slave, either: he was a freedman's son, hard-working, intelligent, and able to read and write a little. It was not at all inconceivable that he could be appointed to supervise the production of liquid fire in Kallinikos' place – without the title, presumably, but with most of the salary. Anna didn't believe he'd conspire to supplant Kallinikos, whom he seemed to admire – but if he were appointed to the job, he certainly wouldn't refuse it.

It made it even more important to solve this latest dispute privately.

She used the north entrance to the palace, made her way to the vestibule of Theodosia's suite, and was admitted by one of her daughter's slave girls. Theodosia was in the main room, an elegant dining room which overlooked the garden. She was reading a book when her mother came in, but she set it down quickly, her face brightening.

'Mother!' she exclaimed, getting to her feet and coming over to clasp hands. 'I didn't expect you this evening!'

At fourteen, Theodosia had delivered on her promise of beauty. Almost as tall as her mother, elegant and graceful, she was dressed this evening in a dark blue stola over a sky-blue tunic. Her hair was braided and lightly covered with a silk veil, immaculately tucked in: it had been a long time since Anna had found any straying wisp to tidy with her own loving fingers. The girl could now read and write better than her mother; she played the lute outstandingly well, and her public manners were faultless. A number of eminent nobles were competing for her hand, and a number of elegant ladies had attached themselves to her in the hopes of benefiting from the favour the Emperor regularly showed her. None of them, so far as Anna knew, were friends.

Maria and Sophia were still running about the streets of

170

Philadelphion, free to giggle or sulk. Theodosia always asked after them, and always listened to their news with far more liveliness and interest than she showed for anything that happened at the court. She had never said outright that she missed her old life, but Anna had watched with grief as all her excitement and all her eagerness for the new one eroded steadily away.

'I wasn't planning to come this evening,' she admitted, 'but I'm afraid we need help again. I'm sorry.'

Theodosia rolled her eyes – the old gesture, which made Anna smile. 'What's Stephanos done *this* time?' she asked, then caught herself. 'No, wait! Where's Basiliskos?'

The slave who'd admitted Anna ran to fetch him. Presently the eunuch hurried in, slightly out of breath and wiping ink from his fingers: Anna immediately guessed that he'd been writing poetry again. He bowed to Theodosia, then greeted Anna with a warm smile.

Of all the misconceptions Anna had had of the court, the suspicion of Basiliskos was, she had decided, the most mistaken. She was extremely glad that Theodosia had ignored her own advice and appointed him. Her fears that he would fiddle the household accounts had been as ignorant as they were misplaced: court eunuchs didn't expect to get rich from embezzling, but from selling access to an important master. Basiliskos had seen instantly that a marriageable cousin of the Emperor had the potential to become a prize courted eagerly by every faction in the palace, and he'd devoted all of his considerable abilities to ensuring that Theodosia fulfilled that potential. He also, however, seemed genuinely devoted to his young mistress: he took immense pains over every detail of her household and wardrobe, he was always furious at any insult to her, and at least half the poetry circulating in her praise was his. Anna had come to suspect that Theodosia's household was the first time he'd had anything even faintly resembling a family since the events in his childhood which had led to him being enslaved, castrated and sold to the sacred palace. She had come to feel almost motherly towards him, and it was hard even to remember how unfathomable she'd found him at first. It had been something of a landmark when they

171

reached the point where he felt able to admit that he did not actually like the scent of sandalwood. The aroma which had clung to him when they first met had come from the clothes chests of the Vestiarion, not the pomade he used on his hair. He preferred floral scents for that, and Anna now made a habit of keeping him well supplied with them.

'Stephanos is making trouble again,' Theodosia told him.

Basiliskos rolled his eyes, just as Theodosia had, and shook his head. 'Unless Stephanos has a new patron, Mistress, he's being very stupid.'

'We need to decide what to do about it,' Theodosia declared resolutely. She sat down on her couch, and gestured for Anna and Basiliskos to be seated as well. 'All right, Mother: what's Stephanos want *this* time?'

Basiliskos listened with a frown as Anna explained the situation at the Arsenal. When she'd finished he sat silently a moment, ink-stained finger against his lips, his frown deepening.

'Well?' Anna asked him.

'I didn't expect this, Mistress,' he said unhappily. 'Lord Stephanos was defeated on this point before.'

'He was *defeated* when I first appealed to my cousin,' Theodosia pointed out impatiently, 'but it hasn't stopped him finding new ways to make trouble. None of it's done him any good, and even Sissinios has finally dropped him, but he still won't stop. He *hates* Kallinikos, and he wants to get back at him so much that he doesn't even care that he's hurting himself, too.'

Basiliskos took the finger from his lips and held it up warningly. 'He hasn't made trouble twice on the *same point*, though,' he said, with the apologetic air he always had when correcting Theodosia. 'I wouldn't expect him to do that, Mistress, unless he really has found himself a new patron, and thinks he can improve on the result he obtained before.'

That was a very uncomfortable thought. Basiliskos had long before explained Stephanos' position and grievance to them. It was no accident that Sissinios the Drungarios had supported Stephanos: they were cousins. It was possible that Stephanos was as efficient as Sissinios claimed he was; on the other hand, collusion between a drungarios and the Magistros of the Arsenal could cover up a multitude of financial sins, and both Sissinios and Stephanos were richer than they had any legitimate right to be. To Basiliskos it was perfectly obvious that the real reason Stephanos had wanted to get rid of Kallinikos was that an independent authority at the Arsenal might interfere with a profitable arrangement for double-billing or embezzlement.

Corruption was so common among imperial officials that it could be taken for granted, but usually it was kept within bounds. In Basiliskos' opinion, the Drungarios was honest: he'd been happy to skim off some of the Arsenal's funds for his private enrichment, but he was willing to forgo the privilege for the sake of a weapon which would help him defend the city. He had broken with Stephanos over the question – not, despite his promise, after the first confrontation, and not after the second and third either, but in the end Stephanos had found himself complaining alone and unsupported. Anna had even dared to hope that the Magistros of the Arsenal would finally resign himself to sharing his post with a rival. Now, however, Basiliskos was suggesting that somebody else had agreed to take Sissinios' place.

'It isn't really the *same* point,' Anna objected, hoping that Basiliskos was wrong. 'He's not saying that his people should do the work; he's just saying he wants control of the ships when it's done.'

'It *is* the same point, Gracious Lady,' Basiliskos insisted. 'Bar a quibble. Lord Stephanos was told by His Sacred Majesty himself that your noble husband was in charge of fitting the siphons. For him to claim that he's still entitled to dictate to your husband's men when they're on a ship defies an imperial judgement! I don't see how he can expect such an insolent claim to succeed, unless he's confident that he has a powerful backer.'

'Have you heard any rumours that he has a new patron?' asked Theodosia.

Basiliskos shook his head glumly. 'He's been looking for support, of course, ever since the most distinguished Drungarios broke with him. I hadn't heard that he'd found anyone.' He looked chagrined. 'I didn't think he *could* find anyone, to tell the truth. None of his other relatives are powerful, and as for people who aren't relatives – what advantage could he offer them? He's been forced to share his office with his enemy, so he can't divert any money!'

'Maybe Theodosia's right, and he just doesn't care any more what sort of damage he does to himself, provided he hurts Kallinikos,' suggested Anna hopefully.

Basiliskos shook his head again. 'Your pardon, my lady, but it seems to me that, unless he has a new patron, Stephanos *cannot* hurt the Magistros with this. I don't think he's stupid enough to risk destroying himself if it won't even harm his enemy.'

'*Won't* it hurt Kallinikos, though?' asked Anna. 'Kallinikos was worried that the Emperor will consider it an action by the workers. And I met the two princes on my way here—'

'Them!' exclaimed Theodosia, with contempt. 'I wouldn't worry about what *they* say about anything.'

'They hear things, though,' replied Anna. 'Heraclius had heard that Kallinikos and Stephanos had quarrelled again. He said the Emperor believes it's because Kallinikos is ambitious. He suggested that the Emperor should get rid of Kallinikos, and appoint one of the workers instead. He said they'd have less trouble that way.'

Theodosia waved that aside. 'My cousin isn't going to dismiss *my stepfather* – the man who *invented* liquid fire – in favour of a *slave*!'

Demetrios isn't actually a slave, Anna thought unhappily, *and I'm less confident than you are of your cousin's perfect justice and wisdom*. She said nothing, however.

Theodosia went on, 'And anyway, anybody who knows Kallinikos *knows* he isn't ambitious. All he really cares about is his alchemy – and you!' She smiled at her mother.

'Oh, but His Sacred Majesty *does* believe Magistros Kallinikos is ambitious,' Basiliskos at once said apologetically. 'He believes *everyone* is ambitious. An emperor would be foolish to believe anything else.' He set the finger against his lips again. 'I'm surprised that Lord Heraclius had heard your news, if it only happened today.'

'I was surprised, too,' Anna admitted. 'Maybe he hadn't heard anything. He could've been talking about the last time.'

The finger tapped against the closed lips. 'If he had heard, though . . . I wonder who he could have heard it *from*?'

'Nobody important associates with *the princes*,' Theodosia said scornfully. 'They're traitors.'

'That was never proved,' Anna pointed out gently.

She pitied the two princes, despite the way they treated her. She couldn't help it: they'd been born to the same situation as her own lost prince. She had some idea what it must be like, to be born in the purple and have 'nobody important' willing to associate with you, and she could imagine the horror of being young and disfigured, though she suspected her imagining fell short of the truth. Of course they were angry. Of course they resented it when they saw the beautiful bastard their brother had raised from obscurity being courted and flattered, while they were pushed aside.

Unlike Theodosius, they had once had something of a role. As boys they had worn the purple and been acclaimed as co-emperors with their elder brother. Five years before, however, the soldiers of the Opsikion theme had mutinied in an attempt to force the Emperor to share his power and his military command with the two princes. Constantine had invited the leaders of the mutiny to the palace for talks, then displayed their bodies on a gibbet: that subdued the rest. In the aftermath he had deposed his brothers and ordered that their noses should be slit, so as to prevent any repetition. Heraclius had been sixteen at the time; Tiberius, only thirteen. Constantine was probably right to suspect his brothers of inciting the mutiny – but there had never been any proof.

'People do associate with them, Mistress,' Basiliskos said, with the apologetic air. 'They were born in the purple. If they married, their wives would become Our Lord Constantine's sisters-in-law, and their children his nieces and nephews. That's a prize worth gaining, however unpleasant the sources.'

Theodosia made a face. 'A husband without a nose! *Yuck!*'

175

'They didn't cut off their *own* noses,' Anna pointed out.

'Don't defend them!' Theodosia commanded fiercely. 'They're horrible.'

She had, Anna knew, tried to be friendly with the princes: the hostility she'd met in response had hurt and offended her. Anna sighed and stopped defending them.

'There are people who court them,' Basiliskos resumed, after a tactful pause. 'Quietly, because, as Your Wisdom pointed out, they're suspected of treason, but they *are* courted. Their servants, too, still have friends among the servants of the Emperor. Your lady mother is right, Mistress: they do hear things. It makes sense to pay attention to what they said and wonder about it.'

'They were going out to dinner when I met them,' said Anna. 'With a friend, they said, in the New Town. The grooms at the stableyard wanted them to take an escort, but they refused it.'

'Ah!' exclaimed Basiliskos, smiling. 'A *secret* meeting!'

Theodosia rolled her eyes. 'Those two don't *have* any secrets!'

Basiliskos shook his head. 'Oh, but they do, Mistress. It's true, His Sacred Majesty has them watched, but he has not ordered them confined. By refusing an escort, they ensured that His Majesty's loyal spies aren't part of their own party. The spies will still observe, know where they're going and who they meet – but they won't know what's said, unless the gentleman they're meeting is also being watched.' He rubbed the finger against his lips. 'Does Lord Stephanos live in the New Town?'

'Yes,' agreed Anna, who'd had the house pointed out to her. 'But, really, you can't think—'

'They knew about a quarrel which occurred only *today*,' Basiliskos pointed out. 'What if they learned about it from Stephanos himself, while arrangements for this dinner were being confirmed?'

'I'm not sure they really *did* know about it,' Anna protested. 'Heraclius could have said it just as a provocation.' Remembering the prince's look of knowing disbelief when she denied the existence of the quarrel, she doubted it. Still

176

trying to reassure herself, though, she went on, 'Or they could have been referring to one of the earlier quarrels. God and his saints know, there've been enough of them.'

Basiliskos shook his head. 'Lady Anna, the last time you went to Our Lord the Emperor was when the question of who was to fit the siphons first became controversial. Since then, has there been any quarrel which you would have asked Our Lord to adjudicate?'

No, there hadn't been. There had been several of the niggling harrassments, which brought Kallinikos home from the Arsenal in a furious temper, but there had been nothing remotely worth bringing to the Emperor. What was more, Anna realized, the question of the siphons had been the first and only serious dispute since Sissinios withdrew his support from Stephanos. Her heart sank. Basiliskos was probably right on both points: Heraclius had been referring to the quarrel which had taken place that day, and Stephanos had some new reason for confidence. The two developments might be unconnected, but there was a good chance they weren't.

'So, what do you suggest?' she asked unhappily. 'All I was really hoping for when I came here was that you knew someone who could reason with Stephanos and get him to back down.'

Basiliskos gave her a fond look. 'I'll do that, of course. I'll try to find someone to go tonight, though, just to see if Stephanos is giving a dinner party.' He smiled, beginning to look pleased with himself. 'That has another advantage, too. If this is merely another provocation, then Stephanos should be willing to back down. Then your noble husband would have his way clear when he arrives in the Arsenal tomorrow morning.'

'What if Stephanos doesn't back down, and the person you send doesn't find out anything about who he's dealing with?' Theodosia asked doubtfully.

The eunuch hesitated. 'Might I suggest a stratagem?'

'Please do!' Anna said at once. 'Your stratagems are always very clever.'

Basiliskos beamed. 'Your noble husband could accede to

the ridiculous demand, and agree that his men are to obey
Stephanos' orders while on the ships, but make it plain that
he is only doing so to speed the vital work. If Stephanos then
gives no orders, all is well . . .'

'He'll find something,' Anna said grimly. 'He'll order
something, just to show that he can.'

'In that case, the men should obey, since your husband
has instructed them to and they would be punished if they
didn't. They should also, however, inform your husband.
Then Magistros Kallinikos could tell Lord Sissinios that
Stephanos has commanded the men to fit the weapon in a
way which is *dangerous* and risks setting fire to the ships
concerned.'

There was a startled silence, and then Theodosia laughed.
'Sissinios is planning to be on one of those ships *himself*! He'd
be *outraged*! We wouldn't have to take it to the Emperor: he'd
do it for us – and it would cost Stephanos his *job*!'

Basiliskos laid his hand over his heart and bowed slightly.
'That *is* the intention, Mistress. I think we have all suffered
enough of Lord Stephanos' complaints.'

'You're wonderful!' Theodosia told him warmly, and the
eunuch blushed.

Ten

When Anna returned to Philadelphion and told her husband the suggested 'stratagem', Kallinikos was reluctant. He did not like the idea of giving Stephanos any authority over his own men. 'What if he punishes them?' he asked unhappily.

'He can't punish them if they *obey* his orders,' Anna pointed out. 'They'd only be in danger if they tried to *refuse* them.'

'What if he tells them to do something that damages the siphons?'

'Is he that stupid?'

'Where the fire's involved, yes!' Kallinikos was sharp and exasperated. 'He doesn't understand anything about it or about the siphons, but he's so conceited he thinks he doesn't need to.'

'How much damage could he do before you caught it?'

Kallinikos hesitated, sucking his upper lip. 'Probably not much,' he admitted. Then he grimaced. 'I *hate* giving in to the son of a whore.'

Anna put her arms around him. 'I know!' she said, kissing him. 'And maybe he'll back down and you won't have to. But if he doesn't back down – this might get rid of him. Think of that!'

Kallinikos snorted. 'If he *does* give the men orders it will probably be about what kind of rest breaks they can take – something that makes life harder for them, but nothing I could possibly claim was a danger to the ships.'

'But if he doesn't order anything worse than that, would it be worth going to the Emperor about anyway? It won't take that long to fit the siphons. The men would only have to put up with it for a couple of weeks.'

Her husband sighed. 'A point,' he admitted. 'No: Basiliskos is right. It's a good way to deal with the problem.' He sighed again, then added, under his voice, 'I just hate giving in to the bastard.'

It was, however, what he was forced to do, because Stephanos did not back down. Kallinikos returned the following evening and reported that he had found the Magistros of the Arsenal unyielding. Accordingly, he had made a speech, to him and to the workers, declaring his willingness to sacrifice his rights in the interests of getting the work completed quickly. The first siphons were now being installed, and Stephanos, as Kallinikos had predicted, had given the workers orders about where they could take their lunch breaks.

'He gloated,' Kallinikos reported in digust. 'I was with the team on *Heraclias* today, and he came up and said, "You're not to eat on board the ships. The sailors have enough of your stinking mess to clean up as it is." He made us all get off and sit on the dockside in the wind and the cold, and then he stood and watched us shivering and gloated. Smug-ugly in white silk, cleaning his spotless fingernails and smirking, may he burn in hell!'

'He didn't say anything, though,' Anna comforted him. 'Probably didn't dare.'

'Hah!' exclaimed Kallinikos, gloomily unconvinced by the flattery.

Anna called on the palace the following morning, after dropping off a load of scented oils at the shop on the Milion. Theodosia was out when she arrived, attending the Empress, but Basiliskos was supervising the household. He greeted Anna with something that seemed uncommonly like relief, and at once drew her into the dining room for confidential discussions.

'I asked Philopoimon to talk to Stephanos,' he informed Anna. 'A friend of mine, in the office of the Logothete of the Stratiotikon.'

She nodded. The Logothete of the Stratiotikon was responsible for military spending, and someone from his office was a good choice as an emissary to the Magistros of the Arsenal.

'I gave him a present for his trouble,' Basiliskos went on, with a questioning look. 'It was that jar of pomade you made for me, with the jasmine and violets . . .'

'I'll give you another tomorrow,' Anna promised him, with a smile.

'I put a nomisma on top of it,' Basiliskos confessed. 'I wanted him to do it at dinner time.'

Anna sighed. A whole gold nomisma seemed a lot for one errand – but court bribes always were expensive, and Basiliskos had a very exact sense of how much was appropriate. 'I'll replace that, too, dear. Go on.'

'Philopoimon was very pleased with it, Gracious Lady. He went straight to Lord Stephanos' house. This was last night, My Lady, after you left; about the second hour of the night. Lord Stephanos was entertaining guests.'

Anna looked at the young eunuch with misgiving. 'Heraclius and Tiberius?'

He nodded.

Anna was shocked and bewildered. 'So, you were right!' After a moment, she went on, 'Surely *they* wouldn't be any use to Stephanos as patrons? They're the last people in the world Our Lord Constantine would listen to!'

'Exactly,' said Basiliskos, nodding. 'Exactly.'

'So . . . ?'

Basiliskos gave her a look of mild exasperation. 'So, Lord Stephanos is acting as a go-between for his new patron, My Lady! The patron wants to negotiate with the princes, probably because he has a marriageable daughter, but he doesn't want the details of his discussions known. He's such an important man that he either has, or fears he has, an imperial spy attached to his household. Stephanos isn't important enough to merit such attention, so he's providing a house where discussions can take place in private.' He frowned. 'Philopoimon didn't overhear anything, and apparently he wasn't supposed to see the princes. He said Stephanos took him out of the room quickly, and sent him off without listening to any of his arguments.' He gave Anna a nervous look. 'I can't think who the patron could be. I haven't heard *anything* about this from *anyone*.'

181

Anna thought about it. 'I don't understand why you're so sure Stephanos wasn't entertaining the princes for some reason of his own,' she confessed at last. She was not really arguing – she trusted that Basiliskos *did* know what he was talking about – but she could not follow his reasoning.

He made uncertain jerking motions with a half-fisted hand. 'Stephanos raises a complaint he raised before and was defeated on. He's so confident about success that he won't even hear out the person I sent to discuss it with him. He him- self can't expect to get anything from the princes: he doesn't have any daughters, and wouldn't be important enough to hope to marry one to them even if he did. He has to be acting on behalf of someone else – and it has to be one of the real powers, someone who can aspire to a marriage alliance with the house of Heraclius, but doesn't want anyone to know he's dealing with suspected traitors until he has it all set up.'

'Maybe the princes have nothing to do with this supposed new patron!' protested Anna. 'Maybe Stephanos' business with them is something completely different.'

'Such as?'

She hesitated again. 'I don't know!' she admitted. 'Maybe he wants to buy something from them. Maybe they own a building next to his house or something.'

'They have very little personal property, Lady Anna,' Basiliskos pointed out. 'Their household is part of the imperial inheritance. They can *use* the palace and the estates their brother's allotted them, but they couldn't *sell* anything without His Sacred Majesty's permission.'

'Maybe they want to buy something from Stephanos, then! They must have *some* money at their disposal. Theodosius had enough to buy me a perfume shop.'

Basiliskos shook his head doubtfully. 'What could Stephanos sell that the princes would want?'

'I don't know! A house or a farm or . . . or anything! Maybe he's in debt and he's offering a good price. If he lost a major source of income when Kallinikos got his cloak, he could easily be in debt. So maybe he needs to sell some of his property, and the princes want to have something which *isn't* under their brother's control.'

Basiliskos considered that. 'It's possible,' he admitted. 'It would be a coincidence, though.'

It would be: Anna silently acknowledged that. 'If he is acting as a go-between,' she asked, after a silence, 'who are the possibilities for the patron?'

The eunuch shook his head. 'I don't know, My Lady. A high official or a general, I suppose. But I haven't heard any rumours about it, and, to tell the truth, I can't think why anyone who's hoping to marry his daughter to a prince would choose *Stephanos* as a go-between. He's been casting about for support ever since the Drungarios dropped him, and the court's treated him as though he were a notorious bankrupt looking for a new loan. If *I* were looking for a go-between, *I* certainly wouldn't choose him. I'd choose some respectable neutral person – a holy and devout churchman, by preference.'

'Why a churchman?' Anna repeated, momentarily distracted.

'They aren't dependent on the Emperor for preferment,' the eunuch replied quickly. 'That means they're less likely to betray you. Besides, a touch of sanctity always adds respectability to an intrigue.'

Anna smiled: the Church through the eyes of a courtier. 'Of course.' For a moment she saw Stephanos, too, through the eyes of Basiliskos: a man who had been halfway up the slick incline of power, but who was now struggling and slipping on the way down; a man whom others on that treacherous slope were beginning to avoid. No, not a good investment for a powerful man who was looking to secure his own place at the top. What did he have that a patron would want?

If Basiliskos was wrong, though, and there *was* no powerful new patron, why had Stephanos stirred up trouble with Kallinikos on a point where he'd already been defeated once already?

'I'll try to find out what the truth is,' Basiliskos promised her. Then he dropped his eyes, cleared his throat, and added, 'How much are you willing to spend on it?'

Anna considered her expenses and the profits of her shops. She was not short of money: in fact, she had more than she

183

needed. It was just as well, though: with a siege approaching, the cost of feeding her household would shoot up, and the profits of her shops would certainly go down. The citizens wouldn't be spending money on perfumes once they were short of food. She was very tempted to give Basiliskos only a token amount to spend on bribes.

She was, however, deeply anxious about Stephanos Skyles. That he hated Kallinikos and would do anything he could to injure him was not in doubt. Had he really found a new patron? She had to know.

'Twenty nomismata,' she decided. 'If you can't find out anything for that, I think we'll have to conclude there's nothing to find.'

'If there is something to find,' the eunuch replied with satisfaction, 'that amount should be enough to find it.'

Anna returned home very thoughtful. She sent Sergios back to the livery stables with the carriage, and went into her workshop.

It was quiet and empty. Berenike, the new helper, must have gone out. The oil of juniper Anna had set her to finish straining had, Anna noted, duly been strained and bottled, and there was no other work waiting. There was not usually much to be done in March, unless one had imported aromatics to prepare, and those were scarcer than ever. Anna wondered what would happen when the city was under siege. It seemed very likely that there would be no roses carted in this summer, no jasmine or sweet lavender: the fashionable scent for the city this year would be the biting smell of Kallinikos' fire. It might be a long time before anyone imported something as frivolous as flowers. Anna sighed, gazing around her empty domain and wondering whether she was really wise to commit so much to Basiliskos for his investigation. She wandered idly through the kitchen and out the back of the house into the garden.

She had always had a small garden for vegetables and kitchen herbs, but when Kallinikos built his workshop, he had argued that a big garden would be invaluable if the expected siege should be prolonged. They had, accordingly, bought all the land surrounding the half-ruined house which they had turned into an alchemy laboratory. A farmer had been hired to plough up the long-neglected ground, and now Georgos, the new gardener, was at work, carefully planting onion sets in the freshly tilled earth. There was a bitter wind, and clouds scudded across a pale sky. Anna glanced up at them, and was suddenly glad of the wind. It was a friend, roughening the seas and holding the Arab fleet secure in the harbour of Cyzicus.

Kallinikos had told her that the siege was likely to be long and fierce. The Caliph Mu'awiya had only a dubious claim to his title. When Othman, the previous caliph, was assassinated, his legitimately appointed successor was Ali, the son-in-law of the Prophet himself. Mu'awiya had suspected Ali of involvement in Othman's murder and opposed him. There had been a war, to the scandal and grief of the whole community of the Faithful, and in the negotiations afterwards, Ali was assassinated. Mu'awiya probably wasn't to blame, but there was no doubt he'd profited, and in the eyes of many Muslims, his power was tainted. He needed to show the world that God was with him: he needed a notable victory. Constantinople, the last bastion of the old empire and the old world order, was the ideal enemy. It was entirely to be expected, Kallinikos had said, that the Caliph would press the siege beyond any sane limit.

Anna drew her cloak around herself more tightly. One month, maybe two, and then the invading fleet would appear on the blue seas of the new season. What did Stephanos think he was doing, playing games with the centrepiece of the city's defence? He'd had the excuse, before, that he hadn't understood the importance of the liquid fire, but that wasn't true now. What did disputes about authority and budgets matter, when there was a storm coming out of the south which could sweep the whole familiar world away?

It didn't make sense to her, no more than the idea of a powerful nobleman choosing at this juncture to become Stephanos' patron. That Stephanos would venture another petty quarrel without such a patron, however, was equally senseless. She hated that senselessness: her mind kept worrying at it, trying to work out what Stephanos hoped to gain. She hoped that Basiliskos would soon turn up some critical fact that threw the whole affair back into the realm of reason.

Her heart had reasons enough to ache, without this new burden. She worried almost constantly about Theodosia. Not only was the girl unhappy, but she was ripe for marriage. Who would the Emperor choose as a husband for her, and how would that man treat a wife who was simultaneously a member of the imperial house and a shopkeeper's bastard? There were other worries, too, about her husband: the risks inherent in his work with fire, the dangerous jealousies swirling through the men around him, the uncertainty of the Emperor's support. And there was another new worry, too, kept carefully secret: a possibility that she was pregnant. The thought of bearing another child was both desperately sweet and agonizing. She had never imagined that marriage could be so comfortable and warm. What she'd felt for Theodosius had been giddily exciting, but *this* was much deeper, much more stable and satisfying. She'd given Theodosius a child, and she longed to present one to Kallinikos – but what might become of that baby, in a city under siege? Dear God, how could she bring a new life into a world where everything was breaking?

In a sheltered patch by the back door, violets were in flower. She bent down, picked one, inhaled the chill fragile sweetness of the scent. No point trying to use them for a perfume: there were barely enough flowers to fill the palm of a hand.

If the siege ended, and the city survived, she would plant the garden full of violets instead of onions. Violets in masses on the ground, roses and jasmine climbing up trellises above them: fresh flowers, fresh scents to feed her workshop. A child, hers and Kallinikos', toddling among them: that would be the future . . . if the city held.

Kallinikos was late back that evening, and when he arrived it was with an appalling banging and clattering. She hurried to the shop door and found him trying to fit an upended tank through the doorway with the aid of three of his workmen. There was a reek of distilled oil and sulphur.

'Holy Mother of God!' she exclaimed, crossing herself.

'Don't just stand there!' snarled Kallinikos. He was crouched over awkwardly under his edge of the tank and very red in the face. 'Help us!'

'Not in the shop!' she exclaimed. 'Holy Immortal, not in the shop with all the glassware, please! Put it in your workshop!'

Kallinikos swore, but he jerked his head at the others, and the tank wobbled back into the road. Anna followed it, and found that a flat-bedded cart, drawn by a pair of sway-backed mules, was waiting by the curb. One of the force pumps lay on it, cushioned with straw. It was dusk now, and a few neighbourhood women and children who'd been fetching water for the evening meal had stopped in the street to stare and ask each other what was going on.

Kallinikos and the men staggered over to the cart and hefted the tank up beside the pump. It made a thick sloshing sound as they set it down.

'Dear God!' exclaimed Anna. She hurried over to her husband, and asked in an undertone, 'It isn't full of fire, is it?'

The men wiped their hands off on their dirty tunics and looked at each other. One of them was Demetrios, the foreman, just as dirty and bedraggled as the slaves – or, for that matter, as Kallinikos himself.

'Yes!' snapped Kallinikos. 'That hell-bound whore Stephanos, that shameless fornicating *dog* . . .' He broke off, too angry to think how to finish his sentence.

'You carried it clear across the city like that?' Anna asked in horror.

'It's *sealed*,' her husband told her. He slapped a cap on one end. 'It won't leak.'

'But it isn't supposed to leave the Arsenal!' protested Anna in a furious whisper. That rule had been imposed the moment the fire became a state secret.

'We *know* that!' Kallinikos roared, going red in the face again. 'But that *whore* . . .'

187

'We installed it on a ship, Lady Anna,' Demetrios interrupted, 'but it wouldn't work. The pump jammed, see? And—' he lowered his voice in response to Anna's frantic hushing gestures, but kept talking at the same rate – 'and we can't take the pump apart on a warship, because when we dismantle it it'll spill the fire that's in the chambers, and we don't want that, and we *absolutely* don't want a spill near the tank, in case, God forbid, somebody should drop a lamp or something. So we took it off the ship and we were bringing it into a fire room in the Arsenal when Stephanos comes up. He says, oh no, you can't put that in the Arsenal now it's been on a ship, it's not Arsenal gear any more, it's naval stores. So the Magistros says, God help us, we can't take apart a pump full of fire in *naval stores*, not with all that rope and tow and timber, one spark and the whole place would burn like Sodom and Gomorrah! But Stephanos says, well, you can't put it in the Arsenal, and the Magistros damns him to hell. So I say, trying to make peace, we can put down a tarpaulin on the deck of the ship, and we can drain the pump and take it apart on that, but Stephanos says no, you can't choke up the deck of a warship like that, I forbid it, and you agreed to obey my orders on the ships. So the Magistros—'

'Decided to bring it here?' finished Anna, cutting him off.

Demetrios grinned, teeth white in a dirty face. He was a tall, sandy-haired man, and Anna liked him, despite the worry about whether the Emperor might assign him to her husband's place. 'After some more cursing, Lady Anna, yes.'

'He told me I should leave the precious thing lying on the dockside, God help us!' exclaimed Kallinikos furiously. '"Cover it up with a canvas," he said, smirking at me, "it'll be fine." A year's work – more than a year's work – a state secret! The damned son of a whore!' He drew a deep breath. 'I told him I was going to go to the Emperor over this. *First thing in the morning!* I bet he *put* something in the pump!'

'He could've done,' offered one of the slaves. 'He could've gone and put something in the pump while we had our lunch break.'

The others nodded. 'We was shivering on the dock then,'

another man declared bitterly. 'He won't let us eat on the ships. He could've done anything to the pump.'

'That pump was working just fine when it was in the workshop,' the first man asserted.

'Why would he want to sabotage a pump?' asked Anna sceptically.

'Make trouble for us,' the other slave volunteered instantly.

'Try to make the Magistros look bad,' Demetrios expanded. 'If we'd left the siphon on the dockside, how much you want to bet we'd come back tomorrow and find it damaged? And you can bet Stephanos would blame *us* for it!'

It sounded only too credible. Anna sighed. 'Well, it'll have to go into the workshop, then.' She looked at her husband. '*Your* workshop, my love. *Not* mine. For one thing, I don't think that tank can fit through our front door.'

He glared at her furiously a moment. Then his shoulders sagged. He drew a deep breath and nodded. 'My workshop,' he agreed.

'We'll need the handcart,' she told him. 'I'll fetch it.'

Deliveries to Kallinikos' workshop were complicated, which was undoubtedly why he'd tried to bring the siphon into the perfume shop instead. Unlike the house and perfumery, the workshop was not on the main road. To reach it, the mule cart had to drive up half a block along the Middle Street and turn right down a narrow alley which ended in the wall of a monastery. Just before that wall, a narrow track between two houses led through into an area of gardens, interspersed with the tumbledown buildings which had been abandoned when the empire began to crumble. Kallinikos' workshop was in one of these.

While the men took the mule cart round by the road, Anna ducked through the house, collecting young Sergios on her way, and fetched the handcart the household used to move heavy jars or garden rubbish. From the house, Kallinikos' workshop was merely a trudge down to the bottom of the garden. She and Sergios wheeled the cart past the laboratory itself and along the track to the alley. The mule cart drew in to meet them, and the men loaded the tank full of fire on to the handcart. Demetrios and one of the slaves stayed with the cart and the pump, and Kallinikos and the other slave wheeled the tank back up the track to the workshop.

This was built into what had been the kitchen of a small house. Most of the house was in the same ruinous state as the others around it: roof fallen in, crumbling brick walls full of collapsed upper floors. The workshop, however, had been shored up and re-roofed, and its whitewashed walls looked stronger and firmer for the decay all around them. Its door – which was, fortunately, wider than that of the perfume shop – was secured with an iron bolt top and bottom, each one fastened with a heavy padlock. Kallinikos kept the keys on a chain around his neck. He fished them out, unlocked the padlocks and drew the bolts, then opened the door. The handcart would not fit through, but with the help of Anna, Sergios and the slave, he managed to unload the tank full of fire and deposit it in the middle of the workshop floor.

The workshop was dimly lit at the best of times – the windows consisted of narrow horizontal bands tucked up under the eaves – and in the growing dusk the room was almost completely dark. Kallinikos and the slave went back to fetch the pump while Anna looked around for lamps. Sergios found one for her, and provided a match. She hesitated before striking it, very aware of the black bulk of the tank full of incendiary in the middle of the room . . . but Kallinikos had said that it was sealed and wouldn't leak. She lit the lamp.

The interior of the workshop sprang up around her in the soft gold light: whitewashed walls, a flagged floor, benches full of equipment, and a stone hearth, cold, at the far end of the room. Everything was clean: Kallinikos had had the workshop built and equipped, but had been too busy to use it. That hadn't prevented him from buying more things for it: there were boxes of sulphur and various salts, sealed jars of quicksilver, pots of tin, antimony, realgar, copper, silver and bronze. There was a range of pots and water baths, ambices of various sizes, and an outrageously expensive kerotakis, all gleamingly new. Anna, looking around it for the first time in weeks, was struck by sadness. Her husband had spent a huge sum on all this, eagerly planning his investigation into the mysterious decay and renewal of sublunar things – and it was all untouched. He had exhausted himself instead at the Arsenal, struggling to provide the liquid fire and a system to deliver it in spite of the constant niggling harrassments of Stephanos Skyles.

Kallinikos and the slave returned with the pump and deposited it beside the tank of fire, then stood back wiping their hands. The slave glanced about himself uneasily, obviously inclined to regard the alchemical apparatus as sorcerous. Kallinikos ignored him, knelt down beside the pump and began checking it over.

Demetrios arrived and stood in the doorway. He glanced about the room curiously, then turned his attention to Kallinikos. 'Sir,' he said in a respectful tone, 'we need to move the cart.'

Kallinikos looked up at him impatiently.

'There's a man come out of one of the houses and complained we're blocking his door,' Demetrios elaborated.

Kallinikos sat back on his heels and gave a sigh of disgust. 'Very *well*! Take the cart and go back to the Arsenal!'

Demetrios hesitated, then came a few steps closer. 'What about the pump, Magistros?'

'I'll have a look at it now.'

'Magistros . . .'

Kallinikos brushed him impatiently aside. 'If what's wrong isn't complicated, I'll fix it myself, and we can take it back to the Arsenal tomorrow morning and put it straight on to the ship.'

'Magistros, what if it *is* complicated? You're tired; we're *all* tired. Just *leave* it tonight, please!'

Kallinikos ran a hand through his hair. 'I'm not going to try to fix it here if it needs reforging! If it's complicated, I'll leave it here and see if the *Emperor* can persuade Stephanos to let us use the Arsenal's damned workshops!'

The foreman grinned. 'That's right, sir! You just leave that pump tonight. And tomorrow, sir – weren't you planning to see the Emperor? Doesn't that mean I should wait until you've finished, before I send the cart to collect the siphon?'

Kallinikos sucked on his upper lip. 'Yes,' he decided.

191

'Though I may not manage to see the Emperor tomorrow. I'll apply for an appointment, but sometimes . . . yes, wait for word from me before you send the cart. If I don't come in, start work on installing the siphon in *Nikephora*.'

'Yes, sir,' agreed Demetrios. 'Good luck!'

'Would you like some food to take with you?' Anna asked the foreman. It was already past the usual time for supper, and she suspected that the workers had missed their evening ration at the Arsenal.

Demetrios grinned and bowed. 'Thank you, Lady Anna. We'll have missed rations, and it's been a long day.'

They left Kallinikos crouched over the pump and made their way back along the narrow track between the houses. It was night now, and growing cold. At the end of the alleyway, the other incendiary workers had unhitched the mules from the cart and were tipping the cart back on its wheels in order to turn it round: the lane was too narrow to turn the vehicle any other way. 'Stop at the house on your way back,' Anna invited them. 'I'll give you some food.'

She went back to the house and organized a package of bread and cheese for the workers, with a bottle of wine and some dried figs. When she presented it to Demetrios at the front of the house, he thanked her warmly.

'Look after the Magistros, too,' he begged her, handing the bundle over to the slaves, who were sitting on the bed of the cart. 'Don't let him work on that pump all night, Lady Anna. He doesn't need to do that: whatever's wrong with it can keep till tomorrow. You tell him to leave it, whatever's wrong with it, and put himself to bed. He needs to get himself a good night's sleep so's he can be all calm and lordly tomorrow when he goes to see the Emperor.'

One of the slaves stifled a guffaw, and Demetrios looked at him sharply.

'Never seen the Magistros calm and lordly,' explained the slave.

'The Magistros is a *gentleman*,' Demetrios told the man reprovingly. 'He's read more books than you have teeth in your head. I'm sure he can look calm and lordly when he wants to.'

192

The slave was not convinced. Anna wasn't either, to tell the truth. 'I'll make sure he gets a good night's sleep,' she promised Demetrios.

'Good,' said the foreman, nodding in satisfaction. 'Good.' He looked at Anna a moment, then added, 'Stephanos Skyles can rot in hell.'

'I wouldn't wish any man in hell, Demetrios,' said Anna, crossing herself. 'I admit, though, I'd be pleased to see Stephanos rotting in idleness and a plain wool cloak, far away from the mastery of the Arsenal.'

Demetrios laughed, then, with a wave, started the mule cart off.

Anna went back into the house. There was a scent of barley soup in the air: Chloe had cooked supper for the household, who had all been waiting to eat until the master had returned.

Anna thought about her husband, crouched over the broken pump in his cold workshop, no doubt raining curses on Stephanos Skyles as he worked. She could ask him to leave the pump and come up to the house for supper, but she already knew that he wouldn't come.

She went into the kitchen and packed up a basket with a pot of soup, some bread, and another bottle of wine. She told the rest of the household they could have their supper, then took her basket down to the bottom of the garden and knocked on the workshop door.

'What?' came her husband's voice from inside.

'I've brought you some supper,' she told him. 'Hot soup.'

There was a silence, and then the door opened. The workshop smelled strongly of the liquid fire, and Kallinikos' hands were shining with the stuff. The pump lay in pieces on the floor behind him. The liquid from its chambers had been drained into a basin.

'Thank you,' said Kallinikos, without much enthusiasm.

Anna came in and set the basket of food down on one of the workbenches. The room was cold, and she chafed her hands together. 'I thought we could share it here,' she said. 'Unless you want to go back to the house, where it's warmer.'

193

Kallinikos looked from her to the basket. 'You're trying to get me away from the siphon, aren't you?'

Of course! she thought. *You're in a state, my love, and you need to calm down.* 'I just want to be with you,' she told him – and that was true, too. 'I'm tired of worrying and being afraid, and I want to be with you.'

Kallinikos looked at her for a long moment. 'Good idea,' he said at last. 'I'd better wash my hands. Fire tastes foul, and it sticks to your fingers worse than garlic.'

He went outside to wash his hands in the garden water butt, then came back in. They sat together on the workbench in the cold, fire-smelling laboratory and ate their bread and soup. Anna loosened her cloak, tossed one end over her husband's shoulders, and snuggled up against him, consolidating their warmth. He put half his own cloak and his arm around her.

'You're being very sweet,' he said, kissing her.

'Mmm,' she agreed, burrowing into his neck. It felt good and comforting. Fun too: a workshop deserted except for the two of them, no servants around to notice what they were up to, just the wind gusting against the eaves . . .

They ended up on the floor, with both cloaks on top of them and a pile of discarded clothing as a mattress. 'Feeling better now?' Anna asked, when they were satisfied and relaxed in one another's arms.

'*Much* better,' Kallinikos agreed, kissing her.

'So, are we going to spend the night here or in bed? It's warmer in bed.'

He laughed. 'I suppose we can go to bed.'

Anna sat up, pulled loose hair out of her face, and tried to free her tunic from underneath her husband's body. She jarred a piece of the pump which lay next to them and steadied it quickly. 'Did you find what was wrong with it?' she asked, with a wary glance at the machine.

Kallinikos sobered abruptly. 'Yes.'

Anna looked at the hollow shell of bronze and iron, the dismantled leather seals and pistons and levers. It was not something she felt she could understand.

Kallinikos got up, slung his cloak around himself, and went over to the pump. Guarding his clean fingers with the edge of his cloak, he picked up from the floor beside it a fragment of metal. 'Found it inside the case, next to the fitting for the handle,' he told Anna. 'It was jamming one of the pistons.' He set the metal fragment down beside her.

Anna examined the piece of metal without touching it. It was a nail, a bent nail. It was easy to imagine someone slipping it into the space around the handle while the workers sat on the dockside eating their lunch.

'Could it have been an accident?' she asked, feeling slightly sick.

Her husband hesitated. 'I wouldn't say that it's *impossible* that it got there by accident,' he conceded. 'It's very, very unlikely, though.'

Would Stephanos *really* have disabled the pump? Was he trying to ensure that it was left overnight on the dockside so that it would suffer some accident he could blame on Kallinikos and the workers. Surely – even granted Kallinikos' ineffective style of complaint – that kind of negligence towards a state secret would hurt Stephanos more than it hurt Kallinikos?

'I don't understand this!' Anna protested unhappily.

'Don't you?' Kallinikos demanded. His face was going red again, and the cords of his throat stood out. 'That corrupted whore Stephanos . . .'

'It doesn't make sense!' Anna objected, cutting him off. 'Yes, I know he hates you, I'm sure he'd love to ruin you – but, my love, it *doesn't make sense*! I know he's baited you until it's *hard* for you to think clearly, but . . . but just *look* at it! He tells you you can't eat lunch on the ship, and then when you agree he takes advantage of it to sabotage a pump. He bars you from fixing it. First he tells you to put it in naval stores – *liquid fire*, in *naval stores*? Then he wants you to leave it out where it might be damaged. It's *stupid*. Even if he does have a new patron, and even if it's somebody *really* powerful, he still couldn't possibly justify that sort of carelessness to the Emperor! Either he's gone mad, or he's up to something we haven't yet worked out – and I *don't* think he's gone mad. He's got some scheme, some new plot to hurt or discredit you. I wish I could understand what it *is*!'

Kallinikos was silent, staring worldlessly at the pump. He began to chew his lower lip. He looked back at Anna, his face now more worried than angry. 'You spoke to Basiliskos this morning,' he said.

Anna nodded and gave him a quick summary of what the eunuch had said.

Kallinikos scratched at his beard, frowning. 'The princes are suspected of treason,' he said in a low voice. 'What if . . .' He trailed off.

Anna felt cold in a way that had nothing to do with the chill of the workshop. 'You don't think Stephanos could have sold them the *fire*?'

'If they really *are* traitors,' Kallinikos whispered, 'wouldn't they want it? They could hand it to the Caliph, tell him that this is the centrepiece of the city's defence, and ask him to appoint them rulers when the empire has fallen.'

'They wouldn't!' exclaimed Anna, numb with shock. 'They're descendants of *Heraclius*! How could they betray . . .'

She stopped. Of course they could betray the empire. Why would they believe in its glory and virtue, after their brother had had them mutilated? Probably they felt that the empire *deserved* to fall. Maybe they felt that Islam was preferable to orthodox hypocrisy.

'But . . . but why would they dream up such a complicated plot to get hold of a siphon?' she asked unsteadily. 'Stephanos buys supplies for you: he must know the recipe for the fire, and that's what's really new and special, isn't it? Lots of people can make pumps!'

Kallinikos glanced at the pump again. 'The siphon *is* a bit special,' he said grimly. 'Liquid fire is thicker than water and it dissolves ordinary sealants like pitch: I had to put a lot of work into the pressure seals and cylinders before I could get the pump to deliver smoothly. Most army engineers don't have the experience with irrigation I do, and they couldn't build one as good. And anyone trying to steal the secret would want a batch of the finished product. Yes, Stephanos could tell them the ingredients we use in roughly the right proportions, but he doesn't have much idea of what we do to blend them. A finished batch would let an enemy engineer know what he was working towards.' He bent abruptly to pick up his tunic. 'We shouldn't keep the fire here tonight,' he said, pulling it on. 'The Arsenal is under guard night and day, and that's where this siphon should be.'

He could be completely wrong, Anna thought, desperately arguing against her sudden conviction that this explained everything. There was no evidence that the princes were traitors, none. It was really much more likely that Stephanos had some scheme they hadn't yet fathomed, or that he had misjudged the limits of what he could get away with, or that he simply didn't care any more what harm he did himself, so long as he could get back at his enemy.

Kallinikos could be wrong . . . but he could be right. Stephanos might have done a deal with the princes, agreed to supply them with a pump and a tank of fire. He could have made arrangements for men to collect the fire from the naval stores – which were more lightly guarded than the Arsenal – or from the dockside.

Or, God save them, from this completely undefended workshop in the heart of the city. He would surely have *known* that Kallinikos wouldn't leave it in naval stores or sitting out on the quay.

Anna got to her feet. 'I'll tell Sergios to fetch the carriage at once.'

Eleven

Anna hurried up the path through the dark garden into the house. The kitchen was empty, lit only by the faintest glow from the banked coals on the hearth: the slaves and servants were all preparing for bed. She ran up the stairs, and found the four women in the room they shared, combing one another's hair by the light of a candle; the men's room was already dark. She stood on the landing, dishevelled, out of breath and agitated, and clapped her hands for attention.

'Sergios!' she cried sharply.

The women all got up and came to the door of their room with their hair loose, staring in amazement and misgiving. After a moment, Sergios came to the door of the room opposite, yawning in an unbelted tunic.

'Go fetch the carriage,' she ordered him. 'Take it down the alley to the access to the master's workshop. We've decided that the things the men brought from the Arsenal this evening aren't safe here, and we're going to take them back there at once.'

Sergios opened and closed his mouth. 'It's *dark*!' he protested. 'The stable will be *closed*, Mistress Anna!'

Anna hesitated. Away from the cold, fire-scented laboratory, on the familiar landing of her own house, the possibilities she and Kallinikos had conjured between them seemed extreme and unreal. Surely it was much more *likely* that Stephanos was entertaining the noseless princes for some ordinary reason? Surely there was no *real* danger that armed men were creeping through the dark of the night with the intention of stealing a state secret from the back garden of a house in Philadelphion?

Could she say, though, that what they'd imagined was *impossible*?

'You'll have to wake them up, then,' she told Sergios ruthlessly. He looked so dismayed that she added, 'You can promise them a bonus for their trouble.'

'Yes, Mistress,' the boy said nervously. 'Can Paul or Georgos come with me?'

He was, obviously, afraid to go out in the dark and face the wrath of the livery-stable owner alone. 'If they're willing!' Anna conceded.

The four women staff had been watching all this open-mouthed. Now Berenike – who, as a servant rather than a slave, had precedence over the others – cleared her throat and asked, 'Should we do anything, Mistress?'

Anna looked at them a moment, then sighed, ashamed to be giving her household so much trouble on a cold night. 'No,' she told Berenike. 'Go to sleep.'

She went downstairs, then pulled her cloak around herself more closely and ventured back out into the garden. The wind was gusting, and a quarter moon shone from a cloud-patched sky. The night smelled of damp earth, fresh onion sets, and manure. She made her way back down the narrow track between the vegetable beds to the workshop.

As she reached it, she heard voices. She stopped and stood still in the windy dark, listening. Men's voices, the words indistinct. Many of them, and they were in the alley, just at the end of the track between the houses.

Her heart beat hard. She ran to the door of the workshop and hurried in.

Kallinikos had been reassembling the pump, and was kneeling over his machine in the middle of the floor, pair of pliers in hand. 'There are men in the alley,' she told him.

He swore, set the pliers down, ran to the door and listened, then swore again. He looked at Anna, his face white above the beard. 'Did you tell Sergios to fetch the carriage?' he asked.

'Yes, but—'

'All right,' he said, not waiting for her to finish. 'You take these . . .' He pulled the chain with the two padlock keys from around his neck and tossed them to her. 'Go out, bolt the door, lock it, and run up to the house. Go!'

'I can't leave you!'

'They won't be able to get in! Get help. Go!'

She wanted to scream, to protest that she would *not* run away, that she would stay with him, whatever became of her. If she stayed, however, she could do nothing to help, while if she ran back to the house she might be able to rouse the neighbourhood. She ran out the door, closed it, bolted it, and began fumbling in the dark with the padlocks and the keys. She was locking the second, lower, bolt into place when there was a shout behind her and footsteps thudded heavily through the darkness.

She jumped up and sprinted for the house. There was another shout, and some of the footsteps diverted after her.

She realized, even as she pounded up the path, that the pursuer was gaining, that he would catch her before she could reach the house. Almost any man could run faster than she could: her long skirts and cloak clung to her legs and hampered her. Even if she reached the house, what then? How much safety would it provide – in exchange for how much danger to her household?

She dodged away from the house and paused a moment to fling the keys out into the garden. The jingle as they landed was almost inaudible over the noise of the keys at her own side. She ran on, off the path now, her feet sinking into the soft earth. The edge of her cloak tripped her, and she stumbled. Her pursuer lunged up from behind her and grabbed her.

She screamed loudly, and was hauled back by strong arms. In a stink of dirt, old sweat and garlic, a hand was clapped over her mouth.

'Shut up!' a rough voice snarled into her ear. 'Shut up!'

She squirmed and struggled, kicking out at her assailant. He took his hand off her mouth and clouted her, knocking her down into the onions and the mud, then grabbed her arms and hauled her to her feet again, shaking her. 'Keep your mouth shut and you won't be hurt!'

She tried to scream again, and he punched her in the chest, knocking the wind out of her. She coughed, whooped for air, thinking with horrified concern of the child that might be growing in her womb. The man dragged her left arm

200

up behind her back, put his right hand over her mouth, and marched her back down the garden towards the workshop.

The light shining from the narrow windows under the eaves was enough to show a substantial number of men gathered in front of the workshop door. One, holding a partly blackened lantern, was bent over the padlocks, inspecting them. Anna counted four others behind him, then spotted a fifth man further back along the track between the houses. That made seven, if she included the one who was holding her. Another man appeared from around the far side of the workshop, where he must have been looking for another entrance. He was better dressed than the others, with a heavy dark cloak and good boots. The rest were in dirty hemp and patched leather, armed with knives and clubs: typical Amastrianon toughs.

'Ha!' said the man in the heavy cloak when he saw Anna. 'We want the keys.'

He would want the keys. Kallinikos had invested in top-quality bolts and padlocks to protect his alchemical supplies, and breaking into the workshop wouldn't be easy.

'I threw them away,' Anna told him, still gasping for breath. 'They're somewhere in the garden. Probably they've been stepped on.'

The man glanced at the dark, muddy expanse of garden, then surveyed her in deep displeasure. Brown hair, a beard that was neatly trimmed, woollen cloak secured with a good bronze pin. When he moved, she glimpsed the outline of a sword under the cloak: no, this was not a robber. This was a man who'd been appointed to hire robbers by somebody who wanted something valuable stolen.

'Search her!' he ordered his men.

One of the robbers came over to pull her cloak off, though the rest continued to study the door. Anna shivered in the cold March wind. The man who'd taken her cloak leered at her, then noticed the keys at her belt. He unfastened the belt, thrust one hand between her legs for a quick feel, then slid the keys off the belt and handed them to the leader, who smiled.

'House keys,' Anna told him, feeling stupidly triumphant.

'Kallinikos had the keys to the workshop, and I've thrown them away.'

The leader ignored her and moved forward to try the keys on the padlocks. It quickly became clear that none of them would fit.

'We've already raised the alarm,' Anna said. 'People should be coming soon. If I were you I'd give up and go before they get here.'

There was a quick look of alarm exchanged among the hired thugs, but the leader just sneered. 'She's lying,' he said confidently. The sneer turned to a look of appraisal. 'You had the household keys,' he commented. 'You're the sorcerer's *wife*, aren't you? Where is he?'

She said nothing, but the man glanced up at the lighted windows. 'In there?'

Anna still said nothing. The robbers' leader went to the door and thumped on it. 'Kallinikos of Heliopolis?' he said. 'We have your wife.' He glanced back at Anna. 'A very fine-looking woman she is, too. If you value her at all, open the door.'

There was a muffled curse from the other side of the door.

'He can't open the door,' Anna said, feeling sick and dizzy with terror. 'No matter what you do to me, he *can't*. It's locked on *this* side, and I threw away the keys.'

The man saw that this was obviously true, and was infuriated. He turned suddenly and hit her, throwing her back against the robber who held her. Everything went grey and pulsed sickeningly. She swallowed blood from a cut lip and tried to get her feet under her again.

'Pick the locks,' the leader ordered the robber who'd been inspecting the padlocks before. 'You said you could.'

'Quicker to jemmy the bolts off,' the robber replied. 'Quality padlocks, there, an' it's hard to pick locks in this cold: it'd take time. In this wind we c'n jemmy the bolts, no trouble. Nobody'd hear a thing.'

'Do it, then,' ordered the leader impatiently.

The robber nodded. Another man came up with a long package wrapped in black cloth, and unwrapped it to reveal a set of crowbars. Quickly the housebreaker worked the ends of two of the bars between the lower bolt and the door. He and his assistant heaved on them: the bolt squealed alarmingly. Anna was sure, however, that the robber was right. None of the noise they'd been making was going to draw attention from the neighbours. The workshop was set well away from the nearest house, and the gusting wind was enough to mask or explain any sound.

'Anna?' came Kallinikos' voice from inside the workshop. 'Anna, are you there?'

Anna swallowed, trying to ease the choking in her throat. 'Yes,' she called back.

'Let her go!' Kallinikos said to the robbers.

The bolt split just then with an explosive crack. The robbers drew the broken pieces out of the sockets and tossed them aside, then inserted the crowbars under the upper bolt.

'I've got the fire,' Kallinikos called, loudly this time, his voice hard. 'I've got a tank of it here, and I've got a lamp. If you want it, you let my wife go!'

The housebreakers looked puzzled. Anna wondered how much they knew about what they were trying to steal. The leader obviously had the whole story, but it seemed unlikely he'd explained everything to his hirelings.

'A moment, a moment!' said the leader, quickly. *He* looked alarmed. 'You in there?'

'I'm here,' replied Kallinikos. A sound came from inside the workshop: the rhythmic clank of a pump handle. Anna felt the hair stand up on the back of her neck. She remembered the large water bath in her workshop blazing with blue-edged fire, and the rag burning under the water. In a desperate agony of imagination she saw Kallinikos burning alive, screaming as the flames of his own creation devoured him.

'Don't do anything stupid,' said the robber leader.

'You let my wife go!' Kallinikos called through the door. His voice was savage. 'You let her go, or, I promise you, you won't get anything from here but ash!'

'We'll let her go, we'll let her go!' the leader exclaimed quickly. 'Don't do anything stupid!' He glanced round at the man holding Anna and snapped his fingers. The man

203

holding her let go. Anna stood where she was, shaking. She felt almost too sick and frightened to move.

'Anna?' Kallinikos called again.

'Yes!' she called back. 'They've let me go.' She glanced round, edged away from the man who'd held her, began backing out through the thick of the group.

'Get back,' Kallinikos shouted to her. 'Go to the house.'

'We let your wife go,' said the robber leader. 'She's unharmed. There's no need to do anything stupid. You know what we want. If you give it to us quietly, nobody will get hurt.'

The pump clanked again, twice. Anna backed away further. She couldn't seem to get enough air, and she was afraid she would faint.

'We're going to open the door,' said the leader.

'Come on in!' Kallinikos cried. There was a note in his voice that made Anna stop in her tracks. It wasn't fear, but a desperate excitement. A man who sounded like that might do anything, anything at all.

The housebreaker and his assistant heaved on their crowbars, and the second bolt shattered. They scattered the fragments and flung open the door.

Over the heads of the robbers Anna glimpsed Kallinikos standing in the middle of his workshop, teeth bared in a grin, eyes wild. In one hand he held the leather hose that was attached to the pump. In the other hand was the lamp.

'Come on in,' he said again.

The leader put his hands up, stepping in front of the others. 'Just give us what we came for,' he said quietly, edging forward. 'Just put the lamp down, and let us take what we want, and you won't be hurt.'

Kallinikos laughed. He moved the lamp so that the flame burned directly under the nozzle of the hose, and with one quick flick of his fingers, released a clamp.

There was a roar like a tree falling, and a blaze of appalling light. Smoke billowed across that light, black and biting, full of the reek of sulphur. Hellfire was released on earth, and men screamed as it caught them. Anna screamed too, wanting to run, but unsure whether she wanted to run away from the conflagration or towards it.

Black shapes stumbled away from the light, bellowing in pain, hair and clothing ablaze. The awful roar of the fire ebbed, then surged again with another clank of the pump. The other robbers reeled back, crying out in horror. Kallinikos appeared in the doorway, holding in his hands a jet of fire, blue-white, edged with poisonous crimson. Howling like a demon, he passed it over the men before him, and they wailed and shrieked as it touched them, turning, running, frantically trying to get away.

A fleeing man crashed into Anna. Fire touched her arm and clung there, blistering agony. A numbed brain threw up a memory of Theodosia bringing in the buckets of mulch from the compost heap, and she spun away, threw herself into the soft earth of the garden, burying the pain in the cold wet soil. Behind her the screaming continued.

She put her hands over her head and lay still, pressing her face against the soil, afraid to look, afraid to breathe. The screaming went on and on, with the sound of running, with thumps and bangs and splutterings. She heard Kallinikos' voice raised in a shout, but couldn't make out what he was saying. *Oh God*, she prayed silently, *Oh God, have mercy, have mercy on us, that we do such things, that we make such things. Oh God, forgive!*

The screaming ebbed into sobs and moans. Anna sat up, shivering convulsively.

The lamp had gone out. The fragmentary moonlight showed ground littered with smouldering, moaning heaps. Someone was bent over one of them, throwing earth on to the last flickering flames. The light of the burning body showed her a black face and glaring eyes, like an attendant devil in a painting of the Day of Judgement.

Anna climbed slowly to her feet, and the black-faced demon looked up at her. It was Kallinikos. 'Anna?' he said uncertainly.

The last flames went out, leaving smoke, and the scent of burned flesh and alchemical fire. Anna stood still, not knowing whether to speak or not, not knowing what to say.

Kallinikos stumbled away from the body, staggered over to her, and threw his arms around her. He buried his face against her neck and held her tightly. He was shaking all over. Slowly, almost without her willing it, her own arms rose and locked around him. The left forearm brushed the rough wool of his cloak, and hurt.

There was a flurry of footsteps, cries of horror, lamplight. Anna lifted her head and saw Sergios standing in the passage-way to the alley, accompanied by Georgos the gardener and several neighbours with lanterns. The wavering light caught on bodies and smoke.

'Master Kallinikos?' asked the boy, utterly appalled.

One of the heaps sat up and raised a pleading hand to the rescuers. 'For the love of God!' the man croaked. 'For the love of God, fetch a priest!'

'Yes,' said Kallinikos, letting go of Anna and walking over towards the rescue party. 'Yes, go and fetch a priest.'

The neighbours were from the houses along the alleyway: they had been disturbed by the screams and the blaze of fire, and had come out to see what was going on just as Sergios arrived with the carriage. Anna was glad of them. While Sergios turned the carriage around and went to fetch a priest, they helped carry the injured robbers through the garden and into the house. The kitchen wasn't big enough for all the men, so they moved them into the workshop. The afternoon's smell of juniper and cedar oils was overlaid by the terrible scent of burned flesh. The neighbours, having done their duty, were eager to get away. Anna thanked them and sent them home.

The entire household was up now, and the women moved about in shocked silence, lighting lamps and fetching medi-cines and blankets.

Three of the robbers were unconscious; one was dead. Of the remaining four, two were severely burned and in great pain, while the other two were merely scorched. All, however, were shaken, shocked beyond words: the fires of hell had blazed out at them, had seized upon and clung to them. When Sergios returned to the house with Father Agapios, the two most lightly injured men at once dropped to their knees and began to gabble confessions: they had sinned, they had committed robbery and fornication and shed innocent blood, and they begged the priest to grant them God's mercy. Agapios, with surprising authority, commanded them to compose themselves and meditate on the divine law, while he saw to their fellows, who needed him more urgently.

Anna had already been doing what she could for the victims: sponging off fabric that had eaten its way into blackened skin, anointing blistered and bleeding flesh with soothing oils, distributing cups of water and wine laced with hellebore to dull the pain. She did not expect the unconscious men to live, and she hoped very much that they would die without regaining consciousness. No one should have to suffer the torture of a death from such appalling burns: the very sight of them brought tears of pity and revulsion. As for the dead man, he was disfigured beyond recognition – though she suspected he was the leader of the party. He had, after all, been in front of the others, and caught the full blast of the fire, and the twisted corpse had a gold ring on its finger and a gold-hilted sword at its side. She forced herself to go over to the body and examine it, but she could find no trace of the man's identity. The gold ring was plain, not a signet or helpfully marked with a name or device, and the sword, though obviously expensive, was similarly anonymous.

Father Agapios began to administer extreme unction to the dying. While he chanted the solemn words over the bodies, Kallinikos came into the workshop. It was only at his reappearance that Anna realized he'd gone upstairs as soon as they reached the house. He had washed his face and hands and put on his cloak with its narrow purple stripe. He made his way over to Anna in silence.

'I'm going to the palace,' he said, bending over to whisper into her ear. 'I want someone else to take charge of this. I've sent Sergios and Georgos to keep an eye on the siphon, but if the robbers start causing any trouble, call them in again.'

Anna nodded numbly. Kallinikos touched her shoulder – then paused, staring at the burn on her forearm. The skin was puckering up in great white blisters.

'I burned *you*?' he protested in horror. 'I told you to go back to the house!'

'I couldn't, when I didn't know what was happening to you,' she replied. 'I was at the back, my love. You didn't . . . it wasn't from the hose. One of them ran into me.'

He was silent a moment. 'I'm sorry,' he said at last, very sadly. 'I'm sorry.'

She couldn't think of anything to say to that, so she caught his hand and kissed it. He kissed her back, on the mouth, then quietly left the room.

Agapios finished his ministrations to the dying and turned to the survivors, taking the confession of each man in turn. Anna tried not to listen. Helena and Zoe came over to her, bringing oil of lavender and bandages, and she allowed them to anoint her forearm and wrap it in clean linen. Her teeth began to chatter, and she realized that she was shivering in an unbelted tunic: her cloak must still be lying on the ground by the workshop. Her keys, too: dear God, those should not be left lying around! She took a blanket from Helena, and ordered the woman to go and check with Sergios and Georgos whether they'd found any keys.

'How did *they* know the master would have the fire *here* tonight?' asked Zoe in a whisper, with a frightened nod at the robbers.

'It was arranged,' Anna replied wearily.

She realized as soon as she'd said it that someone besides Stephanos must have assisted with that arrangement. The robbers had headed straight for the alchemy workshop, despite the fact that the access to it was hard to find and that Kallinikos' own first instinct had been to put the siphon in the house.

She remembered, with a wrench of pain that cut across everything else that had happened, how Demetrios had urged Kallinikos not to work on the pump that night, had told him to leave it in the workshop, and encouraged him not to take it straight back to the Arsenal in the morning. She remembered the foreman begging her to make her husband leave the pump and go to bed. Oh, God! She *liked* Demetrios.

If she mentioned her suspicion, he would certainly be

questioned under torture – in the Noumera Prison, or the Strategion, by a figure like the blunt-faced officer who'd interrogated Anna long ago. And he might be completely innocent. His concern might have been perfectly genuine, and the aftermath merely a coincidence.

The robbers could certainly expect to be tortured. She looked at the man who was now pouring out the tale of his sins to a solemn-faced Agapios, and felt a wave of revulsion. They had just tasted hellfire: should they have to suffer the rack and the hook as well?

She gathered up the blanket around herself and walked over to the nearest robber. He was one of the more severely injured ones; he'd already made his confession, and was now lying quietly, his eyes closed. Most of his hair had been burned away, and his chest and right arm were swathed in bandages. The smell of burning had been swallowed up by the clean scent of lavender oil. Anna knelt down beside him.

'What is your name?' she asked.

The robber opened his eyes and looked at her. The whites of his eyes had turned red; the pupils, dilated by the hellebore he'd been given for the pain, were immense and black. He was probably quite young, though with his singed and bloodied face it was hard to tell. 'Zoilos, My Lady,' he whispered.

'Zoilos,' Anna repeated. 'Do you know what it is that you tried to steal tonight?'

His cracked lips curved in a ghastly imitation of a smile. 'If I'd a known what was in that shed, Lady, I'd never'a come near it in my life.'

'But do you understand what it is you were doing?' she insisted.

He stared at her blankly. He was certainly a robber, Anna told herself, and from the fragments of the confessions she'd been unable to avoid overhearing, theft was the least of the crimes these men had committed. They would have done worse than robbery to Anna herself. They'd been entirely prepared to, to get into the workshop more quickly.

She couldn't help it, though: she still pitied them.

'My husband is an engineer, a Magistros of the Arsenal,' she said. 'He invented a new type of incendiary, which is what he used on you tonight. Our Lord Constantine intends to use it to protect the city from the attack of the heretics: that is a secret belonging to the state. It shouldn't really have been taken out of the Arsenal, but there was some kind of plot to ensure that it was stored in a vulnerable place, just for tonight, when you came to steal it.'

Zoilos stared at her in confusion. The next man, who lay just a little distance away, sat up frowning.

'A *state secret*, Zoilos,' Anna told him. 'You were trying to steal a *state secret* . . . and my husband has gone to report what happened to the palace.'

'Holy God!' said the next man over, and crossed himself. 'She means it was *treason*, Zoilos.'

Confusion gave way to fear. 'I . . . I didn't!' stammered Zoilos. 'Look, we was told it was a *machine*. There's this Syrian sorcerer, we was told, has a machine that somebody else wants, and we was to come here and take it. There wasn't supposed to be nobody around, or if there was, we was s'posed to take care of 'em. It was just . . . just hitting a house! We're no *traitors*; nobody told us about no *treason*!'

The other man, who seemed to be quick to understand, had a hand against his burned mouth, as though he wanted to be sick. 'You think they'll believe that?' he demanded. 'You think they'll believe that, in the Noumera?'

Father Agapios looked round disapprovingly – but both the other robbers were alarmed now, both getting up and coming over. 'What's this about the Noumera?' asked one.

'She says,' the more intelligent robber explained, 'that the . . . that hellish thing, the thing we came to steal – she says it's not a sorcerous machine, it's a secret weapon meant for the heretics, an' there was a plot to get it here tonight, so it could be stolen an' used against the city!'

There was a ripple of shock and dismay among the listeners.

'She says,' the man went on, 'that her husband is an imperial magistros, and he's gone to the palace to report it, right now.' Then he looked at Anna in bewilderment and added, 'I don't know why you're telling us this.'

210

She leaned back on her heels. 'You paid for what you tried to do tonight,' she pointed out. 'You've repented your sins. I thought you should at least have the *chance* to live a better life.' She glanced around the room, then added softly, 'There are only clergy and women in the house right now: the men are down at the bottom of the garden, guarding the machine. If you decided to leave suddenly . . . we couldn't prevent it.'

The spokesman stared at her a moment, then exclaimed fervently, 'God's blessing on you!' He glanced round at his companions, saw their agreement, and extended an arm to the nearest to be helped wincing to his feet.

'Wait, wait!' cried Father Agapios indignantly. 'Will you run away from Christ's mercy?'

'No, Father: from the Emperor's justice,' replied the spokesman.

The man who'd been in the middle of his confession, however, wanted to finish it, and he went back to the corner with the priest and gabbled out a rapid catalogue of his sins while his comrades tried to organize themselves to walk. They were weak and unsteady, and Zoilos obviously couldn't go far, but Anna thought they could manage to get themselves out of danger. The period they'd spent in the house recovering, and the treatment they'd received, meant they were stronger than in the shocked aftermath of the fire – and none of them had been burned on the feet.

The spokesman glanced at the twisted corpse in the corner, then went to Anna. 'You done us a good turn, Lady,' he said, 'an' the fellow there that hired us done us a bad one. I'll tell you what I know, for as much good as it c'n do you. We was hired by that fellow there a week ago, me, an' Zoilos, an' Daniel over there, who's not goin' anywhere on this earth, God have mercy on him. The others was hired separate, and we only met up with 'em this evening. The fellow that hired us said his name was Johannes, though whether it was or not, I don't know.' It was an obvious alias: undoubtedly the most common masculine name in the city. 'He was a gentleman,' the robber continued, 'or I'm a monk. We met him just off the Amastrianon, in a tavern called the Ivy, which is a place

211

where men on the lookout for work in our line often meet up. He told us that his patron had an interest in a machine made by a Syrian sorcerer, an' he said he needed some strong men to break in where it was kept an' carry it off. He gave us a half nomisma, an' promised us as much again when we had the machine, and he said he would send us a message when he wanted us to come and take it. He sent us a message this evenin' sayin' tonight was it, an' we all met up at the Ivy, at about the second hour of the night. He had a cart, my lady – his own, I think, 'cause it was a solid rig an' good horses. We turned it round once we got into that alley, on account of we thought it might have to leave in a hurry, and I guess the bastard drivin' it galloped off when he heard the screamin' start.'

'Did you go straight to the workshop?' Anna asked intently.

The robber began to nod, then winced at the effect of the movement on his burns. 'Straight there. Johannes wasn' altogether sure of the way, though: we missed the turn, first time past, an' had to come back for it. When we got to the bottom of that alley, though, by the wall, he said it was the right place, an' he looked around for the track goin' to your shed, an' found it without any trouble.'

So Johannes had never been to the workshop, but somebody had provided him with a detailed description of how to find it. The timing made it entirely likely that that 'somebody' had been Demetrios. 'Thank you,' said Anna grimly.

The robber bowed, clumsily and painfully. 'My name's Isidoros an' they call me the Weasel. If ever I c'n do you a service, leave a message for me at the Ivy . . . only,' he dropped his eyes, 'only don' go there yourself, 'cause it's no place for respectable women.'

'Thank you, Isidoros,' said Anna. 'I pray that God grants you healing and amendment of life.'

'Amen,' said Isidoros seriously. He took careful hold of Zoilos' good arm, and the two men made their way stiffly and unsteadily out of the workshop. Anna unbolted the front door for them; as she was doing so, the remaining two robbers hurried up from behind, and departed with them.

Agapios appeared as Anna was bolting the door again. 'Daughter,' he said seriously, 'I did not ask what this affair was about when your boy came to fetch me, since I could well understand why I was needed. But . . .' The priest stopped, looking bewildered and anxious, groping for words. 'But . . .'

'I will explain, Father,' Anna told him, and led him back to the kitchen.

Father Agapios was not nearly as quick as Isidoros the Weasel, but he eventually grasped the essentials: Kallinikos had invented a terrifying weapon for the defence of the city, and there had been a plot to steal it, which Kallinikos had foiled with the weapon itself. Agapios approved. To Anna's dismay he even approved of the weapon's existence. ('Thanks be to God, for his vengeance on the arrogance of the heretics!') To her relief, however, he also approved, warmly, the decision to let the surviving robbers go. ('They have learned the fear of death and hell: they must have time to turn away from their sins.') Satisfied, and well pleased with his own priestly work, Agapios blessed her and went home.

The troops from the palace didn't arrive until about an hour later: presumably it had taken Kallinikos some time to find an official who would listen to him in the middle of the night. The men who came were Scholarians, a dozen of them, with a cart. Kallinikos was not with them. The officer in charge had been sent by his own commander, and barely even knew who Kallinikos was, let alone why he hadn't come with them.

The officer had authorization to collect the siphon and return it to the Arsenal; he also had a letter ordering the arrest of the robbers and their transport to the Noumera Prison. He was annoyed to hear that some of the robbers had escaped, but he accepted Anna's explanation that the women in the house had been unable to stop them, and that the men had been posted to stand guard over the siphon. He and his men collected the siphon and packed it carefully on to the cart, then tossed the dead and dying robbers roughly on to the cart-tail behind it. One of the bodies woke up enough to whimper in agony; the others were beyond feeling anything, and made no sound. Anna prayed that the whimperer would soon be like them.

213

Twelve

It was the middle of the morning before Kallinikos returned to the house. Anna, who had fallen asleep at dawn, woke to find her husband sitting on the bed beside her, gazing lovingly down at her face.

She sat up slowly. She was still short of sleep, felt bloated with grief and anger, and her arm hurt. When she was upright she discovered that she also felt sick. She brushed her husband aside, sat groggily still for a moment, then hooked the chamberpot out from under the bed and vomited into it.

Kallinikos was immediately all anxious concern. He told her to lie down, and fetched Helena and Chloe to fuss over her. 'Last night was too much for you,' he said miserably. 'It would be too much for any woman. Those *devils* hit you, and then *I* burned you, and then I abandoned you with those *dogs* still in the house . . .'

'I'm all *right*!' she said irritably.

'No, but I shouldn't have done it! I should've sent Sergios to the palace; I should've stayed and protected you!'

'We were *fine*!' she snapped. 'And you know that nobody at the palace would've listened to Sergios.' She looked him in the eye and added, 'They weren't devils, either. They were just stupid young thugs from the Amastrianon. I *let* them go. I didn't want them to end up in the Noumera.'

There was a startled silence. 'Oh,' said Kallinikos. 'I was told that they'd overpowered the women of the household and escaped.'

'I couldn't very well tell the Scholarians what I just told you, could I?' Anna wiped her face with the cold cloth Helena had brought and lay back in the bed.

'No,' he agreed. After a moment he added ruefully, 'I

214

should have realized. I know you – and I knew they were in no condition to overpower anybody.'

She inspected her worried and unhappy husband. He was still wearing the official cloak he'd put on the night before, but it was very smudged and dirty. When he'd appeared in it the previous night she hadn't noticed that he'd simply draped it on over the dirty tunic he'd been wearing for work at the Arsenal, but by daylight the mismatch was glaring. Apart from an air of exhaustion, however, he seemed unharmed by the night's events. She remembered her nightmare vision of him burning alive, and impulsively reached out and caught his hand.

'When I heard you working the pump last night,' she told him, 'I thought you were pumping the fire out all over the floor. I thought . . . I thought you were going to destroy the siphon, and yourself along with it.'

He sucked his upper lip down and bit it. 'No. I was getting the pressure up in the tank.'

'The fire came out like a fountain,' she whispered. 'Like a torrent of lightning. It was the most frightening thing I've ever seen in my life.'

He sighed. 'We discovered we could do that,' he said matter-of-factly. 'We worked at it.' He rubbed his face. 'Sissinios wanted a way to make the application of the fire more accurate. The stuff is expensive to produce, and pumping it out on to a large area of sea . . . well, it would cost a lot, and we'd use up our supplies very quickly, and it might drift and set fire to our own ships or to buildings on the shore. If you get the pressure up in the tank, get a nozzle on the hose so that it produces a fine spray, and set the fire alight just as it comes out . . . well, you saw.'

'Dear God!'

He squeezed her hand. 'I'm sorry,' he said vaguely. 'I know . . . I know you have a gentle heart, and you hate it. When I saw what it had done . . . I hated it, too. But . . . well. When we knew they were coming, I sat there in the workshop putting the siphon back together, and I was thinking, "Just let them try to take it, just let them try!" And then when they threatened you, I *wanted* them to come in, because I

215

knew what I could do to them. And then . . .' He drew a deep breath. His eyes were abstracted, filled with a terrible elation. 'Then when they came in, and I lit the jet . . . I felt as though I had the mastery of the world. I wielded fire! The first of the elements, the one everything else is made from. When I held it in my hand, and I pointed at my enemies and saw them burn . . . it was glorious!'

He stopped. The gladness ebbed from his face, and he met Anna's eyes again, sober and guilty. 'When I heard those men crying afterwards, though, when I saw the burns I'd given them . . . when I saw that I'd burned *you* . . . then I felt ashamed. Maybe men shouldn't seize power over the divine elements. Maybe it's impious. We are born to a world where all things corrupt and change, and what we create will always be riddled with death.'

Anna did not know what to say to that. She remembered Agapios' enthusiasm for the fire as an instrument of God's vengeance. It did not in any way satisfy her: if God controlled the outcome of wars and approved of Constantinople, why had the Arabs succeeded so well that they were sitting in Cyzicus waiting for a favourable wind? No: she agreed with Kallinikos. Wars were human things, mortal things, product and result of a world of corruption and death. The Christian power was hypocritical and cruel, and the Muslims were tainted, even in their own eyes, by internecine war. The only justification that could be claimed for a weapon like the fire was that the city was desperate and had no other way to defend itself against an attacker bent on its destruction. Kallinikos knew that, and she knew it, so there seemed little point in reminding him of it; in fact, to do so seemed cheap, an arrogant dismissal of the horrors the fire would certainly inflict.

'I use an ambix, too,' she said at last. 'I used the very same ambix you used to invent the fire. I'm seizing power over the elements, too, and *I* don't create things that are full of death. If you were in your workshop trying to turn base metals into gold, you wouldn't, either. I don't think there's anything impious in wanting to understand and use the workings of nature.'

He drew in a deep, unsteady breath, then squeezed her hand again and brushed a lock of hair away from her face. Then he kissed her. 'Thank you,' he told her seriously.

After a moment, he let go of her hand, studied her carefully, and asked, 'Are you really all right?'

'Yes,' she replied at once. 'I'm just tired, and a bit overwhelmed by last night. I'll be fine with a bit of rest.' She thought to wonder if the sickness had anything to do with the suspected pregnancy. The possibility that it might, made her smile. She wouldn't mention it to her husband now, though. It would only upset him more. After a moment, she said, 'You look like you could use a rest, too.'

'I have an audience this afternoon,' he told her. 'I want to consult Basiliskos beforehand. I only came back here to wash and change.'

'Oh.' She thought of Basiliskos, then of Theodosia. Theodosia would undoubtedly have heard something about what had happened. The Scholarians who'd come to collect the siphon would have talked to their friends in the barracks, who would have talked to the palace servants, who would have brought the news to Theodosia's household, probably in a sensational and exaggerated form. She'd be worried.

'I'll come with you,' Anna declared. 'I ought to see Theodosia.'

Kallinikos was doubtful, but yielded to Anna's insistence. She got up and dressed in her court clothes and a good cloak. She also sent Helena to the kitchen to sponge the worst of the dirt off Kallinikos' cloak while he changed into a clean tunic.

They set off for the palace in a hired carriage: their own horses were, apparently, safely stabled and in need of rest. 'I had to leave them tethered by the Scholarians' barracks half the night,' Kallinikos told her disgustedly. 'The grooms at the stables were asleep, and nobody wanted to pay any attention to me. I had to argue with the officer of the watch for ages before he'd even contact his superior, and then *he* wanted to consult Stephanos!'

'Consult *Stephanos*?'

'The Magistros of the Arsenal is responsible for dealing

with theft from the Arsenal,' Kallinikos proclaimed bitterly. 'Eventually I managed to make the fellow understand that I was accusing Stephanos of complicity in the theft, but he still didn't think it was important. *He* thought it was a matter of an official with his hand in the till, and another official trying for a promotion, that was clear. He wouldn't refer me to anybody with real authority. He said it could wait until morning.'

'He sent troops, though.'

Kallinikos nodded, scowling. 'Eventually.'

'I was surprised that you weren't with them.'

'I had to arrange for safe storage for the siphon. I didn't get any additional authority from the palace, so I knew it wasn't going to be easy to get the guards at the Arsenal to take charge of the siphon. I went straight over from the palace, and I was just beginning to make some headway when the Scholarians arrived. It still took another half an hour to settle it, though, and then I had to arrange protection for the rest of our gear. Then I went back to the palace and asked for an audience, and I was told I could have one this afternoon.'

Anna was silent. The hired carriage, drawn by a pair of mangy greys, jolted into the Milion: the horses, unused to the route, did not slow down. Anna noted that her perfume shop was open and that there were customers in it.

'Did you see Demetrios?' she asked at last.

Kallinikos looked at her quickly, then looked away, and she saw that he had exactly the suspicion she did.

'One of the robbers spoke to me before he left,' she said in a low voice. She relayed what Isidoros the Weasel had said.

'Demetrios is a *friend*,' said Kallinikos, in a strained voice. 'We've been working hard together all year, and we get on well. He's a very good foreman. The men respect him. I don't believe he was part of it.'

Anna said nothing.

'Even if he did know something was going to happen,' Kallinikos continued defensively, 'he was trying to get me out of the way, to protect me.'

'If the siphon had been taken last night,' Anna pointed out, 'it would have been taken out of *your* hands, after *you* removed it from the Arsenal against the rules. You *would*

218

have lost your job, and Demetrios almost certainly would have been appointed in your place.'

Kallinikos grimaced. 'He deserves promotion,' he said quietly. 'He deserves it, and he wants it. He used to believe I could get it for him, but he's seen that I'm no use as a patron and advocate. I can't even defend my own position, let alone secure anything for him.' He met Anna's eyes. 'I can't send him to the Noumera! It's only a *suspicion*, for Christ's sake!'

'I don't want to send him to the Noumera either,' Anna replied, 'but I don't want him to stay where he is. If he's betrayed you once, and if he guesses that you suspect it – that's dangerous. *Did* you put him in charge of the siphon when you returned it to the Arsenal last night?'

'No,' admitted Kallinikos miserably. 'I got it into a store-room, and I locked the door and sealed it with my own seal.'

'Good.' After a moment Anna went on, 'Couldn't you give him a recommendation for a position somewhere else?'

Her husband chewed on his lip. The carriage rattled up to the Bronze Gate, and he reined the horses to a halt. 'I'll see if I can think of one,' he said, in a whisper, then turned an insincere smile on the guards.

They managed to leave the hired carriage in the stables of the Boukoleon, and made their way to the north wing of the palace. Anna was feeling a little wobbly still, but her stomach had settled again.

Theodosia greeted her mother with a relieved shriek and ran across the room to hug her. 'I've been so *worried*!' she exclaimed, gazing into Anna's face. 'I heard this morning that you were attacked by robbers, and there was a fire, and the robbers tied you up . . .'

'No, no, no!' protested Anna, kissing her on the cheek. 'There were robbers, darling, but they never tied us up. As for the fire – the liquid fire was what they were after, but Kallinikos used it to fight them off.'

Theodosia looked at Kallinikos sharply, then went and hugged him, too. 'You'll have to tell me about it,' she ordered. 'Basiliskos, too, of course. He's out, right now, trying to answer the question you set him, about whether Stephanos has a new patron.'

'I'm beginning to think Stephanos doesn't,' said Anna, earning a sharp look of her own.

Kallinikos cleared his throat. 'I have an audience this afternoon . . .' he began.

'Oh, dear!' exclaimed Theodosia in alarm.

Kallinikos gave her an anxious look. 'Why, "oh dear"?'

'Your *cloak*,' replied Theodosia, rolling her eyes. 'It's *filthy*. And your *hair*! You can't *possibly* go to an audience looking like *that*!'

'Isn't what I have to say more important than my haircut?'

'Nobody will *listen* to what you say while you have that haircut! Dora!' Theodosia summoned one of her attendants with a snap of the fingers. 'Dora, my stepfather has an audience this afternoon. Can you give him a haircut, please? And send Lalis to find Basiliskos. I think we're going to need him.'

Kallinikos was firmly sat down and barbered, and his cloak was taken off for another, and more thorough, sponging. Lalis, however, did not succeed in locating Basiliskos. Anna was slightly concerned that the eunuch might have run into trouble in his inquiries, but she told herself that he was an experienced courtier and knew how to go about his business discreetly.

Theodosia's household brought them a light meal, and Kallinikos – rather reluctantly – recounted the previous night's events, without mentioning his suspicion of Demetrios. Theodosia was both appalled and delighted. 'I never thought Stephanos would actually *betray the city*!' she exclaimed appreciatively; and then, eagerly, 'And you think the princes are behind it?'

'I don't think we can prove anything,' said Anna warningly. 'Not unless Stephanos testifies against them.'

'They can *make* him tell the truth,' Theodosia declared savagely. 'They ought to!'

Anna stared at her daughter a moment in shock. She had brought her up to be considerate and kind. 'Do you know what you're *saying*?' she asked in dismay. 'Do you know what they *do* to people, to "make them tell the truth"?'

Theodosia looked mulish. 'Stephanos deserves it!'

Kallinikos shook his head. 'They won't torture Stephanos. He's an imperial magistros and a cousin of the Drungarios, even if Sissinios has dropped him. Men of that rank aren't tortured unless there's a real suspicion that they were plotting against the Emperor, and this is only the attempted theft of a siphon. There isn't even any real evidence to link him to it: he'll point out that *he* intended to keep the siphon at the Arsenal, and *I* was the one who took it out. I'm going to be in almost as much trouble over this as he is.' He sucked his lip down again. 'Stephanos will claim that *anyone* at the Arsenal could have seen the siphon being carted off and found out where it was going. There's nothing to connect him or the princes to the attack last night. The robbers are dead or escaped, and the man who hired them is burnt beyond recognition.' He scratched unhappily at his beard. 'I wish Basiliskos were here. I wanted to ask him what I should *say* to the Emperor about it – whether I should come out with everything I suspect, or whether I should just say what happened and leave it at that.'

'When is your audience?' asked Theodosia, trying to be helpful.

'The eighth hour,' Kallinikos replied glumly.

'But it must be almost that *now*!' exclaimed Theodosia, jumping up in alarm.

Kallinikos nodded. 'I ought to get over to the Octagon. Thank you for the lunch. Umm. Where's my cloak?'

Theodosia waved a hand to her slaves to fetch it. 'I'll come with you,' she said, her face hard. 'It's not right, if you're going to be in trouble because *Stephanos* is committing treason. I'll *tell* my cousin that.'

Kallinikos' cloak was damp, and the wind was cold: he was shivering by the time they reached the Octagon. They were in fact still slightly early for the audience – the seventh hour hadn't ended – and the guards stopped them in a cold antechamber. Theodosia at once ordered them to find her somewhere warmer to wait. The Scholarians scrambled to

221

obey: the Emperor's cousin could not be required to wait in a public hall, not least because it would be immodest to leave her exposed to the gaze of anyone who passed by. Their party was, accordingly, escorted to the office of one of the eunuchs of the household – and then, almost immediately escorted back again, and admitted to the audience chamber of the Octagon.

Stephanos must have arrived while they were trooping back and forth to the office, because when they entered the hall he was there, standing before the imperial throne, his white cloak with its narrow purple stripe immaculate and gleaming. Just behind him, looking hunched, anxious, and out of place in his best woollens, was Demetrios.

Anna hadn't known what to expect of this audience; she hadn't been sure whether anyone would be there other than Kallinikos and the Emperor. She had been worried that she and Theodosia would be immediately dismissed. At the sight of Demetrios, however, her heart gave a double hammer of rage and dismay. The foreman had no right to be there, and certainly had no right to be there *with Stephanos*. This audience was potentially much more dangerous than they'd expected.

Theodosia swished confidently to the front of their own party, stalked across the hall to the space before the throne, and made her formal prostration to Christ's viceroy on earth. She rose to her feet again while Anna and Kallinikos were still down.

'Forgive me,' she said, smiling hopefully at her cousin. 'My mother and stepfather came to visit me before my stepfather's audience with Your Majesty. I was very worried by what they told me, and I would like it very much if you allowed me to join them, Master. Please?'

Constantine looked less than pleased, but he sighed and gestured to his right. 'You and your mother may stand there,' he said. 'But this is serious business, little cousin. You must keep that lively tongue of yours still.'

'*Thank you*, Master!' exclaimed Theodosia. She took Anna's arm and hurried her over to the side, leaving Kallinikos to stand before the throne next to Stephanos and Demetrios.

222

Constantine leaned back and rested his hands on his knees, surveying the men in front of him. Anna, scanning the room in the momentary silence, took note that none of the higher court officials was present. There were half a dozen eunuchs of the Emperor's inner household – bodyguards and attendants – and another half-dozen of the domestic guard. A notary stood against the wall by the apse, with a notebook to take down the proceedings: that was all.

'Kallinikos of Heliopolis,' said the Emperor formally. 'You requested this audience.'

Kallinikos bowed deeply. 'Yes, Master. Your Majesty entrusted me with the charge of the liquid fire I invented for the defence of the city, which you have ordered classed as a secret of the state. Last night, as Your Majesty is probably aware, an attempt was made to steal a tank of the fire and one of the siphons for applying it.' Kallinikos paused, then drew a deep breath, straightened his shoulders, and said determinedly, 'The circumstances make me suspect that my colleague, Lord Stephanos Skyles, was involved in that attempt. I therefore petition Your Majesty to dismiss him from his office.'

Constantine raised his eyebrows. 'At least you come to the point,' he observed.

Stephanos bowed. 'Your Majesty . . .' he began.

Constantine silenced him with a wave of the hand. 'I did indeed hear of this treasonous attempt,' he told Kallinikos. 'It was reported to me, however, that you had used your authority as a magistros to remove the fire from the safety of the Arsenal to your own unprotected house in the city.' He paused, then went on, more graciously, 'It was also reported to me that you overcame the robbers by means of the fire, and at once took steps to return it to safety – which I take as clear evidence that you were not engaged in treason. Nonetheless, it was surely an error of judgement to remove such a valuable weapon from a place where it was secure, to a place where any spy could try to seize it.'

'Your Majesty,' said Kallinikos, 'I had a damaged siphon on my hands which Stephanos Skyles refused to admit into the Arsenal stores. He demanded instead that I leave it

223

either in naval stores – which I considered a grave danger to the materials kept there, Your Majesty! – or else lying on the dockside, where I believed it was at risk of further damage. I—'

'He's lying!' interrupted Stephanos. 'I never refused to admit the siphon to the Arsenal; indeed, I urged him to put it there. He insisted on taking it home to repair in his own workshop.'

There was a moment of silence. Kallinikos stared at Stephanos, his face reddening.

'I have brought along the foreman of the work gang to confirm what I say,' continued Stephanos, with a confident wave towards Demetrios.

Demetrios looked at the floor. 'Lord Stephanos speaks the truth, Your Majesty,' he declared.

'You *whore!*' choked Kallinikos, glaring at his foreman in outraged anguish. He whirled back to the Emperor, who was watching the scene with narrowed eyes. 'Your Majesty, *they* are lying! Stephanos is lying to protect himself, and he's prevailed somehow on my foreman to join him, but it's a *lie.*'

'Do you have any witnesses?' asked Constantine.

'The whole work gang heard! Holy Mother of God, we were standing there on the quayside shouting at one another for half an hour! Stephanos refused, totally *refused*, to let me take the siphon back into the Arsenal. What's more—'

'*I* can produce witnesses,' said Stephanos coolly. 'They will confirm what I say.'

'False witnesses!' cried Kallinikos furiously. 'Witnesses you've bribed and threatened into saying what you tell them to!'

Anna stepped out from the side and prostrated herself. Constantine, looking annoyed, impatiently gestured for her to rise.

'Your Majesty,' she said earnestly. 'Yesterday afternoon Demetrios here helped my husband take the siphon back to our house. While they were unloading it, he himself told me that Stephanos had forbidden my husband to repair the siphon in the Arsenal, and that he'd urged him to put it in naval stores or leave it on the dockside. I and several members of

224

my household heard this. I know that we are not impartial witnesses – but neither are slaves from the Arsenal, who are under Stephanos' authority.'

'A point,' conceded Constantine, 'but not, I fear, evidence to prove your husband's assertion one way or the other.'

'The reason that siphon was damaged,' said Kallinikos, in a thick voice, 'was that *somebody* dropped a nail into the workings.'

'Your men were careless,' Stephanos replied, with vicious satisfaction. 'That hardly implicates *me*.'

Kallinikos glared. 'That pump was working fine before lunch! And *you* ordered us off the ship during lunch.' He turned back to the Emperor. 'He'd insisted, Your Majesty, that he could give us orders while we were working on the ships, in defiance of your own judgement that *I* was in charge of the work. I accepted his interference because the work is so urgent and I didn't want to cause any more delay, but he abused that!'

'A nail in the pump workings!' scoffed Stephanos. 'Is that *really* likely to have come from my hand, rather than from one of your . . . *fellow workers*?' He spat out the last with all the disdain of an aristocrat for men who get their hands dirty. He, too, turned back to the Emperor. 'As to my giving orders to his men – am I to be blamed because I instructed them to eat their lunches on the dockside, rather than on deck? Does this arrogant fellow really think that is so important a violation of his sovereign authority that it deserves *your* august attention? Listen to him! He boasts of the *sacrifice* he made in allowing such an outrageous order, rather than appealing to you to overrule it!' He gestured disdainfully. 'Surely he's condemned by his own pettiness! Master, Kallinikos disregarded my advice and removed the siphon from the Arsenal. Some spy saw him do it and attempted to steal the precious thing. *He* is the one who put this secret at risk, and it is only through God's good favour to Your Majesty that it didn't fall into the hands of the enemy. He knows this himself: it's why he's come up with these slanders against *me*. If anyone ought to be dismissed, it's this ambitious and vainglorious Syrian!'

'Your Majesty!' cried Anna, seeing the Emperor hesitate. 'Your Majesty, the attempt to steal the fire was *not* a matter of a watching spy making the most of an opportunity! Your Majesty, some of the robbers survived the attack on us last night, and we brought them into the house while my husband went to fetch men to arrest them. I heard them talking about what had happened. They said that they were hired *a week* ago, by a man whom they knew as Johannes. They believed him to be a gentleman – and, in fact, last night, I thought the man who led them was a gentleman, because he dressed and spoke like one. The robbers were told that what they were stealing was a magical machine made by a Syrian sorcerer, and they were given a half nomisma and told to assemble for the robbery when they received a message, which they did last night. Your Majesty, this attack was *planned* at least a week ago. Someone *arranged* for the siphon to leave the Arsenal!'

'Your Majesty!' objected Stephanos. 'This woman knows very well that the robbers have fled, apart from those who were dying, and that no one can question them to see if this story she's telling is true.' He gave Anna a glare of bitter spite. 'And you know, Master, that this is a clever, quick-witted woman, *well* able to invent a convincing lie when she needs one.'

'My mother is *not* a liar!' exclaimed Theodosia indignantly. She turned to Constantine. 'Master, will you let him insult her like that?'

'I meant no insult!' protested Stephanos hastily, before the Emperor could respond. 'For a wife to hurry to the support of her husband must, indeed, count as a virtue.' He bowed to Theodosia.

Constantine was scowling. 'I am greatly tempted to dismiss *both* of you!' he snapped. 'The only thing that's clear about this affair is that we nearly lost the weapon I rely upon as the pillar of the city's defence – that, and that two magistroi cannot live together peacefully in one Arsenal. This continual wrangling has delayed and bedevilled the development of the weapon from the beginning, and now it appears to have jeopardized its security completely. Perhaps I—'

He broke off: his chamberlain Andreas had just entered the room in a hurry. 'What is it?' he demanded, his voice sharp with alarm.

Andreas made his way to the throne and prostrated himself. 'Master,' he fluted, standing up again, 'I apologize for my intrusion, but some information has just come to light which has a bearing on the very matter you have under your consideration.'

Theodosia clapped her hands. 'God protects the innocent!'

Andreas gave her a withering look, then turned expectant eyes on the Emperor.

'What is this information?' Constantine asked suspiciously.

'I will have the bearers admitted, if Your Majesty pleases.'

'Very well!' The Emperor flicked a hand.

Andreas prostrated himself again and hurried back through the audience chamber. The others watched him uneasily. Anna noticed that Demetrios looked white and sick. He caught her eyes on him, and looked away quickly.

She ached, suddenly, to take him aside and whisper, *Look, we know what you did, but we weren't going to tell anyone. You don't have to turn to Stephanos for protection. We always liked you, and we don't want to send you to the Noumera!*

It could not be done. It could not be done, before the Emperor's eyes, and probably Demetrios wouldn't believe her anyway. She stared at the foreman's bowed head and asked herself if she'd really tell all she knew, and send him to the torturers, if the Emperor decided to dismiss her husband.

Andreas exited the audience chamber, then re-entered it, bringing two others with him. One of them Anna recognized immediately, with relief and surprise, as Basiliskos. The other was an officer of the Scholarians who also looked familiar – Leontios was the name, she recalled at last. The young guardsman who'd accompanied her on her first venture to the Octagon.

Basiliskos caught her eye as he marched into the chamber behind Andreas – her eyes, and Theodosia's. He smiled quickly in reassurance. Then his face became a mask of

227

serene reverence. He stopped the requisite three paces from the Emperor and made the prostration with all the grace of a man who'd been brought up to it. Behind him, the Scholarian Leontios dropped on to his face far more clumsily, partly impeded by the long thin bundle he was carrying in his arms.

Basiliskos got to his feet and waited, his eyes downcast.

'You're my cousin's chamberlain, aren't you?' asked Constantine.

'I am indeed honoured that Your Sacred Majesty remembers me!' agreed Basiliskos delightedly. 'Master, I am mortified that I should interrupt you and the stepfather of my beloved mistress in the middle of your exalted business, but—'

'Get to the point!' snapped the Emperor. 'Andreas said this was relevant to the case!'

Basiliskos bowed deeply. 'And he spoke truly, Master. Most Exalted and Praiseworthy of all Lords, some days ago Lady Anna, the mother of my beloved mistress, came to our household asking advice. She said that her husband, the most sagacious Magistros Kallinikos, had been vexed by a new harrassment from his wicked colleague Stephanos Skyles. Although you, in your divine wisdom, had allotted the task of installing siphons for liquid fire to Kallinikos, Stephanos insolently refused to acknowledge your sublime authority, and insisted upon a spurious right to order the work teams whenever they were on a ship. Lady Anna was troubled by this, and feared that his boldness in defying your sacred decree meant that Stephanos had obtained a new patron to support him in his wicked persecution of the Most Distinguished Kallinikos . . .'

'I *know* this!' snarled Constantine. 'Come to the point!'

Basiliskos looked hurt. Anna made a mental note to tell him how much she admired 'insolently refused to acknowledge your sublime authority'.

'Lady Anna asked me to investigate and see whether Stephanos had a new patron,' the eunuch said, reluctantly coming to the point. 'I couldn't find even a rumour of one. However, I did discover that he was meeting with your brothers. If your loyal spies have not yet reported this to you, you can easily ask to them to confirm it.'

Constantine's scowl vanished, and his changeable eyes became still. 'Go on,' he said, in a soft chill voice.

Dear God! thought Anna. She hadn't realized how much the Emperor feared and distrusted his brothers. The fact that they were involved obviously put the whole business into a different, and far more critical, category.

Basiliskos bowed. 'My immediate suspicion was that he was acting as a go-between for a powerful new patron – though I was puzzled, for now that his incorrigible viciousness has become apparent and his own cousin has turned away from him, I could not see why any powerful patron would adopt him. I decided to investigate another possibility, one suggested by the wise Lady Anna: that perhaps the princes were negotiating with Lord Stephanos because they wished to buy something from him. What, I asked myself, might they want to buy from such a man?'

'Your Majesty!' interrupted Stephanos, now sweating with anxiety. 'It is, surely, no crime to entertain your brothers to supper?'

'What *did* they want with you?' asked Constantine softly.

'A piece of land!' exclaimed Stephanos. 'A piece of land, Your Majesty, which they wish to purchase for a charitable foundation – for a *monastery*, Master, which they are hoping to found for the glory of God and the benefit of their souls.'

The Emperor's eyes narrowed. 'We shall see,' he remarked. 'Have you more information, Basiliskos?'

Basiliskos bowed again. 'If I had had no more than that, Lord of the World, I would have been ashamed to interrupt you. When I went to pursue my inquiries this morning, however, I learned of what transpired last night. Amid my anguish at the thought of the threat to the parents of my dear mistress, and my relief that they had surmounted it in safety, a question occurred to me: was this connected to the puzzling behaviour of Stephanos? What, I asked myself again, might the princes hope to buy from a man known to be disaffected, a man who has lost status, patronage, and perhaps money because of Your Majesty's appointment of Kallinikos – a man who has access to a weapon you have declared to be a secret, and hope to use to shield the city against the onslaught of the heretics?'

'Your Majesty!' protested Stephanos desperately. 'The eunuch *slanders* me!'

'Does he?' asked Constantine. 'It seems to me a fair description. Go on, Basiliskos.'

Basiliskos once more bowed deeply. 'It seemed to me that what I needed to do was question the prisoners taken during the attack on Magistros Kallinikos, to learn who might have recruited them. Accordingly, I hurried to the Noumera Prison, hoping that I might learn something – but I discovered, alas, that the prisoners were dead, all but one, who was expiring even as I arrived. I therefore asked to speak to the guardsmen who were charged with disposing of the criminals' bodies. I hoped – though without real expectation – that one of those bodies might have some clue as to who the dead men had been, and to whom they owed allegiance. This loyal guardsman, Leontios, was in charge of the burial detail. He can vouch for the fact that what we have brought you was indeed found on the body of one of the dead robbers who assaulted the house of Magistros Kallinikos last night.'

'Enough eloquence!' exclaimed the Emperor. 'Let's see it!'

Basiliskos bowed again and gestured Leontios forward. The young man swallowed nervously and stepped forward, the bundle in his hands. He bowed clumsily and extended it to the Emperor.

Constantine snatched it impatiently and unwrapped it. It was a sword, a gold-hilted sword in a sheath of burned and blackened leather. Anna remembered that she had seen it before, at the side of a disfigured corpse.

The Emperor drew the sword, struggling a little to get it free of the warped leather of the sheath. Flakes of charcoal fell over his purple cloak, and the scent of burning was released, together with the piercing sulphur stink of the fire. The blade came free at last, and he swung it through the still air of the audience chamber, a hiss and a shimmer of polished metal. He set the point down on the floor between his feet and clasped his hands together on the hilt.

'Whose?' he asked Basiliskos, his voice hard.

Basiliskos bowed. 'When I sent to the house of Count Johannes Eukrates, his people reported that he went out last night, and had not returned. They were greatly alarmed for him.'

'Have you shown them the body?'

Basiliskos made a deprecating gesture. 'There was not time . . . and, Master, I fear that even his wife would not recognize it.'

Constantine let out his breath slowly through his teeth. He stared at the sword in his hands. Then he looked up, directly at Stephanos.

'A piece of land?' he asked softly. 'A piece of land – or a siphon, which they could exchange for a throne?'

'Your Majesty,' panted Stephanos, 'I swear . . .'

'No,' said Constantine gently. 'Don't swear. Let your yes be yes, and your no be no. The quarrelling between yourself and Magistros Kallinikos has been incessant, and I have blamed you both for it. I think now that perhaps that was a mistake. When you said that you urged Kallinikos to store this damaged siphon in the Arsenal – that was a lie, wasn't it?'

Stephanos stammered and said nothing. The Emperor turned his dark hazel eyes to Demetrios. 'You supported the Magistros of the Arsenal,' he said gently. 'Do you still?'

Demetrios dropped to his face on the floor. 'Mercy!' he pleaded.

'Take him to the Noumera,' Constantine ordered. 'Have him questioned. Arrest Stephanos Skyles, on suspicion of treason, pending the result of inquiries. The rest of you are dismissed.'

Thirteen

T he gold-hilted sword, Basiliskos explained later, was the sort presented to high-ranking military officers on their appointment: he had seen many such items distributed, and had recognized it instantly. So, of course, had the Emperor, who had presented the weapons. Most of the men who had received them were on the frontiers, trying to defend the empire's flanks from one or another division of the enemy armies. A dozen or so were in Constantinople, and Basiliskos knew the names of all of them from his years in the Office of the Vestiarion. Johannes Eukrates had been dismissed from his command five years before, though he had been allowed to retain his rank. He had been an officer in one of the units involved in the Opsikion mutiny on behalf of the princes; there had been no evidence that he had personally supported the mutiny, but he hadn't tried to stop it, either, and had paid the price. He had been the first and most obvious candidate for the sword's owner, and it had been an easy matter for Basiliskos to determine that he was missing.

'It was perfectly straightforward,' Basiliskos told them with satisfaction. 'The answer was obvious, once I asked the right question.'

'You're wonderful,' Theodosia told him warmly. 'I don't know what we would have done without you. My cousin was getting ready to dismiss Stephanos *and* Kallinikos. I would have burst into tears and begged, of course, but I don't know whether it would have worked.'

Basiliskos beamed at her. 'I am glad to have been of service, Mistress! I did hope that I was doing the right thing when I interrupted. I *thought* that Magistros Kallinikos ought to have a strong case, but then I thought, well—' he hesitated delicately – 'he doesn't always *present* his case very well, if he'll excuse my speaking so bluntly.'

'I know I don't,' Kallinikos said heavily. 'I'm in your debt.'

Basiliskos coughed. 'Um, you're in the Most Illustrious Andreas' debt, My Lord. I promised him ten nomismata on your behalf, if he would interrupt the audience.'

'*Ten nomismata!*' exclaimed Kallinikos in horror. 'People *live* on less than that! Ten nomismata for one interruption?'

Basiliskos looked apologetic. 'He *is* the chamberlain, My Lord.'

'Money well spent,' said Anna, taking her husband's hand. 'Thank you, Basiliskos. We're *all* in your debt.'

The eunuch looked shy, and pleased with himself, and very contented.

The household of Johannes Eukrates eventually confirmed that the sword was his, identified the body from the ring and the boots, and claimed it for Christian burial. They denied all knowledge of what Johannes had been doing in the company of robbers who were attacking a workshop in Philadelphion. The family estates were, nevertheless, confiscated as the penalty for his treason. He had, Anna learned, a wife and three children who lost their livelihood in that; she hoped that the woman had family to go to, because otherwise they would starve.

Demetrios confessed under torture that Stephanos had promised to put him in charge of incendiaries in exchange for help in stealing the siphon; he denied, however, that he had been involved in treason, and claimed that the plan had been intended solely to discredit Kallinikos. Stephanos, confronted with his testimony, eventually claimed the same. The two princes indignantly protested their innocence, and denied any connection between themselves and Johannes Eukrates. They might have met him socially, they conceded, but they had no idea why he'd been trying to steal a siphon. If there was a plot, they insisted, it was a plot to discredit *them*, and it originated with Theodosia and her household.

The Emperor obviously believed it no more than he'd believed their protestations after the mutiny of the Opsikion.

233

He had them confined to their palace and allowed them out only under guard. He did not, however, formally charge them with treason, probably because he didn't want to become as unpopular as his father had been after the murder of Theodosius. He officially accepted the version of events that the attempt to steal the siphon had been Stephanos' plot to discredit Kallinikos, and that the participation of a high-ranking supporter of the princes was a coincidence. He stripped Stephanos of his rank and sentenced him to exile – though, since no ships were likely to set sail from Constantinople for some time, the sentence was suspended. Demetrios, however, who had no powerful connections to protect him, was executed.

As soon as he was officially notified of the foreman's death, Kallinikos led his workers to the Noumera, collected the body, and paid for a funeral for it. He sat through the service in the Church of the Theotokos with a stony face, but refused to discuss the death even with Anna.

The following day, Kallinikos was summoned to the Octagon, where the Emperor offered him the post of Magistros of the Arsenal. He turned it down.

'I told him I don't *want* it,' Kallinikos informed Anna afterwards, in some distress. 'He just didn't understand. He said, "Isn't this what you've been trying to get all along?" and when I said no, I never wanted it, he looked at me like he was trying to work out why I was lying. I thought he *realized* now that all the quarrelling was because Stephanos was trying to get rid of me!'

'Basiliskos said that the Emperor believes everybody is ambitious,' Anna told him. 'I suppose he finds it hard to accept that you aren't. I hope you gave him a good excuse.' She was nervous about the refusal, afraid that the Emperor might have been offended.

'I told him that I don't know much about swords and spears and catapults, let alone invoicing and stock-keeping, that I feared that I would serve him badly. I said that at a time of war the Arsenal really needs an able and experienced person in charge, not a complete novice. I said he had honoured me enough by making me Magistros of Fire, and that I was well content with that. I said I hoped to have more time for my own work.'

'Oh,' said Anna, unhappily. 'Did you tell him you meant alchemy?'

'Yes. When he asked.'

'Oh.'

'Actually, it seemed to make sense to him. He looked very knowing. I suppose he couldn't understand my turning down a promotion for ordinary reasons, but believed I might do so if I thought I could make the elixir and turn lead into gold.' Kallinikos shrugged. 'Which I can't, at the moment, though I suppose I might be able to one day.'

Anna frowned. 'I don't want you to get a reputation as a sorcerer!'

'I'm *not*. Alchemy is a research into the *natural* processes of—'

'My love, *I know* you're not. But a lot of people think of alchemy as akin to sorcery. Those robbers were told you were a Syrian *sorcerer*. I don't like it.'

Kallinikos sighed heavily. 'I don't either,' he admitted. 'But I can't help it. Some people at the Arsenal think the liquid fire is sorcerous as well, and if I didn't have that achievement to point to, I'd've been sent to Cherson long ago.' He brightened slightly and said, 'If there's any trouble over the alchemy, I'll get Basiliskos on it.'

There was no immediate need to call on Basiliskos, however. The Emperor apparently accepted Kallinikos' refusal calmly, and appointed an experienced courtier from the office of the Stratiotikon as the new Magistros of the Arsenal. By this stage all the working siphons had been installed on their destined ships, despite the absence of a foreman. Kallinikos and his team set to work brewing up more of the fire.

Early in April the weather improved, the cold winds and rain giving way to balmy sunshine and calm seas. It was the weather that all the city had dreaded for months, and, sure enough, the omen was fulfilled: the Arab fleet sailed from Cyzicus.

The rumour of the sailing arrived in the city a few hours before the fleet itself. Crowds from every neighbourhood made their way down to the southern and eastern sides of the city and up on to the sea walls, where they stood straining their eyes at the blue haze to the south. When the first ships were sighted, that news, too, raced along every street. The churches filled up, and the populace prayed for the safety of the city, or at least – if it pleased God – for the survival of their own households.

Anna tried to keep working during the morning, but at noon, after closing the shop, she took the whole household down to the Church of the Theotokos. Most of the neighbourhood was there, and Father Agapios had organized a recitation of psalms and prayers. There was a certain degree of comfort in the familiar words, and in the packed crowd repeating the same responses in heartfelt unison. A certain degree of comfort – but Anna still felt chilled at heart. God had not saved Theodosius. God had not given victory to Constantinople for many years. The enemy fleet far outnumbered the imperial ships; the enemy armies, the imperial ones. The Arabs were experienced soldiers, well trained, well supplied, courageous, filled with faith in their religion and led by able generals. What did Constantinople have to give it hope?

Strong walls, and her husband's fire. Would it really be enough?

When the prayers were over, she did not stay in the church. Instead she went back to the house, sent Sergios for the carriage, and put on her court dress. She drove the mares down a strangely quiet Middle Street, through the Bronze Gate to the palace of Boukoleon.

Theodosia was not in her suite, but one of the slaves directed Anna to another part of the palace: a balcony overlooking the sea. Anna arrived on it to see her daughter and most of her daughter's household leaning on the balustrade. Beyond them, the water of the Sea of Marmara shone in the late afternoon sun. Ships were scattered across it, black against the light: the armies of Islam, arrived at last.

Theodosia glanced round as her mother stepped on to the balcony, then moved aside to give her a place to stand. Basiliskos, who had been standing next to her, bowed, but for once did not say anything. He was very pale, though Theodosia looked calm and dignified. *A princess*, Anna thought wonderingly, gazing at her daughter. *She really is a princess of the house of Heraclius.*

'They're all on this side of the city,' Theodosia told Anna quietly, with a wave at the ships. 'Some of them are going west along the coast towards the Hebdomon, but none of them have tried to enter the Golden Horn.'

The inlet of the Golden Horn, on the north side of Constantinople, was protected by a heavy boom which could be lifted to bar the passage of ships: it was also protected by catapults situated in the towers of the sea walls flanking it, with more catapults in the forts of Galata, on the other side of the Horn. The 'Thracian', or southern, side of the city was obviously a more vulnerable target.

Theodosia's face bore a very adult expression of resolution and regret. 'My cousin summoned me this morning, when we heard the news,' she informed her mother in a low voice. 'He wanted me to know that he'd tried to arrange for me to marry Yazid, the son of the Caliph. He said he sent envoys last autumn, to the Caliph in Damascus and to Yazid in Cyzicus, offering peace on fair terms, with the marriage as part of the settlement. The Caliph told him that if the empire wanted peace we should surrender and accept the rule of God and his Faithful. Yazid told him to expect his answer when the winds were favourable.'

Anna looked out at the black ships. She imagined her precious daughter married to the man who commanded them. Then she tried to imagine what would happen if the city fell. There were so *many* ships, so impossibly many. Was there enough fire to sink all of them?

'I don't think this is a wedding party,' said Theodosia quietly.

'I don't think it is,' Anna agreed.

The girl sighed. 'I would've married Yazid very happily,' she said wistfully, 'if it saved the city. I would have been very proud if I could do that.'

'I would have gone with you,' volunteered Basiliskos.

Theodosia smiled at him affectionately. 'I know. That's what would have made it bearable.'

The eunuch smiled back. Anna had a sudden vision of them in ten years' time: Theodosia a great lady of the empire, Basiliskos the head of her staff, the two of them intriguing and manoeuvring to advance the interests of their own party up the slope of power. A princess, yes. Her daughter had left Anna's own world, and, for all her love, was never going to come back to it.

Maybe that was true of all children.

Theodosia gazed out at the ships and bit her lip. 'I wish Yazid had agreed. A lot of people are going to die.'

'God is with us,' Anna replied. 'Whether we live or die.'

Theodosia sighed again, then reached over and clasped her mother's hand. 'I'm glad you're here,' she whispered. 'I'm scared.'

'Me too,' replied Anna, and squeezed the hand.

They watched the slow movement of the ships westward. The vessels closer to the shore had stepped their masts and were moving under the power of their oars, though in the distance the sea was patched with sails. The sails were going down, though, as the enemy fleet prepared for battle. The southern shore of the city was dotted with harbours – all defended, but still, places where the ships could hope to put in. Those harbours began with the imperial port of Boukoleon, just below them, and ran as far west as the harbour of the Hebdomon, seven miles away. Beyond that the coast became steeper and more rugged and there were no good landing places. The enemy fleet would try to force its way in and establish a beachhead from which it could disembark troops.

Basiliskos glanced nervously at Anna. 'Is Magistros Kallinikos at the Arsenal?'

Anna nodded. 'I imagine he's checking that everything works.' She did imagine it: Kallinikos in his dirty tunic and leather apron, surrounded by his workers, going from one ship to another, inspecting the pumps, topping up the tanks of fire, giving a few last-minute instructions to the sailors.

A dozen or so of the ships had separated from the rest

238

and were coming closer. They were dromons – large biremes which could carry up to three hundred men, including a unit of marines. Now that they were nearer, it was possible to see that they'd been painted green, and had only looked black against the brilliance of the sea. They flew banners decorated with crescent moons. Their masts had been taken down, and the heavy bronze rams fixed to their prows nosed hungrily through the water as the oars flashed regularly along their sides.

'Mistress,' said Basiliskos respectfully. 'Maybe we'd better go in.' He glanced anxiously at the ships. 'They may have artillery on board.'

Theodosia shook her head impatiently. '*We* have artillery on the walls, and it's much bigger than anything anyone could fit on a ship. If the enemy come close enough to shoot at us, they'll have to do it under a barrage from our catapults. We'll watch a little longer. I want to see Kallinikos' fire.'

One of her attendants cried out suddenly and pointed: imperial ships had left the harbour of the Kontoskalion and were rowing out to meet the enemy. There were dromons and the smaller chelands and some light galleys, red and black, flying the eagle standard inherited from the legions of Rome under the crossed chi-rho monogram of Christ. Several of the ships turned east towards the Boukoleon; the rest matched the main flow of the enemy to the west.

Anna heard distant cheering as the ships rowed along the shore. The walls were lined with people, soldiers and citizens, come to watch the attack. She craned her neck, trying to see the sea wall at the foot of the slope below the balcony, but it was hidden by trees and by the slope itself. More cheers, however, indicated that it, too, held an audience.

The imperial ships arriving to protect the Boukoleon consisted of three chelands, two dromons, and two light thirty-oared galleys. They looked no match for the ships now rowing to meet them – ten dromons, Anna counted, and three chelands. On the other hand, the imperial ships had the support of the catapult batteries on the sea-walls – and the fire. As the ships drew nearer, Anna saw that both of the fragile-looking galleys were equipped with siphons: the new bronze fittings for the hoses glinted at the highest point of their prows, and she could just make out the squat shape of the tanks amidships. One of the chelands was equipped as well.

Four of the Arab ships speeded up, moving ahead of their fellows as their oarsmen picked up the stroke. It was clear at once that they were manoeuvring to catch the imperial dromons broadside – the killing strike for a ship equipped with a ram. Water whitened at their prows. The other Arab dromons swung round, trying to get into positions that would allow them to ram if the imperial ships turned aside from the threat, while the chelands hung back, waiting their turn. All of them were still out of range of the artillery on the walls.

The imperial dromons slowed down; the two galleys and the cheland with the siphon wheeled to face the attackers. It was oddly beautiful to watch: two dance troupes, approaching one another across the stage of a theatre, taking their positions with elegance and grace as they prepared to put on a display.

The galleys and their larger companion began to move at ramming speed, oars flashing as they closed, quickly now, with the approaching dromons. The dromons disdained to respond, choosing to hold their courses towards their imperial opposites rather than turn aside to deal with opponents they outmatched so completely. The other imperial ships had turned, and more of the Arab ships began to close in.

The galleys slipped sideways, preparing to pass the dromons to the left and the right; the cheland was slightly behind them, aiming for a third ship. The Arab dromons, larger and unable to change course as quickly, at once shipped the oars on their threatened flanks, obviously expecting the common tactic of attempting to strip an enemy's oars by a glancing blow of the ram. They were completely unprepared for the fire.

It flashed from the swivelled hose, a torrent of light and a plume of smoke; it flooded along shipped oars and decking, and it left flames leaping in its wake. They were too far away, on the balcony, to hear the roar of the discharge or the screams of pain and terror, but they could see how the ships staggered, swung around as the oars stopped, first on one side, then on both. Tiny figures appeared on the side of the stricken ships: men, leaping into the sea, unaware that this fire burned so fiercely that the sea itself couldn't put it out.

From the wall down the hill rose the sound of cheering, astonished and joyful.

The fire ships turned, one to the left, two to the right, leaving their victims behind and bearing down instead on the Arab dromons on the flanks. The fourth of the attacking dromons, which had escaped the fire, found itself facing two imperial ships of its own weight. It rowed on towards them bravely, but the remaining imperial cheland sped in suddenly from the side, ramming it across the stern and then disengaging. The dromon laboured and began to sink.

The other three were burning, and the galleys ran eagerly towards the attackers on the flanks. These turned heavily, wallowing as they tried to bring their rams to bear and build up speed enough to manoeuvre. The fire ships darted past them, vomiting flame. Even where the fire fell short of its target, still it drifted, burning on the surface of the water, catching at oars, carried by currents and the light breeze towards the enemy. The enemy turned away from it in terror.

Anna watched, exhilarated and sickened. Glancing down the coast, she saw more ships burning, saw the Arab fleet falling back, giving up the attack. All along the walls, the citizens cheered.

Theodosia let out a long breath. 'I knew it!' she exclaimed in fierce joy. 'I knew, the moment I saw the fire burning on our water bath, I *knew* it was important. And look!' She flung a hand out towards the burning ships. 'Look!'

Anna crossed herself.

The imperial fleet did not press its advantage. Still outnumbered, and probably out of fire, the ships retreated to their harbour at the Kontoskalion. The Arab ships anchored at sea, and the onlookers on the walls could make out the small boats going back and forth as the captains conferred. They did not move again, though, as the afternoon light began to fade.

'Will you stay and have supper?' asked Theodosia.

Anna shook her head. 'No, thank you, darling. I ought to go home.'

Theodosia hugged her. 'Kiss Kallinikos for me, and tell him he's a hero and the saviour of the city.'

Anna smiled weakly. She felt extraordinarily weary, despite having done nothing for hours but stand and watch. 'I'll do that,' she promised.

The church bells were ringing all over the city as she drove home, and the streets were crowded. When she reached Philadelphion, some of the neighbours recognized her and began to cheer.

'It's Kallinikos' wife!' they cried. 'Kallinikos, the master of the fire!'

State secret or not, there had been rumours. The neighbours all knew that Kallinikos worked in the Arsenal on incendiaries, that he'd been made magistros because he'd done something special. The whole city had seen now, what that thing was. The people of Philadelphion crowded around the carriage, cheering and clapping their hands. Anna smiled at them uncertainly and tried to keep control of the nervous mares.

Then someone began to sing, 'Kallinike, tenella kallinike!' – an old song of triumph. Honey and Nutmeg rolled their eyes and pranced, and Anna reined them in hard while the crowd around her laughed and shouted and clapped and sang: 'Beautiful is victory, beautiful is victory!'

Stunned and bewildered, she eventually managed to get back to the house. Sergios was on the doorstep, dancing with Zoe. She called him over, gave him charge of the carriage, and got out. She waved to the neighbours, tried to thank them, then gave up all hope of making herself heard and instead went inside, closing the door behind her.

Kallinikos arrived about half an hour later to a new wave of cheers and singing. He came in and slumped down at the kitchen table, dishevelled and exhausted. 'God and all his saints!' he exclaimed, looking at Anna in disbelief. 'Did you hear that!'

She nodded. 'They sang it for me, too.' She came over and

put her arms around him, leaning her cheek against his hair. 'Theodosia says to tell you you're a hero and the saviour of the city.'

He looked blank, then leaned his head back to kiss her. 'It's better than being a sorcerer, which is what the fleet seems to believe.' He let his breath out very slowly. 'It worked better than I expected.'

'The fleet thinks you're a sorcerer?' Anna asked with concern.

'*Their* sorcerer,' he said quickly. 'Nobody's threatening to arrest me. Dear God!' He sucked his lip down. 'It worked better than I expected. It makes the most terrible sound, you know, a sort of roaring, and the smell is . . . it frightens people. It frightens *me*, and I know exactly how it works. It terrified the enemy.'

'I was watching with Theodosia, from the Boukoleon. We saw.'

He looked up at her grimly. 'They'll get over being terrified, you know.' He caught her hand, then pulled her round on to his lap and put his arms around her. 'It isn't victory yet, you know,' he said seriously. 'It won't be, not this year, probably not next. They have a secure base for their fleet in Cyzicus and more ships than we do. They didn't know about the fire today, but they will tomorrow. They'll come up with some countermeasures. Sand buckets, shields of wet hide. That sort of thing.'

'Will those work?'

He hesitated. 'It will certainly *help* them. It won't make them safe. Thank God *they* don't have the fire!'

She stroked his beard, found the burn scar that fitted the tip of her finger.

'I'll be glad when it's over,' he said abruptly. 'This thing I've made . . . now that I've made it . . .' He stopped.

'What?'

He grimaced. 'They're calling it by my name. "Kallinikos' fire." I see it, and I ask myself, is that what I want my name to mean?'

'I don't think we could hold the Arabs off without it,' Anna said quietly. 'You *have* saved the city, my darling.'

He sighed. 'I wish, though . . . I wish I could make something *different*. I wish I could find the elixir.'

She smiled a little at the hope. 'And turn lead into gold?'

He shrugged. 'It would do that. Among other things.'

'Has anyone ever *really* found such a thing?'

'Oh, yes!' exclaimed Kallinikos in surprise. 'Apollonios of Tyana, and Zosimus and Maria the Jewess – they're all supposed to have made the elixir, and they've all written about it.'

'So why isn't there a gold-making industry in every town in the empire?' Anna asked sceptically.

'Because the process is difficult,' said Kallinikos seriously. 'And the instructions are expressed philosophically and mystically, in metaphors.' He paused, then went on, with sudden passion, 'The elixir, you understand, is the substance by which nature renews itself. All things below the circle of the moon are subject to change and to decay. If there were no countervailing principle in nature, all the world would be completely corrupted within a few generations. It isn't: we struggle on, constantly beset by sin and death, but constantly striving for love and life – and sometimes we even find them, for a while. So it has to exist, the elixir. A ferment in the corruption, capable of turning base metals into noble ones, of healing and renewing life. Should we expect it to be easy to find?'

'No,' whispered Anna, watching his face.

'But isn't it worth searching for?'

'I suppose so,' she said. She thought of his clean workshop, the shelves of equipment: the jars of sulphur and salt, the flasks of mercury. 'But is it something you can find in a workshop?' she asked slowly. 'From the way you talk about it, it sounds almost as though you're looking for the Holy Spirit.'

'It has to be a natural principle!' Kallinikos insisted. 'The Holy Spirit, so we're taught, is God's gift to believers, but this isn't something only for believers. The whole *world* is constantly dying, but it constantly renews itself. Maybe the elixir comes from God the Creator, but it has to be a natural principle, something you can isolate and preserve, if you search for it in the right way.'

244

She thought of the child in her womb. She was almost certain now that it was indeed growing there, through some natural miracle, some elixir of life and renewal. She kissed him.

He kissed her. 'Anyway,' he said, with determination. 'That's what I want to do now: search for the elixir. You'll stick to transforming rose petals?'

'It's a lot easier,' she told him, and leaned her head against his shoulder. 'I have all the elixir I want already.'

Historical Epilogue

The essential underpinning of this story is taken from history: the Arab conquest of the Byzantine empire in the seventh century was halted when a Syrian refugee to Constantinople discovered the weapon now known as Greek fire. It must be admitted, however, that seventh-century Byzantine history is notably muddled and debatable. The nature of Greek fire is also debatable, though it's clear that the Byzantines considered it a secret weapon. The Arab states did eventually get hold of the recipe, but not until a couple of centuries later.

I'm aware that in writing about the first great clash between Islam and the West, I am commenting on a conflict that is still raging. Let me say plainly that I am not anti-Islamic. Medieval Islam was undoubtedly more humane, tolerant and civilized than medieval Christianity; its subjects were better off, and the world owes much to it. When I have characters refer to Muslims as 'heretics' and 'enemies of God', I am reflecting the language of seventh-century Greeks, not my own views at all. However, there can be no doubt that in the seventh century the Arabs were engaged in *conquest*, and I can't help but sympathize with the people who found themselves under attack by an enemy who was interested in nothing short of their complete subjugation. (Let me add that, yes, I agree the Crusades were even worse, and the Crusaders much nastier. The history of relations between Islam and the West appears to be thirteen centuries of hatred and misrepresentation, with no end in sight. It is immensely depressing.)

At any rate, that first Arab siege is reported to have lasted some years – two to eight years, depending on your source. When it was over, the Caliph Mu'awiya agreed a thirty-year peace in which he ceded all the territory he had recently acquired in Asia Minor and the Greek islands, and agreed to pay the Byzantine emperor three thousand pieces of gold, fifty slaves and fifty horses a year. However you interpret that, it looks like a significant Arab defeat.

The story of Theodosius, and that of the noseless princes, are both historical – though, I confess, it's likely that the princes didn't lose their noses until 681. (Theophanes the Confessor, the best source, places the event in 669, but A.N. Stratos in *Byzantium in the Seventh Century* convincingly argues for the later date on the basis of numismatic and Western evidence.) The picture of Greek alchemy is based on ancient sources – and, yes, Graeco-Roman alchemists *did* employ distillation, which was *not* invented by the Arabs, whatever you may read to the contrary! I'm afraid that my picture of seventh-century perfume-making is based on much shakier evidence. Certainly it was a major industry, and certainly perfumes were generally oil-based rather than alcohol-based as they are today (alcohol, strangely enough, probably *was* an Arab invention). I couldn't find much discussion of the technical processes, however, though I encountered numerous works which waxed lyrical about the materials. I did what I could with what I could find.

To close, a few self-defensive comments for the scholars. I know perfectly well that the Latin title is *magister*, not *magistros*: the Byzantines Hellenized it. Next, that word 'Byzantine': I haven't used it in the book because the Byzantines never did. Nor did they call themselves 'Greek' – so obviously they didn't call their secret weapon 'Greek fire', and I've tried to reflect this, too. Finally, in referring to the Emperor 'Constans the Bearded' I'm guilty of an amalgamation. Traditionally the man in question was known as 'Constans II', and 'Constantine the Bearded' was believed to be his son. However, modern scholarship has shown that 'Constans' also used the name 'Constantine', and that the epithet 'Pogonatos' – 'the Bearded' – properly attached to him, not to Constantine IV.

Modern scholarship is indeed a wonderful thing. I think I'll stick to fiction: it's much clearer.